JAMES AYLOTT

Tales From

The Beach House

A NOVEL

BEAUTIFUL ARCH
St Louis, Missouri

ISBN: 978-0-578-47956-9

Library of Congress Control Number: 2019903109

Literary Editing by Lesley Upton.

Flamingo Cover Art Copyright © Solomon Thurman.

Printed by Lightning Source LLC.

First printing edition 2019.

Beautiful Arch LLC.
St Louis, Missouri.

A Declaration of Fiction

* * *

The "Florida Man" and "Florida Woman" news items that are the foreword for each chapter are sourced from the credited media outlets.

With Thanks

I dedicate this book to The Bermuda Inn, Huge Organs, The Green Owl (original location), Boston's (before the remodel), Elwood's and all the other Delray Beach institutions that succumbed to progress.

Thanks to Dean Krystek of World Link Literary for giving me the confidence to take this project to the next level.

A big thank you goes to my family scattered around the globe and especially to Little Girl and Little Rainbow.

Contents

June 14th 2018, from the Tampa Bay Times

FLORIDA MAN ARRESTED AFTER CALLING COPS TO GET HIS METH TESTED

A Florida man called the sheriff's office after growing suspicious that the meth he had smoked was the wrong drug. The concerned caller experienced a "violent reaction" to the narcotics he had purchased. He asked the sheriff's office to test the substance so that he could press charges against the dealer for selling him the incorrect drug. Detectives invited the man to the their office so they could conduct a quality test. The Florida man showed them a clear substance wrapped in aluminum foil. When it tested positive as methamphetamine, he was arrested and sent to jail.

Greetings from FloriDuh!

The great state of Florida, with low taxes and longevity of life, distorts the shitty universal "death and taxes" certainties of regular existence and replaces them with a localized model of normality. For in the Sunshine State, the real certainties in life are that a real-estate bust will follow a real-estate boom, and that sooner rather than later a hurricane will not only come a-knocking at the trailer park door but will most likely blow it off its hinges.

Florida, with its perfect climate for four months of the year and an insufferable one for the other eight, is the rogue state of the Union. The "upper forty-nine" laugh out loud when Florida mangles elections, or causes cruel and unusual punishment at its executions. Most Floridians see election irregularity as divine intervention, and "Old Sparky", as the Tallahassee chair is affectionately tagged, the pinnacle of old-fashioned justice.

It has been said that the rule for living in Florida is that you can only come to the State if you are not normal. Its loose laws and cheap real estate make it a Mecca for those trying to hide from the authorities, or those wanting to make a new life after messing up their prior existence someplace else. Gun legislation is lax – at your typical big-box store it's easier to buy a semi-automatic and ammo than a six-pack of beer, while getting a concealed permit to carry a gun is often a simpler process than obtaining a driving license. To service the criminal elements that make Florida their home, a huge industry of lawyers, bounty hunters, bail bondsmen, plastic surgeons and shrinks thrive and make a good living off the wild dwellers of this American geographical appendage.

The southern tip of the State, with its majority Hispanic Spanish-speaking population, chaotic infrastructure and civic corruption, feels like an extension of Latin America. Ironically, Florida becomes more Southern in "state-of-mind" the further north in "state-of-being" you go. Fifty miles past Vero Beach and a few clicks inland from Highway 95, you are as deep in Dixie as rural Alabama. The State's central hinterland is neither here nor there, with a blend of rough-and-ready rednecks hiding from civilization, intermingled with fixed-income retirees in their gated colonies who are enjoying their golden years in the style befitting their luck and choices in life.

Sprinkled throughout the more pleasant parts of the State are a few million aged Jews, who, en masse, could easily constitute either one of the Lost Tribes of Israel or the biggest-ever *Golden Girls* convention. A Diaspora of New Yorkers, who never fail to make themselves stand out at any beachside bar when the Jets or Yankees pop up on the television, reside in the counties of Broward, Brevard and Palm Beach. Put these strange migrant colonies together and you have a mass of people bound only by the nature of their transiency, and the self-realization that they are dwelling in a land deemed unfit for human habitation by Mother Nature.

Florida was built on imagination and swamp drainage, and fueled by greed and scams. Idyllic towns with marketable names such as Seaside, Celebration, Niceville, Cocoa Beach, Siesta Key, Crystal River and Harmony are dotted around its sub-tropical 105,000 square miles. Often these border more eccentrically tagged communities, like Two Egg, Pancake, Couch, Fluffy Landing, Lone Cabbage, Spuds and Possum Branch. One of the most affluent towns in America, Boca Raton, means, "rat's mouth" when translated from dreamy Spanish to functional English. Peel back the veneer of tropical weather, sandy beaches and kooky-named communities, and it can be scary to think what might be lurking beyond that fiery maroon sunset backdrop with its intermittent dramatic electric sparks.

South Florida's Delray Beach, branded by its Chamber of Commerce as "Village By The Sea", is a modern-day boomtown. Its twentieth-century origins revolved around the pineapple industry. In 1920, following development of the Everglades and the subsequent lowering of the water table, the pineapple industry collapsed. A rampant land-speculation boom in the early 1920s, followed by a land bust at the decade's end, started and then stunted the town's growth. Air conditioning in the 1950s led to Delray's renaissance as a tourist destination and retiree haven. Somewhere between the 1980s, when locals labeled Delray "Dull-Ray", and today, the city became one of the hippest towns in Florida.

With gentrification, spurred on by ambitious mayors, ravenous developers and crooked politicians, came the gradual loss of Delray's "Old Florida" way of life. Historic bars were bulldozed and replaced by multi-story parking lots. Noir diners, with their bathroom stench of rancid steaming piss, became a thing of the past, and were swapped for bland, climate-controlled, Febreze-odor restrooms buried in eateries ripped out of the cookie-cutter design book. Traditional black neighborhoods were devastated by eminent domain, with the hastily raised lots often not even built on. Eviction was simply a ploy to move along people labeled as "undesirables." By the turn of the 21st century there was no "wrong side of the tracks," as the old Flagler East Coast line that used to divide Delray's haves and have-nots would denote. The entire city had morphed into prime real estate.

Today, tourism, development and rehabs are the driving force of Delray's economy, with rehab facilities being the most profitable, fastest growing and least susceptible industry to economic recession. With cozy names like Beachcomber

Rehabilitation and Beachway Therapy, these pricey crutches to those in need can cost more per night than a suite at Palm Beach's ritzy Breakers hotel. The Delray industrial detox complex was not only good business that topped up the city coffers, but it also created a steady supply of cheap labor. The town's dirty little secret was that most of the bar staff and waiters who worked up and down "The Avenue," as the lively main commercial drag along Atlantic was called, were either currently attending "Twelve-Step," or freshly out and in "Recovery." Aside from their twitchy tics, they made willing and reliable workers, in a State notorious for boasting a work-shy population.

The Beach House apartments stand as a testament to a rapidly vanishing Florida. The low-rise building is situated on Delray's breezy coastal barrier island, two blocks north of Atlantic Avenue and a block east of A1A. It was constructed in the early 1950s on a generous corner double lot, in a subdivision created from an abandoned pineapple plantation.

Originally built as a motel catering to bargain-hunting tourists wanting a taste of Florida on a budget, the building is painted in a delightful pastel-green color. It stands two stories high and contains twelve identically sized studio apartments situated around a shallow U-shape courtyard that is surrounded by lushly landscaped grounds. In the front garden facing southwest sits a compact kidney-shaped swimming pool encircled by loungers, chairs and tables that boast permanently filled ashtrays. Two coconut-bearing palm trees flank the pathway that leads from Andrews Avenue to the building's cobbled patio area. To the right of the entrance stands a regal Barbadian mango tree, the fruit of which brings much delight to local foxes. At the center of the patio stands a sun-faded oversized plastic flamingo statue that is tasked with being The Beach House's official mascot. To the building's rear, accessed by an often-muddy pathway, is a tiny laundry room affectionately tagged by residents as "The Club Room." It is home to a rusting coin-operated washer and dryer that is battered, abused and barely clinging onto life, and at every homeowners' meeting it faces the threat of forced retirement to the Miami landfill. Facing east is a swinging sign weathered by salt air and strong winds that notates, in a fat, bright-pink Bauhaus font, that you are at The Beach House.

For the first thirty years of The Beach House's existence, this little slice of the Florida dream could be yours for under forty bucks a night. Today, a motel of that caliber would be marketed as boutique, eco certified and rustic. Then, it was just small, basic and affordable. In the late 1980s, Sharon and Ted Wainright from Paducah, Kentucky, the motel's third owners, were looking to cash out and retire to Belize (as that is where people who have had their fill of Florida go) so they sold the motel. The buyers, seemingly folksy Sid and Wendee Goldberg, from Portsmouth, New Hampshire, bought the operation. The Wainrights believed they had passed the baton of family-run "Southern hospitality" to a like-minded husband-and-wife team. Little did they know that this sweet couple wasn't interested in taking care of the Wainrights "Baby", and only wanted to make a quick profit-making flip. A day after taking title, Sid and Wendee filed paperwork with the city, and following a fresh lick of paint and a scattering of new bathroom fixtures, transformed the old motel into self-described "Luxury Condos." They marketed the development in the spirit of the go-getting '80s as "Yuppie Beach Living for the Gordon Gekkos of the Gold Coast!" The Goldbergs made an easy killing on their deal and headed out west to the Nature Coast. They repeated this process all over Florida until they had finally made enough money to buy a small chain of motels in the Panhandle.

Sid and Wendee Goldberg's luxury condo conversion wasn't much more than papering over the cracks. Thirty years later this was more apparent than ever, with the building's cracks becoming so big that there wasn't an emulsion thick enough even to attempt to cover them up. At heart The Beach House was still an old slab-and-block motel, complete with underpowered air conditioning, unreliable plumbing, paper-thin walls that held no secrets and humming-bird-sized roaches that a battalion of Terminix men couldn't control. The term "Luxury", to describe living at The Beach House, was rarely even muttered by those dubious local realtors with tendencies of glorious embellishment.

As for its residents, even in its late '80s incarnation as a blue-chip-certified collection of swanky condos, it was never quite able to shake off and deter the oddities that typically reside or call a place of this ilk home. The current owners, mostly hands-off absentee landlords at best and hands-on slumlords at worse, in many cases made their tenants look aristocratic. Today, The Beach House, with its twelve little units, houses a mixture of strange and eclectic souls, each with their different problems, vexing quixotic lives, cheap scams, dodgy hustles, secret hidden pasts and future chronicles to be told.

In recent months The Beach House, in a rare fit of owner enthusiasm, has been repainted a different shade of green tagged cheerfully by the paint producer "Lasting Thoughts." The apartment doors and framing trim now gleam loudly in a new flamingo-pink hue – that is, every door except that of Apartment #5. This isolated entry is a filthy version of what was once, in better days, brilliant white. The door and its surrounding frame don't match any other part of the building. At Apartment #5 the blinds are always closed, the indigenous lizards stay well clear and the "welcome" signage was wiped clean from the doormat long ago.

February 6th 2015, from KTVI Palm Beach County

FLORIDA MAN CAUGHT IN SEX ACT WITH PET CHIHUAHUA

A Florida man was arrested after his wife caught him having sex with their pet Chihuahua. The sixty-one-year-old man from Wellington pleaded guilty to animal cruelty and sexual activity with a dog. The man was caught in the act by his wife on their home-security surveillance cameras. Florida is the number-one State in the country for the most severe animal crimes.

Apartment #1 Greyhound Departure

"Why wouldn't I? Hello!" said Tim Flanders, talking to his own reflection in a dirty cracked mirror as he set himself up for another Greyhound, his potent vodka-and- grapefruit cocktail of choice. It was an hour before the nightly rerun block of *Two and a Half Men* started, and plenty of time to knock back another adult beverage. Tim set his body clock to these daily Charlie Sheen reruns and it didn't matter that he had seen them all before and knew every word of the dialogue by heart.

Another day in Paradise or was it really Hell? Flashed through his medicated mind as he pondered what mistakes in life had been made to end up living in a somewhat shabby three-hundred-and-ninety-six-square-foot studio apartment. Was this place karma for screwing all those bored Boca housewives? Surely that was the divine right of being a professional tennis instructor in South Florida? Besides, Tim's rule had always been they had to make the first move, which must be, at the very least, a dispensation of sorts.

"Where did I fuck up?" he asked himself aloud, unable to hear his own question over the din of the apartment's strained air con.

Tim took a lazy slurp of his drink. In the background, a blonde presenter on *Fox News* was debating the issue of the day. Tim had reached the age of fifty-two, and at this stage of life he hadn't expected to be living in what was essentially a space smaller than a tract home garage. He should be living the "good life" by now or at the very least an easy life in a comfortable setting.

Technically, Tim was a millionaire. Legally by right he was "rich," although from a glance at his bank statement he was certainly penniless. Tim didn't ask for much. He was low-maintenance, really, with the five-hundred-and-sixty-two-square-feet and one bedroom at the Windward East complex being all he desired. Those condos, a block nearer to the ocean, came with daily maid service and a pool heated to a balmy seventy-eight degrees all-year-round. The Beach House's pool, due to the cheapness of the Homeowners' Association, was bitterly cold come November.

Of course, he required the touch of a woman, but that had always come easy for him. In recent years, the quality and mileage on some of the rides were functional but not always low. Tim always had at least one girl available on speed dial, even if it was only the fallback sucking-and-fucking from crazy

Precious. She was harder to get rid of than a dose of Bangkok clap, but she was good in bed and a wizard in the kitchen.

Tim stood in his kitchen and poured a freshly made cocktail into a Palm Beach Club polystyrene to-go cup. He shuffled through the living room/bedroom combined space and out of his front door. He repositioned himself on the well-worn plastic chair that sat outside his apartment's main window. It was a perfect-as-they-come evening, with a breeze blowing onshore from the direction of Bimini. As he took a sip from his cup he noticed a Volvo station wagon pulling up to the parking strip in front of The Beach House. Even in his hazy high he could see a "hot tamale", as he affectionately tagged an attractive woman, exiting from the vehicle.

An initial glance revealed she had strong Mediterranean features, long straight black hair, a petite stature and perky breasts that were primed for an easy escape out of a stylishly loose floral dress. The woman made a beeline in his direction along the brick patio that led from the street to the building. Tim wondered if one of the guys had ordered in an escort girl. That routinely occurred around these parts. It wouldn't be a shocker if this young beauty left in exactly sixty minutes counting crumpled bills on the way back to her car. Although she wasn't wearing the "chase-me fuck-me high heels" that were standard call-girl fare and her makeup was modest, anything was possible and the pimp-free digital-empowered hookers of today came in all shapes and sizes. Possibly she was saving money by driving an old car and putting the funds into a retirement account. This wasn't the nineteen '80s any more; fiscal responsibility was all the rage and modern prostitutes were some of the most astute business people alive.

The beautiful young woman was heading straight towards him and evidently didn't have an immediate appointment in any other direction but his. As they made eye contact she gave him a broad smile. Tim still had no recollection of who she could be. He was stoned and drunk, but had evolved to function under these regular circumstances so this unfamiliarity wasn't from a cerebral lapse. The woman was now close enough so he could smell her perfume, a fragrance recognized from the kept ladies at the clubs he worked at.

Do I owe her money? Have I knocked up her sister? Flashed through his head.

Am I her father? Is this her?

Tim began to mentally panic.

Tim had been born into a New England military family, where the detail of not being admitted to West Point was a shame drilled into him at all family gatherings. Not that getting a tennis scholarship to Florida State was bad, but it wasn't what generations of Flanders men did. Tim's tour of duty at the Tallahassee campus known locally as "The Yale of the South", due to the University of Florida snagging the "The Harvard of the South" moniker, was the best time of his life. Back then, he had a full head of lush brown hair, copious amounts of easily obtainable drugs, bountiful women and his tennis was in its prime. It wasn't the creaking game he attempted to play and teach now, but full-speed tennis with power shots and without the constant pain that now dogged his every movement. An Atlantic Coast Conference championship in '78 was the pinnacle of his college career. That year, Georgia was packed with talent and the underdog Seminoles ran the table – which was quite a feat considering how much dope the team had collectively smoked before games. Those were the days before drug testing had become a part of collegiate sports and AIDS curtailed after-game delights.

Upon graduation, Tim became semi-pro and worked small satellite tournaments along the East Coast. He was very nearly good enough, but found it hard to be competitive in the professionalism of tennis in the early '80s. After a year of toil and being unable to make it out of feeder events, he was rescued by a prestigious Californian country club that required his youth and skill to set up a new tennis center. His five successful years there abruptly ended when a Japanese corporate buying spree gobbled up this club. New overlords took a different direction and Tim was surplus to requirements.

A friendly club member who worked on Wall Street suggested he become a bond trader and arranged an introduction. Bond trading was much like tennis – steely nerves, a bit of bluff and skillful movements conducted with the brutal necessity of speed. But ten years of high-octane cocaine-fueled living in Manhattan was as much as he could take. Flush with Wall Street cash, he headed back to Florida and returned to the world of tennis, albeit at a personally slower pace than the game he left a decade before.

For the next fifteen years Tim enjoyed a successful career third act working the ritzy Jewish clubs of affluent Palm Beach. As he could never quite crack the gentile clubs, he was always thankful to the Jews for not discriminating. The members loved him. Not only was he a great tennis coach, but also more importantly he was a fantastic teacher of the game. He had ample well-paid work along with generous tips. He was a favorite with ladies of a certain age and, luckily for him, their husbands often turned a blind eye. He had all the women he could want and many he really didn't.

Tim rented the beautiful Delray Beach waterfront guesthouse of Shelly Goldwyn, a fabulously wealthy widowed GOP donor. The arrangement was ideal for him. Her Florida season was three weeks a year, with the remainder being split between Palm Springs and Rhode Island. So, for the duration of her short stay in Delray, Tim would keep a low profile. For the other forty-nine weeks he had the grounds and pool to himself in return for "keeping an eye on the house." This situation was bliss, and Tim truly felt content and at home.

But as always in life all good things ultimately come to an end. Out of the blue, his landlady, fed up with escalating property taxes, sold her house and booted Tim out from his comfortable digs. Ms. Goldwyn became a full-time dweller on a residential cruise ship and spent her days with like-minded people floating around the world legally avoiding taxes and bragging to anyone who would listen about how well she did it.

Tim scrambled to find a new home. Rents had skyrocketed while he had been living in the inflation-free zone of the Goldwyn guesthouse. Tim's earnings had also been declining as younger coaches were gradually poaching his gigs. A "For Rent" sign, the relatively low price of $850 a month and the dire need to find a place to hang his tennis whites were the perfect combination of conditions that saw Tim and his eight boxes of possessions quietly slip into Apartment #1 of The Beach House.

This change of living circumstances was a culture shock for Tim, who was accustomed to the luxurious surroundings of Mrs. Goldwyn's, and before that his swanky New York apartment. The general appearance of The Beach House was on the shabby side and showed visible evidence of corner-cutting landlords. The laundry facilities were downright ghetto in his opinion – collecting quarters and lining up to use a rusted coin-operated machine was not his style. Then there were the chain-smoking fellow residents who seemingly enjoyed congregating outside his apartment door at all hours of the day and night. The neighborly symphony of muted guttural groans, domestic abuse screams and whimpering underpowered air-conditioning units became the soundtrack to his new life.

Tim had landed with a thud in the American limbo land somewhere between the lower middle class and the upper lower class. The next rung down the ladder would be a trailer park and not in the prime location of Briny Breezes. This wasn't a world he wanted to get used to and he said to himself it would only be temporary, so there was no need to panic. At the same time, his creaking body and his diminishing earnings were telling him that tennis was a younger man's business and he didn't have a long-term game to give. Tim's remedy for his swirling malady of ills and the newfound circumstances was a self-prescribed combination of Percocet, vodka and marijuana – not necessary in that order – but as living at The Beach House went from weeks to years, this self-medication was dispensed in far greater doses.

The strange beautiful woman was now stood directly in front of him.

Tim had a daughter he had never met and hadn't even known existed until last year. Katie was her name. He had learnt that she was a Harvard pre-med student and there had been threats that his newly discovered kin would make a surprise visit. This girl didn't look much like him or his ex-wife, the mother of that child.

Tim wiped his brow and rapidly sobered up – as you do for a cop who has just pulled you over with intentions of making you "walk the line."

"I'm Angel. I just bought Apartment #2. It looks like I'll be your new neighbor," the female said, as she introduced herself with an accent a relieved Tim placed as suburban New Jersey.

Tim gave her a more diligent but possibly too obvious second look-over. The loose lightweight summer dress she wore, the expensive handbag by her side and that glorious beaming smile finished off a truly natural package that a man of any age would instantly fall in love with. With years of experience in reading people, Tim could tell she was an independent spirit who relied on no one but herself. Although he was greatly relieved to find that this woman wasn't newfound flesh and blood seeking fatherly support, Tim realized the problematic scenario Angel had presented to his desperate world. On the macro level, a beauty moving into The Beach House always threw the delicate man-to-woman equilibrium into a dangerous state of flux. On the micro level, having Angel as an immediate neighbor would leave him as the most obvious victim of collateral damage.

Tim was concerned about the toxic combination of a beauty living next door, gentleman callers visiting, noisy nocturnal pleasures following, and the Beach House's thin and unforgiving walls. This cocktail of low-rent living played havoc with sleep patterns, and with all he was currently dealing with Tim didn't need additional stress. The textbook remedy for all but the most extreme "monkey-love" would be to crank up the AC unit to full power and let its aged inefficiency eradicate the din. However, it was only March and Tim liked the windows open at night to capture the pleasant trade winds. The other factor was that times were tough around Apartment #1 and his budget couldn't handle a bloated FPL utility bill. In Tim's opinion, the bachelor stoner guys who passed out by 10 pm made ideal neighbors, especially when they shared their weed. He made a mental note-to-self that he would go to Publix and pick up a box of heavy-duty earplugs.

Not exactly the most responsive guy, and I believe he is staring straight at my breasts, Angel thought to herself as she waited for Tim to continue with the initiated dialogue as per the protocol of conversational norms. Angel could tell that the man, who was dressed in crisp tennis whites and precariously propped up in a chair in front of her, was fired-up on something more than just booze. From his appearance and a sun-weathered face, she wasn't sure if he was a younger man who looked older than his years or an older man who looked young for his years. What she was able to establish for certain, though, was that this was a deeply troubled individual.

"The door over there!" Angel said pointing to the lone front door that wasn't flamingo pink as a way of trying to break the dead air and distract Tim's gaze that was fixated on her chest. "Why's it a different color from all the others?"

Tim finally looked her in the eye and replied, "That's a long story for another day when I have myself a clearer head!" Following another pregnant pause and a further scan of Angel's entire body, he added, "My name is Tim Flanders. Welcome to The Beach House, new neighbor. May I pour you a cocktail?"

"Tonight no, but thank you, Tim. I'll definitely take you up on that offer in the future. I just got my keys and want to see exactly what I now own," she replied while rattling the key to her just-purchased abode.

Angel moved in front of her new door and struggled with the unfamiliar rusted lock. After some wiggling of the key and a dose of elbow grease, the door finally opened. She entered it without looking back at Tim, shutting the door speedily behind her with a scraping thud. The sound of the dead bolt fastening echoed loudly around the courtyard.

Tim sat in his chair sipping at what was by now just ice. The sun was setting in the west and casting long defined shadows behind The Beach House's brace of palm trees and its unique flamingo statue. There was still plenty of time before *Two and a Half Men* would air. *Possibly tonight?* That was the thought running through Tim's head, as it had on many occasions recently.

Tim stood upright slowly and stretched his aching bones. The pain through his spine now throbbed with even the slightest of movements. He shuffled back into his apartment and entered the kitchen area. Opening up the vintage fridge, he reached for a Mormon-family-sized bottle of vodka. He mixed it with grapefruit juice and a token ration of ice to make himself a fresh Greyhound. Taking a soothing gulp, he walked around the small apartment, home to his worldly possessions. Hanging over the sagging Murphy bed was the famous 1970s poster of the pantyless tennis player sexily lifting up her short skirt to reveal a bare bottom. He loved that picture. It had vigilantly followed him from the highs of his life, the dorm room in Tallahassee and the penthouse in Manhattan, to the lows of his life, a failing body and living at The Beach House. Resting on the side of his cracked white leather sofa was his collection of tennis rackets, from the wooden Slazengers of the '70s with their small heads, right up to the current space-age composites he used daily. Stacked between the sofa and the door was a weathered mahogany deckchair that he hauled out to the beach most days.

A lone built-in closet that was nestled between the main room and the grubby bathroom was the location for his wardrobe. En masse, it passed Wimbledon's strict dress code. Tim was traditional, and as far as he was concerned tennis was to be played on grass and in white. The only outfit in the closet not suitable for a game of tennis was a lone grey business suit. The last time he had worn this was five years ago, on the day of his fiftieth birthday. Then he had visited the Palm Beach law offices of Finklestein & Smithshlog in order to sign the paperwork needed to collect an inheritance. Tim's sister, a wealthy businesswoman who was slowly dying of cancer, realized her brother's sagging future earning potential and so changed her will to leave him $2,000,000. This fraction of her large estate was collectable once Tim reached fifty. By then, she had hoped her brother would be mature enough to spend the money wisely.

On the day of his half centennial, Tim, who was dressed in his freshly pressed suit, triumphantly walked into the lawyer's office to collect his inheritance. In his head he had sensibly allocated the entire amount in a manner that his sister would be proud of. He had a realtor lined up to buy for cash a condo at Windward East. His sole lavish purchase would be a new BMW 5 Series, which was intended to replace a twenty-year-old Nissan that Tim affectionately labeled "The Haitian Mobile." Tim had learnt from his losses with safe-as-they-come General Motors' bonds, which had become worthless during the "Great Recession", and planned to place the balance of his inheritance in Treasuries. Tim's simple needs of home-cooked tenderloin steaks and happy-hour beverages could easily be met on the annual returns these bonds yielded. This strategy was exactly the same way the well-divorced Boca women did it – tax-free dividends, a polished BMW and a house owned outright. It had taken Tim a large portion of his free time over several years to refine this plan. Each night he made a toast to his sister and thanked her for not instantly giving him the money, as without this forced time-out he would have blown the lot lightning-fast.

Unfortunately, on the day of Tim's fiftieth birthday, it wasn't the seven-digit cashier's check he had expected waiting at the law offices, but his scheming brother-in-law flanked by a pair of $400-an-hour legal eagles. The iceless glass of water they offered him was the extent of their warmth and generosity. The bulldog attorneys sat him down and told him he was not getting the inheritance. They methodically explained that the final will was written while his sister was in an "unfit state" and under "heavy medication." They claimed the modified document she had signed was thus not valid and, in fact, he was not getting anything whatsoever. The $2,000,000, along with the other $15,000,000 his sister had in assets, would all go to her extremely wealthy and speedily remarried husband. That was their final word and there wouldn't be any negotiations on offer. His brother-in-law knew Tim couldn't afford to fight back.

Tim painfully lowered himself down on the sofa while balancing a cocktail in his hand. Much like the rest of his apartment, the sofa was in need of a deep clean. Another *Fox News* bubblehead blonde, made easier on the eye with a soft-filter lens, was riling up a prime-time audience with the latest liberal antics from California.

Tim attended to a slender pile of freshly arrived mail. Among the items was a note from his landlord reminding him that rent was past due. Tim had become the recipient of regular threatening correspondence from the IRS, resulting from a large tax bill he owed from his prior moneymaking days. Their language in today's correspondence was less than friendly, and in addition to their rude demands they had recently helped themselves to his checking account. Tim had now resorted to using a stash can hidden in the freezer as a primary banking facility. There was also a letter from his doctor. This he filed in the trashcan, which was where he filed all his medical correspondence.

Tim took two Percocet pills, washing them down with a Greyhound chaser. He slowly shunted back to the kitchen and refilled his cup with another drink. Upon returning to the living area of his apartment he retrieved a pre-made joint hidden in his secret cache of medicinal narcotics under the Murphy bed. He wedged the "Camberwell Carrot" behind his ear, much as a tradesman would his essential go-to pencil. With a tight grip on his beverage, Tim exited his apartment without bothering to lock the door. He stumbled along the pathway that meandered in a southerly direction to Thomas Lane.

Looking behind him as he walked away from The Beach House he could see Gabriel, the owner of Apartment #5, standing shirtless outside his dirty unpainted door. Gabriel was conducting his favorite hobby of eye-banging any woman who dared to visit the pool. Today's unfortunate victim was Colleen from Apartment #7. She lay in her skimpy yellow bikini catching the last rays of the day, blissfully unaware of the lusty gazes of her deviant neighbor. Tim heard in the distance the muffled shouting of Rebecca and Shane from Apartment #9. They were in the middle of a roaring drunken domestic. You could set your watch to the loud make-up sex that would be audible from outside their apartment within the hour.

Tim walked slowly and painfully from The Beach House in the direction of the sea. Brenda Smith, a local lawyer, was waxing a Lexus in front of her craftsman cottage. Tim returned her friendly wave. He'd known her for over twenty years. He remembered when she was a hot, young sassy single thing that he desperately wanted to bed, but she couldn't be cracked – she was an ice queen back then. Those days were long gone. Brenda had since married, had kids, divorced messily and was now in a long-term relationship with a woman. Now all manly and dressed like a guy, Brenda was certainly wearing the pants in that happy household. Time and the harsh Florida sun hadn't done her former good looks any favors.

With his cocktail in his hand and playing real-life Frogger, Tim precariously ambled across A1A, narrowly avoiding the speeding cars that constantly thundered down this scenic artery. Safely across, he eased into one of the grey concrete benches that punctuated the boardwalk. The throbbing pain searing down his back, as it did every evening, was unbearable, and he now found it difficult to walk with any ease. To a casual onlooker, Tim's motions of movement were like those of a crab. Constantly stooping over, unable to straighten his back and every motion in short spurts with ugly pauses. Tim's body was physically shot. A lifetime of tennis could do this to you.

From his golden-hour perch, Tim watched the Atlantic Ocean smash onto the pristine shore. Just enough of a breeze was coming from offshore to keep the mosquitoes inland. There were still a few swimmers out enjoying the waves. A lone paddle boarder was visible as a dot on the horizon. On the sand, slender teenage girls hammed it up for selfies, their fun only spoilt by the poor bandwidth slowing down the time it took to share these images with the world.

Tim looked over his shoulder and could see the manicured glory of Windward East, where he should have been living by now. A couple sat on their balcony sipping from champagne glasses. He was envious, but not jealous. Tim looked back at the ocean. It was a picture-postcard "Greetings from Florida" sort of day. Of the thousands of sunsets he had witnessed, maybe this ranked among the best – although he said that every day.

His old-tech flip phone vibrated with a text from Precious: *Dinner my place?* Precious, who in his heart he loved dearly, was a true culinary wonder. An invite from her would usually be accepted speedily, without a second thought, just in case she changed her mind. Always on the menu would be a wonderful entrée, and for dessert a customary blow job.

Tim snapped the phone shut without sending a reply and slipped it into his pocket. Taking the joint parked behind his ear, he lit it up from a Delray Beach Chamber of Commerce matchbook. He took a deep drag from the toke. The medical-quality marijuana shipped in from a friend in Michigan would ease the pain for at least a short time. The mornings were the hardest because by then the good stuff from the night before had worn off and the pain would be kicking in with full vigor, ready to brutalize another day.

It was a month ago that Tim had finally gone to visit the doctor. He had already figured out what the problem was. A man knows when his junk is in trouble. It was the "Big C." Tim's only slight hope was medical attention he truly couldn't afford. The doctor gave him a couple of years, maybe more if he cut out the booze. The quality of life would be poor, pain would be certain. He had friends who had died an agonizing death in this manner.

Tim inhaled the last of the joint and washed it down with the balance of his drink. He looked at his first-generation Casio digital watch. He had twenty minutes to make it back for the start of *Two and a Half Men*. He hated to miss the beginning of the show. It didn't matter that he'd seen them all before. The last minutes of sunlight were rapidly ceding to darkness. Stragglers from the beach were shaking sand from towels and making their way back to the roadside. Traffic was backing up on A1A. A heavily tattooed senior citizen in a convertible blasted out Jimmy Buffett's *Margaritaville* as he drove north towards Ocean Ridge.

Floating on a glorious high, Tim stared towards the horizon. Bulging barrel clouds headed for land. Tim reached into the fanny pack that was attached to his crisp white shorts and pulled out a silver Smith & Wesson 686. He usually kept the gun next to his bed for home protection. With intention, he placed the barrel into his mouth.

Tim was broke and his body was falling apart. In addition to creaking joints, he now had cancer devouring him from the inside. How could he be anything but a burden to those around him? The incoming salvos of life served at Tim were coming in so fast that even in his glory days he couldn't have made clean returns to keep himself in the game. A tennis player knows when he has lost the momentum on the court and without a miracle it's game, set and match. The inner military upbringing was telling him to die with honor and dignity – and to do it quickly. Thinking back, he had made many mistakes. He had a great wife when he lived in California, but of course he couldn't keep his pecker in his pants. If he had, maybe he would now know his daughter. That brother-in-law had fucked him over and this was the thought he couldn't get out of his head. He had often planned taking this gun to New York and blowing that prick away.

Slowly falling apart in poverty was not a way to go. Tim thought again about tonight's episodes of *Two and a Half Men* and if he should go home and watch them. Maybe do this some other day or maybe never. Tim's life was not flashing before him like he expected it would. All he saw in his high was a hallucination of Charlie Harper wearing a Pompano Diamond Strikes bowling shirt, telling him to go home and have another drink and stay alive. "Winner," the vision kept repeating. Tim contemplated that maybe the final formality of "it all flashed before my eyes" was only reserved for those who have no control over the outcome.

Another minute of soulful contemplation could not deliver a workable permutation or a logical way forward. Tim squeezed the trigger of the pistol. The hollow-point bullet entered his mouth faster than the speed of sound, and exited with such momentum that his entire head exploded instantaneously. Brain and remnants were scattered over a wide radius. Tim's headless body slumped to the ground. Blood streamed onto the concrete.

On the ground next to Tim's slumped body lay one of his business cards that read:

Mr. Timothy Flanders

Wishes To Apologize For

His Behavior on the Day/Evening

Of _____

Tel 561-212-1826

A woman rollerblading along the cycle path screamed.

A man across the street heard the gunshot and called 911.

A light rainsquall started unloading precipitation on the gruesome scene.

The yellow police tape that indicated the extent of the gory incident would be up for many days while city workers cleaned up the mess.

The spent bullet lodged high in a palm tree a block south and wasn't ever recovered by forensics.

April 2nd 2014, from the Tampa Bay Times

FLORIDA MAN MISTAKES DEAD WOMAN FOR APRIL FOOL'S MANNEQUIN

A Florida man at a Tampa Bay apartment complex for seniors nonchalantly disposed of the body of a resident who'd jumped 16 stories to her death. The worker mistakenly thought that her corpse was actually a mannequin left over from an April Fool's prank. He decided the blood he saw underneath the body was red paint and then dumped the dead woman in the complex trash bins.

Apartment #2 Angel of Death

Angel Mancini's peculiar job was made easier by a self-diagnosed and fully embraced infliction of obsessive-compulsive disorder. In many ways, the successful conduct of this job was not even feasible without some variation of maladjusted eccentricity or a fully implemented "Monty Pythonesque" outlook on life. Each night, Angel was ritually asleep no later than 9 p.m. A pressed uniform sat ready at the end of her bed and a homemade lunch waited in the fridge. She would sleep for exactly eight hours and always with her Siamese cat Halo snuggled by her side. Each day, Angel clocked into a suburban office complex at exactly 7 a.m., and she hadn't once turned up late for work. In the "death and taxes" quotation, you could say her job was as steady a gig as being an IRS agent, minus the grief of customer feedback. Remarkably, Angel had never suffered from nightmares and fortunately didn't ever dream about work.

Aside from her personal excitement of being a first-time homeowner, the day after Angel bought Apartment #2 of The Beach House was in all but one way like any other. Following a breathtaking scenic sunrise drive, Angel arrived at her office and immediately picked up her task sheet for the day. Detailed on this official document was a set of jobs that needed to be completed during her eight-hour shift. Angel then entered a cool, climate-controlled room in the basement and unlocked a numbered drawer that corresponded with her written list. The drawer, when fully opened, revealed a long, gray, airtight, polyester bag. Angel slid this weighty sack onto a sterile medical gurney and wheeled it into her private examination room. Once unzipped, the bag revealed a fresh human corpse that required her professional expertise. Angel was a Forensic Examiner at the Palm Beach County Coroner's Office. Had his head not been missing in its entirety, she would have instantly recognized Mr. Timothy Flanders, her new next-door neighbor, as being her first patron that particular day.

Cause of death was obvious, Angel thought to herself, as she inspected with a knife and tweezers what remained of the spinal cord. Angel's favorite tool of her job, a skull-opening pulsating power saw, wouldn't be needed for this case. Nor would an in-depth examination to determine cause of death. The head was clean off, with the few fragments of skull and brain tissue the crime scene team had managed to collect sitting in a separate evidence bag next to the body. These remnants showed all the signs of a close-range firearm discharge from a single hollow-point shell and matched exactly the police report sat on her desk.

Angel had examined many suicides over the years and this was a clean and decisive act. Often you could tell from the state of the skull that there had been a last-minute change of plan, culminating in a slow and agonizing finale for the victim. Angel would have a boring job if every cadaver were this easy to establish a reason for death. She filled in the bureaucratic paperwork and swiftly photographed the body from every angle. Angel made a grisly business look simple and effortless. Tim Flanders would be just one of many corpses that would pass through her watch today. The subsequent bodies had heads attached, a few required opening up with the pulsating power saw and none others she personally knew.

Angel was raised in Hallandale Beach, an aspirational enclave of Floridian suburban sprawl. Her family lineage was pure Italian. It had taken generations of slow migration for the clan to make their way from Newark, the fresh-off-the-boat first stop, and down the East Coast, ultimately finding their way to the Sunshine State. Although they had lived all their lives in Florida, the family apparently worked especially hard to retain their New Jersey twangs. Angel's father was a low-level company man with a large blue-chip corporation based in Miami. Her mother was a middle school teacher and homemaker. The family was strict Catholic in the modern twisted notion. Angel was exclusively educated at parochial schools as it was deemed a necessity by her parents to avoid the Godless Florida public education system.

As a child, Angel had always been fascinated by death and dying. It was more than the obligatory rebellious teen phase of listening to heavy-metal music and burying teddy bears in the back garden. Her "calling", as she would phrase it, came at the age of fourteen when her grandma unexpectedly died. As per family tradition, there was to be an open-casket wake. This funeral, with its Catholic pomp, a beautified body sat centre stage and its entire glorious morbid splendor, captivated young Angel. From that day on she knew she wanted to pursue a career in the world of death. Angel was a smart cookie and identified this to be a financially savvy move. Florida was a place where people came to die, and a job in the back end of the death business was always going to provide steady employment.

While her friends babysat and worked at beach cafés through school for their flash-cash, Angel took a weekend job at a funeral home. She started as an assistant at the front desk and quickly moved up to the position of body embalmer. Mortuary homes typically have a high staff turnover and are only able to attract employees who couldn't usually hold down a job at the local Waffle House. Angel took great pride in her work and she was the best employee they ever had. Her specialty was making dead bodies look like Hollywood stars for the coffin. By the time Angel graduated High School, she held the title of Deputy Funeral Director. Cincinnati College of Mortuary Science would be where she earned her undergraduate degree, and she finished this a semester early, debt free, with honors.

Angel's fascination with making the dead look good was merely a roadway to what she really wanted to do. Her ambition was to find out exactly how and why people died. A further two years of graduate schooling in New York would see her become a qualified Forensic Investigator. Shortly after certification, she landed a job at the Palm Beach County Coroner's Office. Angel's family approved of her career path, although her mother not so secretly dreamed she would marry into European royalty – an Italian prince, to be precise.

In Palm Beach County, if you die and are not in the presence or under the care of a medical professional you are promptly deposited at the morgue. Florida State law dictates that you must be examined for a cause of death within twenty-four hours. Angel's job as Forensic Investigator was to slice, splice, photograph and document every aspect of the body and verify a precise cause of death. This in itself was a challenge and required thoroughness and tremendous skill. To cut open a body, a specially designed pulsating power saw was used to sever hard bone without causing damage to soft tissue. This was Angel's go-to tool of choice and she prided herself on being able to crack open a cranium with just two incisions. Angel's other specialism was cleaning up bodies beautifully at the conclusion of a full autopsy. With her funeral-home experience, Angel knew the difference a clean autopsy could make at an open-casket service. Upon completion of her work, she would have the individual stitched up and reconstructed so they looked just as good or even better than they did when she first rolled them out of the cooler. Angel loved what she did, even if her daily visual was death and the accompanying smell was often indescribably grotesque.

At the prime age of twenty-seven and with a solid career, Angel couldn't understand why she was so unlucky in love. Her driving license statistics listed her as five foot two inches, one-hundred-and-six pounds with hazel-colored eyes. Her mirror reflection showed long black hair, naturally brown skin and a proportioned bikini-ready body. A casual onlooker might have suspicions that her breasts were possibly just too good to be real, and possibly they were just that. Angel dressed well, with many of her garments carefully collected at vintage boutique stores. She wasn't a supermodel, and in Florida there were plenty of those around, but she possessed a natural look that fully deserved the admiring glances that came her way.

Angel lived an obsessively healthy lifestyle. She had never smoked – but who would if they cut open the black diseased lungs of those who'd died of cancer on a daily basis. Angel ate well and knew not only what clogged arteries looked like but also exactly how they ruthlessly killed you. Angel was a lover of the beach, but factor 50 and sunset dips were her way, as she'd seen first-hand the gruesome effects of skin cancer. As well as a strict regime of clean living, she enjoyed the virtue of safe living. Angel knew the parts of South Florida that were dangerous by linking the bloodied and bullet-holed gang bangers that she ran autopsies on with local newspaper reports. She then stayed clear of those urban regions.

Most of her friends were Southern girls who had a gun in their apartment, or in their handbags, and sometimes both. In her educated opinion, pepper spray and limited karate were all the protection a woman needed. Angel had witnessed first-hand on the slab that being killed with your own weapon was a more likely scenario than using it safely for self-defense. She could easily afford a new car, but her ride of choice was a station wagon older than she was. As dangerous as I-95 was, Angel had never had anyone in the morgue extracted from the wreckage of a solid old Volvo. Drugs were a big no-no in her world, as she knew from toxicology reports that narcotics alone often wouldn't kill you but the junk dealers added did. What a way to die, she would say to herself when she was opening up the mostly "too young" who had succumbed to an overdose. Angel knew she was mortal, but her aim was to not end up in her office as a punter – even if that meant, when cycling, she would wear a motorcycle helmet, a luminous vest and be the lone person to make a full halt at stop signs.

Angel's neurotic tics came at a cost, with a flatlined love life being one of the most prominent. She was hit on at bars and there were always guys at the beach asking for her number, but that wasn't what she wanted. Angel was looking for a connection, for love, the sort of romance that occurred in nineties' Tom Hanks and Meg Ryan movies. The pool of eligible bachelors wasn't exactly rich in South Florida between the crooks, drug dealers and assorted deadbeats who called the State home. The physically attractive men who entered her realm often came too late, with their first and last date being in the morgue. When this happened, Angel would fantasize as she cut open their rib cages and prodded their groins with a scalpel that this man could have been her Mr. Right. All she could do, though, was investigate how they'd died, wonder how they might have lived and speculate what could have been if they'd previously met. If Angel were in a rom-com movie, the hot guy lying on the table would unexpectedly spring to life in that brief moment of time after she'd ashamedly and unprofessionally checked out his whopping manhood and seconds before she was about to open him up with a revved and roaring power saw. Of course, this ripped Lazarus would be sensitive, kind, good to his mother and worship cats. Angel had never come across anyone with a pulse in the morgue, although she knew from her training that it was more than an urban myth.

The non-stop round of friends' bachelorette parties and baby showers she attended had turned from a slight financial drain to an embarrassing barrage of boring talk, with everyone constantly saying: "It'll be your turn next, Angel." The single guys at work all adored her, but Angel's blinkered vision couldn't see past their strange eccentricities, which mostly mirrored her own and were an obvious side effect that came with cutting up the dead for a living. Angel went on dates set up by friends, but they didn't seem to go far. A combination of her cautious safe approach, in a fast-paced, swipe-right dating scene and her bizarre workplace tales from the crypt, had the effect of creating second-date excuses from suitors. Angel started to believe that maybe the smell of formaldehyde and death followed her and scared live men away. Was it in her eyes? Often she'd be out for dinner and look over at a couple or a family and think to herself that maybe they'd be waiting for her in the office the following day and that she was some sort of freak, or even an Angel of Death?

Wanting an upgrade from rental living, a financially secure Angel decided to make a jump onto the Florida property ladder. Sammy Glades, a lizard-skinned, gator loafer-wearing realtor with unsuspected motives, assisted Angel with her search. Apartment #2 of The Beach House, one block from the beach and two blocks away from the buzz of Atlantic Avenue, was exactly what she was looking for. The oversized flamingo statue that sat in the courtyard appealed to her inner nerd and was the deciding factor. Apartment #2 had been a recent foreclosure, it was less than a third of the price at the height of the frothy market. The mortgage payments would be cheaper than her current rental, so the purchase made financial sense. As she closed on the paperwork, Glades assured Angel that she was already up thirty grand and this purchase was a terrific investment. Little did she know that this sale was an inside scam and Glades had bought the property from the bank shortly before showing it to her. The scheming realtor had doubled his money via this quick flip.

It was unfortunate that Angel's first acquaintance at The Beach House had arrived at her office in a state of rigor mortis just hours after they'd met. She didn't take this as a bad omen, but viewed it as an odd coincidence and promised the situation wouldn't reinforce any personal paranoia. The mood around The Beach House after Tim's suicide was downbeat. He was a popular guy and all of Delray Beach mourned. Angel never told any of the other residents that she herself performed and signed off on Tim's autopsy, and thankfully nobody asked.

Tim's landlord was quick to empty out the apartment. He was unhappy to lose a month's rent, but looking at the glass half full, he was relieved that Tim had the decency not to do the deed in his unit. He would've had to search hard and wide for some incredibly strong-willed Haitians to clean up what would've been a horrific mess. Not to mention the personal liability if the bullet had gone through the wall and heaven forbid injured someone in an adjacent unit. After a thorough hose-down and a brisk paint job, Apartment #1 was speedily put up for lease. Bob, a New York retiree whose claim to fame was that he'd invented the Long Island Iced Tea, became Angel's new neighbor.

Angel had her little piece of tropical paradise redecorated in a traditional Florida style. The walls were painted pastel blue and an accent of pink crown molding was added. She finished the hardwood floors in a dark teak color. Angel bought a new pair of oversized wicker chairs and an antique coffee table for furnishings. She had a Murphy bed custom built into the long wall of the studio's enthusiastically labeled great room. Local Delray scenes adorned the walls and plantation shutters finished off the classic look. During the day when she was at work, Halo her cat slept in a Coroner's Office storage box after refusing to use any of the fancy kitty baskets she had purchased. Angel had an old retro stereo system that played her favorite country music on vinyl, and she was quite partial to belting out Taylor Swift and early Shania Twain tracks. Angel didn't have a television and went out of her way to avoid the local evening news, as it always had a chance of spoiling the surprise of what might be waiting for her at work the next day. However, she was an avid reader of newspapers and took both *The Palm Beach Post* and *Sun-Sentinel*. Angel prided herself on doing all her own housework and kept the apartment industrially clean and to the same sterile standards of her examination room.

Initially, Angel felt like a fish out of water at The Beach House and found it difficult to relate to her neighbors. Her first and last meeting with Tim Flanders was the tip of the iceberg in terms of bizarreness. Although she easily settled into her personal space of Apartment #2, the manic craziness outside those four walls was something different altogether and would take an adjustment on her part to settle in. Angel quickly became aware that some of the men at The Beach House seemed to be stalking her. She could barely put a towel down by the pool before an apartment door would open and one of the guys would non-coincidentally come down to "hang out" with her. Many times two would arrive at the same time and they would race each other for the closest seat. Bodie was a bartender at a local pub, Jacob was a married schoolteacher attending rehab and Ethan a middle-aged chain-smoking wood worker. There was also an older gentleman who looked very much like Rod Stewart. And they had all asked her out on a date within days of moving in.

Angel also made a point of avoiding a neighbor by the name of Pete, after being told that he worked for the Florida-based tabloids. Her cautious instincts perceived he might try to use her for the inside scoop at the Coroner's Office. After all, they did have the occasional celebrity stiff enter the building. Pete seemed mysterious, but on the whole not quite as creepy as most of the other male residents. At the very least, during the few times she had briefly seen him exit his apartment, it was evident that he possessed a shirt. In contrast, Gabriel from Apartment #5, the one with the non-matching door, was sans upper-torso garments at all times. This man, gluttonous belly bulging, would stand outside his front door and gawk at Angel whenever she left her apartment, returned home from work or dared to venture outside. Angel was convinced that each time she was poolside, even if Gabriel wasn't at his front door, he was peeping at her from behind the blinds. A spooked Angel carefully carved out a position at the pool where Gabriel's vantage points were obscured by shrubbery. She was told he had a wife, but this woman was constantly holed up in the apartment and she hadn't yet seen her.

The "ladies" who called The Beach House home were another subspecies of Florida life altogether. Physically outnumbered by men in terms of mass, they commanded more than their Beach House share of drama, gossip and air. Angel noticed how many of these women personally entertained a steady stream of gentleman callers, with the style of the entertainments evident from the noises that echoed around the courtyard at random times of both day and night. If these gals weren't busy screwing, they were certainly screaming and of course sometimes both. Angry encounters ranged from drunken yelling down the phone to objects bouncing off walls during fights. When things got out of control, police call-outs were a regular occurrence. Angel sometimes wondered if she was the only woman in the building who even held down a full-time job.

Colleen, from Apartment #7, spent her downtime before and after "appointments" of an undetermined nature sitting at the pool, doe-eyed, courting attention and playing the men of the building off each other. Angel was certain she had some sort of trust fund, as she hadn't talked about work in the past, present or future tenses. Rebecca, the better half of the Apartment #9 household, bantered big about having an easy system to make stock-market riches. Evidently she hadn't implemented it, as each month she was scrambling to pay her half of the rent from the small amount of money she made from part-time jobs. Emily, from Apartment #11, worked at a beachfront bar as a waitress. Angel was certain from the variety and quantity of men that exited her place that a "night with Emily" must be on the "specials" menu. Then of course there was Bessie, wife of Gabriel. Angel hadn't actually ever seen her, and with the strange vibe she got from Gabriel she wouldn't be surprised at all if Bessie was in pieces stored in the freezer.

The women at The Beach House were initially frosty towards Angel. She believed they felt threatened by a young professional woman moving into the building and rustling away some of the in-house male attention they thrived on – not that Angel was intentionally courting any of it at all.

Angel's induction to The Beach House wasn't at all what she expected and she felt like she didn't quite fit into the funky scene. Angel couldn't decide if that was because of her untraditional career path or because she actually had a career at all. There was certainly a core of transiency and aimlessness holed up in those other eleven little units. Almost every day when she came home from work awaiting in the courtyard was a throng of residents and their collective entourages smoking, drinking, taking drugs and generally living it up. She began to question if any of them even had real jobs. Yes, some of them drove worker vans, but she saw little evidence of them actually going to work. If they did, it must be at the most for half days. Angel had a job and a career, and needed to keep regular hours, but everyone else seemed to be on party time 24/7. Angel had comprehended very quickly that her neighbors at The Beach House were an odd assortment of strange and bizarre characters.

Angel eventually learnt the story behind the mismatched door of Apartment #5. It was the result of an escalating dispute between Bessie, Gabriel and the other Beach House apartment owners. It started a few years ago when Bessie, then newly elected president of the condominium association, using her mandated authority, started handing out citations for violations of minor rules. At first these were dished out to renters for small infractions, like using the washing machine after 10 pm or parking in the visitor's space for more than twenty-four hours. Bessie proclaimed: "The rules are there for a reason and enforcement is essential to maintain order." Bessie reminded the other owners that her actions were being conducted in the all-important interest of maintaining "property values."

Angry tenants complained to their landlords about the Draconian decrees that infringed upon their civil liberties. These owners, who wanted no more bother than cashing a monthly check, formally complained, citing a continued harassment of their tenants as unacceptable. Bessie and Gabriel upped their "New Sheriff" roles and vigorously carried on with their clean up operation. They brought in more rules and commenced with the enforcement of other regulations previously buried deep in the mostly unread condo articles of incorporation. Each new regulation would sinisterly be posted on the laundry-room notice board in the middle of the night. Towels left on loungers unattended would be seized and destroyed. Music was not to be played loud on public holidays. In an Orwellian move, a video camera was mounted in the laundry room to provide evidence used in assistance for the naming, shaming and fining of those residents who didn't clean out the lint tray in a satisfactory manner.

The rule that finally proved to be one too far was the implementation of the "overnight guest registry book". Officially, this log, which was administered by Bessie and Gabriel, was to be kept for security purposes and to be readily available in the event of a fire so authorities could establish an exact head count. However, it was seen by the residents as an impediment to their carefree way of life and the official documenting of their personal sexploits, as many of the overnight visitors who stumbled into the building could be termed "dirty stopovers." Not only did residents not want guests to be logged into any guest books, but also their hosts rarely had any recollection of their actual names.

The final straw came when a lady friend of Randy Showers, from Apartment #12, tried to make a discreet early morning exit. Gabriel, seeing an unregistered car parked in front of the building, staked himself out on the patio waiting to pounce on this undocumented visitor. As Randy's date, which happened to be someone else's wife, did her sunrise walk of shame, Gabriel, clipboard in hand, conducted a full-court press interrogation. The screaming and yelling that broke out woke up the entire building and it took the combined efforts of several residents to hold back Randy, who was seconds away from administering serious bodily harm to Gabriel. Soon enough, there was an emergency homeowners' meeting called. In the following coup, Gabriel and Bessie were booted from their seats of power and replaced by a junta of absentee owners.

Bessie and Gabriel, not taking their dethronement as a lost battle but the start of a war, retreated into their three-hundred-and-ninety-six-square-foot bunker. The bitter pair plotted a guerilla-style campaign against the board of The Beach House and anyone else that happened to get in their way.

The latest maneuver was to fight the legality of the building's much-needed repainting. Gabriel had a legal injunction that dictated his front door was part of the personal property of Apartment #5 and not within the jurisdiction of the condominium common grounds. He did this by exploiting a mistake in the poorly written rules and regulations. Due to this, the painting of his front door was technically an illegal act. The painter backed off from doing his job when confronted by a shirtless, court-paper-waving Gabriel. A grubby and filthy white door has since remained. A second suit they filed argued that the building had been repainted in colors that varied from the original scheme. A local ordinance Bessie and Gabriel had found said that a building within the city limits of Delray Beach couldn't change its exterior color without first getting approval from the city's planning department. The condo association had not followed this procedure, and Bessie and Gabriel were asking a judge for financial damages and the building to be repainted in its old color scheme. Angel didn't recall Sammy Glades disclosing any of this mess during the escrow process. What she hadn't realized was that the slippery realtor, eager to make a clean sale, had binned a large chunk of the minutes from the last few association meetings. He had considered these legal notes as dysfunctional and an obvious hindrance in clinching a speedy sale.

After a few months of living at The Beach House, Angel's life had settled into a new rhythm and she began to slowly transform as a person. She even warmed to a few of her fellow residents, although some still creeped her out and the couple from Apartment #5 were on another level of crazy altogether. Every now and then Angel would chill after work and partake in the occasional beer on the patio with whoever might be there. Without even noticing, she began to shake off her OCD neurosis. Some nights she even stayed up past 10 p.m., and on occasion she was spotted cycling around town without a crash helmet.

Angel felt happy in life and truly blessed. She began to feel that The Beach House would become a special place for her. She had a fantastic career, even if you couldn't talk about it over the dinner table, and she was now a homeowner, albeit a small slither of real estate in what at best could be described as a "transitional pocket" of zip code 33483. Angel was independent and financially stable and not at all worried about money.

The final piece of the puzzle for Angel was to find love. A soul mate would be ideal, but she knew the odds of that happening were stacked against her. Her biggest worry was ending up like a sun-baked Bridget Jones with nothing but a cat to keep her warm at night while she obsessed over gray hairs as her circle of friends transitioned their status to happily married. It was late spring in South Florida and Angel felt it was the perfect moment to seize the day and launch her own personal love quest. She wanted to settle down and possibly have an opportunity to bring some life into her world of death.

November 27th 2014, from the Tampa Bay Times

A FLORIDA MAN ACCIDENTALLY SHOT HIMSELF TO DEATH AFTER THREATENING TO KILL HIS GIRLFRIEND'S DOG

A Florida man picked up a revolver and threatened to shoot his girlfriend's dog, Police said. He then pulled back the hammer on the gun to emphasize his threat. As he tried to release the hammer, the gun fired while he had it pointed at his face. He was pronounced dead at the scene. The man had originally gotten into an argument with his girlfriend over a misplaced cigarette lighter.

Apartment #3 Atlantic Crossing

If I listened long enough to you
I'd find a way to believe that it's all true
Knowing that you lied, straight-faced, while I cried...

As the band with its aged mop-haired singer stood center stage and belted out a rendition of Rod Stewart's *Reason to Believe*, the railroad crossing lights on Atlantic Avenue began flashing furiously to the beat of roaring bells. This beautiful sound of Americana warned that a freight train was fast approaching Delray Beach on the tracks of the Florida East Coast Railway.

In a sing-off with the train's ferocity the band stood no chance and instinctively wound down the song they'd started a mere thirty seconds before. The whole of Elwood's, or whatever they now called the old gas station turned restaurant on the corner of Atlantic and NE 3rd, groaned and shook from the vibrations of the never-ending train. The sound was unbearable at this short distance, even though they had recently modernized the level crossing in an effort to lessen its monstrous growl. These whistle-blowing rumbling trains were so loud they could be heard a mile away at The Beach House.

Rodney Sawdust preferred Elwood's before it was gentrified as part of the wave of so-called progress that had swept through town like a biblical plague. In its old incarnation the toilets smelt of steaming urine and the only beer on tap was domestic. There was no air conditioning and atmospheric cigarette smoke legally lingered. Some things had managed to remain as they were, though, as Elwood's was still at heart a biker bar.

Rodney looked out at the crowd of mostly college kids, tourists and a few older locals, the bikers being much too cool to be seen at a Rod Stewart tribute show. He was lucky to have this steady Tuesday night gig. Tonight, Rodney was just a soundtrack for this crowd and far removed from being a main attraction, but it looked like all in attendance were having a blast. The train roared on, with extra locomotive engines mid-section indicating this was one of those two-mile beasts headed for the Port of Miami. It could easily take fifteen minutes to pass through town.

Rodney Sawdust, formerly Ian Sawdust, was born in the early 1930s to a working-class family in the British city of Southampton. He grew up during the Second World War

German bombing campaign over England, and his earliest memory was of being thrown into an Anderson shelter that sat in the back garden giving protection against the deadly blitz bombing raids. His father was killed on Gold Beach during the D-Day landings. His mother, hastily remarried badly to a man who thought nothing of using the lash as a parenting aid. Brutal economic austerity followed the end of war. Rodney's only escape from the grimness of the time was via Hollywood movies. He spent his school days dreaming about going to America and making himself a career in show business.

Ian left school at the age of fifteen without qualifications and took a position with the Cunard shipping line. His initial job was as a waiter on the New York route. He would always recall that first time arriving in Manhattan by sea. The Statue of Liberty was larger than life, the Empire State Building, at the time the tallest building in the world, dominated the smoke-filled skyline. The boundless optimism that New York oozed was truly inspiring. By the early 1960s, planes had made passenger liners unprofitable and transportation by sea morphed into leisure cruising. Ian auditioned for a role within Cunard's expanding talent and entertainment team. Before he knew it, a microphone was thrust into his hand and he was doing a routine as part of the ship's variety act. Following one performance, an agent from California slipped him a business card and the next thing he knew he was working the Vegas club scene. He married a showgirl called Betsey, got a Green Card and for a while lived a suburban life in North Las Vegas.

Comedy, as many things, is a young man's game. It was the early 1980s and he thought he was still funny and had it in him, but the management and possibly the audience didn't. Ian lost his spot at the Sahara, his agent dumped him and his wife left him for head of security at the Aladdin. Ian bolted from Vegas and took the train to Branson, Missouri. He figured being a former big Vegas fish in a small Branson pond would give him a fresh start. It didn't happen. The comedy of 1985, even in the Midwest, had gone edgy and urban, while Ian's style was pure old-school slapstick. At the age of forty-six Ian was a divorced singleton working as a manager of a family restaurant in Kansas City.

Stopping for an after-work pint at his local English pub turned out to be Ian's salvation. His drinking hole had jumped on an '80s bandwagon by shipping in a state-of-the-art karaoke machine from Japan. After warming up with several pints of strong bitter, he grabbed hold of the microphone and, with a random selection of song choice, belted out Rod Stewart's *Maggie May*. He was so good that the entire bar begged for an encore. His follow up, Stewart's version of *Drift Away*, had the house in tears. Ian was just a few years older than Rod, and with a fantastic head of hair and an English accent (Rod Stewart was a plastic Scotsman born in London) looked and sounded like the great man himself. Ian's voice was a little less gravelly, and actually sounded better than the real deal. Ian took this warm reception as a good omen. He subsequently quit his manger job at the Kansas City eatery and made his return to the world of showbiz as a Rod Stewart tribute artist.

In the late '80s Ian legally changed his first name to Rodney for career purposes and left the "Paris of the Plains" for Palm Beach County. South Florida not only had a great tradition of live music but was also the part-time residence of Rod Stewart. The real Rod had even attended one of his shows. He carried a photograph of the two of them together in his wallet that had been taken at the performance. Rod Stewart loved the concert and joined Sawdust on a duet of *Downtown Train* for the show's encore. At seventy-five, Rodney Sawdust still had it in him. He worked a steady four days a week performing shows from Vero Beach in the north down to Lauderdale by the Sea to the South. On occasion, he ventured over to Naples and entertained the little old ladies of the west coast. Even in his golden years he looked the spitting image of Rod Stewart. For kicks, he would sometimes go down to South Beach and let the local paparazzi corps follow him around and take pictures, as they believed he really was Rod Stewart.

With the train still grinding through town, Rodney reverted to some of his old comedy gags to help fill the dead air. It didn't go down well with the young crowd, who, out of embarrassment for him, stared into their drinks at best or totally ignored him at worse. Even the bearded hipster bar manager gave him a death stare that read, "Cut the comedy pronto."

Whether he liked it or not, Rodney was stuck in that entertainer's purgatory of being successful because of someone else, but actually having more talent than the person he was able to professionally imitate. He had written his own songs, but no one wanted to hear them – all they wanted was Rod Stewart classics rolled out in quick succession. This was the kind of issue he didn't like to think about too much, otherwise it would slowly eat him up from the inside. Rodney just had to keep calm, carry on and realize where and how his bread was barely buttered.

Finally, the train passed through town. The barriers raised and the backed-up traffic and crowds on Atlantic could continue on their way. The band started up and Rodney belted out what they wanted to hear. His set tonight would be starting with *Reason to Believe* and, some fifteen songs later, finishing off with *Maggie May*. He would always come back for an encore whether the crowd asked for it, deserved it or wanted it.

The great thing about gigs at Elwood's was that afterwards Rodney would let the band pack up the gear and he could walk home to The Beach House. It was late spring, hot but not yet sticky, so at this time of year it was a comfortable stroll. He would usually make a detour for a nightcap at one of the local bars. Walking down the now quiet Atlantic Avenue, he passed by the old Colony Hotel before making his way over the Intracoastal Drawbridge. He waved to Jimmy, a by-choice homeless man with a signature spider's-web tattoo covering his entire face. He was sitting on his regular bench just east of the bridge.

Now in his sixties, Jimmy never traveled without a top-of-the-range laptop computer. He plugged it into a city sidewalk power point that, by design, was meant to juice up the street's palm-tree illuminations. Jimmy wasted away his night's courtesy of the town's Wi-Fi playing *Call of Duty*. Few knew that Jimmy was ranked twelfth in the world at this video game, and fewer still that he was a three tour of duty Vietnam Green Beret. He suffered constantly from nightmares relating to his time in 'Nam. Jimmy was personally haunted by the unforgettable sound a Viet Cong trooper made when he slit his throat in hand-to-hand combat. Playing a war simulation video game was, for him, remedial therapy.

Rodney walked through the door of The Blue Anchor. This was Palm Beach County's most famous British pub. The exterior paneling had been shipped over piece by piece from an old London public house that legend said was frequented by Jack the Ripper. Its battered interior and grubby carpet was so authentic that on a stormy day, when looking out of its stained-glass windows, the brain was tricked into thinking you were actually in England.

Bodie, who lived in Apartment #8 of The Beach House, was tending bar tonight, so the drinks would be stiff and cost no more than a tip. Bodie was bulky enough to break up bar brawls, and with his mild-mannered disposition was well suited to dealing with drunks. He was not fat, just big – the kind of large man that American hormone-infused food had been churning out for decades. His hair was thin and his skin, for Florida living, paler than it ought to be. His face exuded an element of despair and hopelessness that could easily be exploited by a carnie fortune-teller. Bodie had the manner and look of a man suited to serving a life sentence of pub work, although if that were to be his final judgment it was for a crime he didn't commit.

Bodie dressed sharp and always wore a big smile. He greeted Rodney with a wave and automatically poured him his regular – a pint of Newcastle Brown. The Blue Anchor was one of Rodney's favorite haunts. Not only was the beer warm like it was meant to be, but it came in an imperial pint, not the shrunken American one that was technically a pre-independence English colonial pint. Rodney thought it was odd that everything in America was bigger and better – except a simple pint of beer.

Rodney supped his ale and, like the old horndog he was, scanned the bar for female options. It was late and a weekday, so at best the goods would be limited. In the far corner of the room near the dartboard he saw a dressed-up Angel Mancini, who had recently moved next door to him at The Beach House. She was sat with a group of her gorgeously well-dressed girlfriends. Rodney thought there was something very hot about her. Partly it was the freaky job that was a turn-on, partly it was that cute little body he had seen poolside and partly it was that they shared a common wall. Angel was always so magically dressed the various times he had encountered her out on the town, all glam in her vintage understated outfits. Rodney had half-heartedly asked her on a date when she first moved in. His problem was he was a little too much method cover artist for the realities of the actual world. Sometimes he would come back from a gig all fired up and in the zone, and really think he could do what Rod Stewart could. So, at seventy-five, he would often embarrass himself and hit on girls that the real Rod Stewart might well be able to bed. He, though, an aging Rod Stewart impersonator, had little chance of scoring with any of these prospective conquests. Angel had been gracious or maybe just shocked by his advances, but hadn't seemed to hold it against him and was cordial when they crossed paths. Rodney knew he was a good soul and in the grand scheme of life would tag himself a "harmless old geezer." As hot as Angel was, though, he did hope that when his time came, he wouldn't end up being sliced and diced by her in the morgue.

"Little bit quiet tonight?" said Rodney to Bodie, who was lazily drying glasses behind the bar.

"Mid-week, end of season," Bodie answered, while noticing that Rodney was looking intensely with deep concentration towards Angel and her surrounding cohort.

A party of late twenties, early thirties preppy-looking men that Rodney assumed to be wealthy from their perfect teeth, designer threads and over-confidence entered the pub. After scoping the scene they planted themselves at the opposite side of the bar from Rodney and adjacent to Angel's party. In a move that reeked of Palm Beach arrogance, they sent a round of drinks over to the girl's table. Personal introductions by the men speedily followed. From Rodney's position he could tell the ladies warmly welcomed these overtures and both parties became absorbed in flirtatious chatter. Rodney followed up his pint with a free-poured whiskey on the rocks. Buzzed, he left a tip for Bodie and eased slowly off the barstool. He waved towards Angel as he left The Blue Anchor, but she was captivated by flatteries from new friends and didn't notice. Rodney, envious of these guys with their youth and gusto for life, exited into the night.

After leaving The Blue Anchor, Rodney staggered east on Atlantic. Taking a left at Andrews Avenue, he passed the dapper homeless guy who kept unofficial guard at the corner real-estate office from a city bench. Rumor had it that this well-dress indigent had a day job and money, but liked barrier-island living without the hassle of paying rent. Whatever the reason, this man was a permanent fixture at the corner. A flash of brilliant lightning stole the street's darkness. Thunder sounding more like a B-52 carpet-bombing campaign than a natural oddity was prompt enough to indicate imminent trouble. A belting tropical downpour broke the still air. This was one of those violent Florida storms that hit you before you knew it, and even though Rodney was only two blocks from home it would be impossible to outrun.

Out of breath, drenched but not cold, Rodney arrived at the door of his apartment. As he closed it, visible from behind the building's flamingo mascot he saw Pete, his other next-door neighbor, making the dash from his vehicle towards apartment #4. Pete, who was laden with camera equipment and oversized luggage, had been away on assignment for several weeks. It must have been to a far-flung sunny destination as he'd acquired a deep tan that no sensible Floridian would volunteer for. Rodney admired his neighbor, as out of all the people holed up at The Beach House he figured Pete was the one living the dream.

Rodney stripped off, tossing the sodden clothes into his shower cube and changed into something dry. He took a bottle of Red Stripe from the fridge and sat down in the leather armchair that gobbled up one corner of his apartment. Taking a swig from the beer, he looked around at the three-hundred-and-ninety-six-square-feet of airspace that, for seven hundred a month, he called his own. An Englishman's home is his castle, but this place barely scraped in as a crumbling Martello tower on the fortress scale.

The little unit contained his entire worldly belongings. *What did he have to show for his life?* Rodney asked himself. *A few pieces of old beaten up furniture at best!* Rodney slept on a pull-down bed that, much like him, had seen better days. Even that was not his, as it came with the apartment courtesy of the landlord. A forty-inch flat-screen TV, no doubt outdated by the time he'd unpacked it from the box, hung opposite his bed. That he owned, albeit after a year of layaway. On the one free wall not taken up by furniture was a collection of personal photos that illustrated the story of his life in a mixture of black and white and faded color. There was Ian as a child in England, and on the cruise ships performing as a young man. Among the dozens of photos was a lone wedding photograph buried behind fishing-trip snaps from the Bahamas. Of course, in the collection there was that photo of him with Rod Stewart. There wasn't much space on that wall for any more pictures, but perhaps there didn't need to be.

Rodney looked into the long mirror that was in the hallway. The artificial light on his face really showed his age. He glanced over at the "Flamingos of Florida" calendar hanging on the wall and saw he had a gig in Lake Worth the following day. He knew there was always a friendly crowd at that venue. Rodney finished off the last of the beer, throwing the bottle into the trashcan. Above it hung a dusty framed signed copy of the artwork for Rod Stewart's seminal 1975 album *Atlantic Crossing*.

Rodney reached over to the old turntable that sat next to his bed and put on a 12-inch vinyl record. He pulled the Murphy bed down flat and laid on it, looking up at the peeling ceiling. A camouflaged lizard, almost unnoticed, was sleeping in the corner of the room. Rodney pressed start on the record player.

When are you gonna come down

When are going to land

I should have stayed on the farm

I should have listened to my old man...

The opening lines of Elton John's *Goodbye Yellow Brick Road* tenderly played through the crackle of the vintage vinyl.

If truth be told, Rodney – or Ian, as the persona he was never able to shake out of his soul, and the one that he still dreamt as nightly – didn't really care much for the music of Rod Stewart. He didn't even possess any Rod Stewart records in his extensive collection. In fact, he detested Rod Stewart's music.

However, he was thankful and forever grateful for the modest third career that had allowed him to eke out a shabby middle-class American dream. Yet this was just kind of a cool job in entertainment and not really a passion. If Ian hadn't, by chance, stumbled upon his Rod Stewart voice or personal likeness, and transformed it into a paying job, he might still be working in that Kansas City restaurant. Possibly he would have made his way to Florida anyway as most English people in America seem to, and maybe he would have found a cashier's position at Publix or become a Team Member at Walmart.

Ian really liked the music of Elton John. Now that for him was musicianship. Elton with Bernie Taupin constructed the lyrics and tunes together. They were proper writers, professionals, a partnership and a team. Rod Stewart had most of his material written by other people or just covered songs, but he was good and a master of what he did. Then there were the five wives and eight children. That showed great swordsmanship, willingness to spread your genes to the wider world, tolerance of divorce payments and logistical expertise in juggling obligations. Ian did admire this side of Rod Stewart and wished he had a fraction of that pulling power. The mansions all over the world were a slick touch. This was a man who had the castles. Take all that away, though, strip it down to the artistry and Stewart didn't have the subtle musicianship of Reginald Dwight, aka Elton John. If Ian had the skill and the look, and could do it all again, he would do it this time as an Elton John cover artist. Well, apart from the gay business, which as a traditional "meat and two-veg" Englishman he'd no time for. Ian's cover shows would stop in the mid-1980s when people assumed but didn't know that Elton was homosexual. Of course, by then, the best music of Elton John, much like that of Rod Stewart, was all in the rear-view mirror anyway.

In between the dead time that separated *Goodbye Yellow Brick Road* and *This Song Has No Title*, a freight train could be heard rumbling through town to the east and the storm thundering its way west.

March 16ᵗʰ 2014, from the Orlando Sentinel

FLORIDA MAN DRESSES UP AS RAMBO, SHOOTS UP BAR AND STILL GETS ASS KICKED

A Florida man who did not enjoy his nice evening at a Palm Beach bar returned later all decked out in Rambo gear, lugging what the Sheriff's Office described as an "Uzi-style assault rifle" and a pair of hunting knives. The man challenged several patrons inside the lounge. Two customers stopped the Flagler County resident and grabbed the barrel of the gun, and one or two shots were fired. Two men subsequently wrestled him to the ground and knocked him unconscious. The faux Rambo was charged by the Sheriff's department with two counts of aggravated assault with a deadly weapon, and two counts of aggravated battery with a deadly weapon.

Apartment #4 Dirty Laundry

In his thirty-five years of existence on this planet, Pete Alexander had a poor track record with women. He had previously been in love twice and on both occasions had his heart broken. There was Manhattan Helen, with whom he'd had a high-octane transcontinental romance. It started with casual flirtations in Los Angeles following an introduction from a mutual friend. It moved onto arguing and hate in Europe after a serendipitous bumping into each other on the London Underground. A year later, from nowhere, it unexpectedly blossomed into love and debauchery on the South American continent – pure *Romancing the Stone* with a whirlwind engagement to follow. As fast as they found steamy love in the jungle, it all turned to icy-hate somewhere in New York City. Helen's mother was the catalyst of the paralysis, because a paparazzo photographer, without an Ivy League degree, who opted for blue-cheese dressing on his salad, wasn't ever going to be good enough for her daughter.

Then there was hippy Marie from San Francisco. They dated forever, but she couldn't deal with Pete's crazy travel schedule and crazier still work hours. It didn't help that she was Bay Area born and bred, and had no inclination of leaving that land of fog and hills. Pete was bound at the hip to Tinseltown, the city of the stars, the place he made his lucre. Marie wouldn't believe Pete when he said that he was on a long stakeout or the phone service in the canyons cut out. Those three-hundred-and-sixty-five miles that separated them might as well have been a light year. Jealousy, distance and timing killed it. For Pete, finding love again had proved much harder than bagging celebrity scoops.

Pete was raised in a middle-class Long Beach household. After graduating from High School, he studied photojournalism at Malibu's Pepperdine University. He finished college in the late '90s with a stack of student loans that a lifetime of news photography couldn't repay, so he had to think fast and find a way to clear his debts. Observing a posting for "Trainee Paparazzo Photographer Wanted", he made a hard ninety-degree career pivot away from his newsman dreams. Pete was hired as an apprentice to a bushy-haired photographer of Levant lineage who had the unfortunate problem on stakeouts of being mistaken for a terrorist. This lack of blending in with the environment often led to police call-outs, SWAT raids and ultimately "game over" on undercover news stories.

Pete was a perfect fix for the veteran paparazzo in need of a stealthy wingman who could blend in with his surroundings, as in appearance he was ordinary in every possible way. He sported average hair, was an average height, and owned an average body weight. In terms of complexion, Pete was a non-descript variety of generic white. His everyday dress style was what could be termed "Californian normcore." He was simply someone who didn't draw the remotest element of attention. All this blandness was useful, because being too good looking, too ugly, too short, too tall, too fat, too well dressed or any other deviation of regular had the side effect of marking your card, getting yourself noticed and making you stick out. And these were all unwanted side effects in a profession where stealth was the key to success. Pete's regular, boring, unthreatening look was to be an occupational asset in every possible way.

Pete had other positive skills he brought to the job. Not only did he have a background in journalism and the technical ability to work a camera, but he also possessed a plethora of contacts in the celebrity-rich stomping ground of Malibu. Pete knew, or knew of, all the important players who resided in the "Bu", as locals tagged their famous town. Through student connections, Pete was on good terms with the drug dealers, who in that part of the world serviced a predominantly A-list clientele. Pete's student peer group included celebrity spawn studying easy majors who wouldn't think twice about dishing dirt on their famous friends and family in return for cash. Although he found the most reliable of his sources proved to be the poor students on partial scholarship studying challenging degrees such as physics, business and pre-med. Out of financial necessity they often worked at local stores and proved to be motivated sources for celebrity sightings and gossip. They appreciated and depended on the money that came in return for these tips. Through Pete's numerous contacts, he had the twenty-seven miles of scenic Malibu wired.

Pete's specialty was long-lens photography and undercover surveillance. He had the patience to sit for hours on end waiting for that big payday money shot. He detested the street photographers with their "short-and-flash" ambush style of shooting. Those guys were ruining the business in Los Angeles and gave skilled paparazzo like him a terrible rap. For Pete, the sign of a job well done came when the first time a celebrity realized they had been "papped" was when he or she was standing in the line at the supermarket and saw themselves splashed on the pages of the magazine they were guiltily gawking. Within two years of starting as a paparazzo photographer, Pete was in business for himself, had paid off his student loans and had purchased a condo in Santa Monica. He considered buying in Malibu, and could have easily afforded to, but his sensible motto was "best not to shit where you eat!"

Pete knew it was time to escape from Los Angeles when actor-turned-politician Arnold Schwarzenegger introduced questionably unconstitutional privacy legislation. Florida, being lawless by nature and nurture, had no privacy laws on the books or any intention of creating them. Compared to California, there were only a few photographers working that part of the world so it presented opportunities. Pete sold his pad and headed east to the Sunshine State. He also hoped and believed the change of location might kick-start his low-yield love life. Those women in California all wanted to be stars, or friends of the stars. They sighed and gasped when average-looking harmless Pete revealed his not so average, in their view, harmful and disgusting profession.

There had been a wishful belief by the jet set that what happened in Florida stayed in Florida. Once Pete landed "in-country", he made sure that wasn't the case, and anything and everything that went down in his patch was speedily made available for public consumption. In the world of paparazzi photography, the more celebrity skin on display, the higher dollar value a picture fetches. Florida's searing heat made shirtless and bikini the quintessential local couture, and it was a place where stars felt relaxed, carefree and safe from the constraints of Hollywood. That steaming humidity seemingly acted as an aphrodisiac that stoked illicit affairs and encouraged crazy antics. For in Florida, stars not only got into trouble but they would get into the kind of big life-changing trouble that fitted neatly onto tabloid headlines.

Tabloid journalism was in the DNA of South Florida, with Palm Beach County being the historical base for all the supermarket tabloids. For Pete, living in the belly of the beast of the dirty laundry business didn't hurt. He would frequently wine and dine with the boozy hacks of the *National Enquirer* at their favorite spot, The Hawaiian Tiki bar in Lantana. Pete spent his first year of Florida living in the insanity that is Miami Beach, as he believed the location would be ideal to cover the close-by celebrity action. However, he quickly realized that high-value targets were popping up all over Florida and the Caribbean. Pete found he was spending more time on the tarmac of Miami International Airport and riding on the turnpike than he did working South Beach.

A tip about Sofia Vergara took Pete to Delray Beach for the first time. The *Modern Family* actress was dating a low-level city politician and he dashed up there to chase a lead that their relationship had hit the skids. Pete instantly fell for this slice of old Florida charm, and after a brief hunt bought Apartment #4 of The Beach House. The place was modest, and he could have bought bigger, but for a guy who spent his life on the road or hiding in a bush, this was about as much space as he needed. Pete redecorated the pad in a jazzy style, and for furnishings he went mid-century modern. Upon completion, the interior of Apartment #4 looked like a miniature version of the *A Clockwork Orange* house sans the "ultra violence."

When not on assignment, Pete decompressed in the laid-back bubble that was The Beach House. He found the residents an odd, somewhat transitional group of individuals who, between them, had managed to attract more than their fair share of life's hard knocks. Pete would like to think that in a time of need this group would do anything for you, but in reality they'd be too stoned or drunk when push came to shove to be of any practical use. However, he knew their intentions were good and occasionally even one of them would come up with a solid story lead.

When Angel Mancini presented herself at the fringes of Pete's world, it turned his life upside down. Upon first encountering Angel, with her porcelain olive skin, toned body and chic dress sense ripped straight from the pages of *Glamour* magazine he was intrigued. Angel was gorgeous – not the faux beauty of the celebrities he chased each day, but a down-to-earth look that would be near impossible for a Beverly Hills plastic surgeon to replicate. When he saw her from his window on that first day, as she was moving in her possessions, he was infused with that manic feeling he often felt on the job. It was the belief that if you missed the shot, you had most likely lost the chance to break that once-in-a-lifetime story and pissed away a unique opportunity that had been placed before you.

It was certainly love – or maybe lust – at first sight for Pete, although Angel had barely acknowledged him, saying no more than "Hello" the few times their paths had crossed. This was often the case for Pete, as he found that his average looks and mannerisms didn't draw attention or interest from those of the opposite sex. After Ethan from Apartment #6 had revealed Angel's bizarre vocation, Pete's interest moved up an additional Defcon level. It wasn't the fact he thought Angel could unethically land him an exclusive on the next Anna Nicole Smith-style celebrity corpse, but that finally he'd found someone in a profession that was more misunderstood than his own. Pete was now smitten, in full pursuit mode and was more determined than ever to win the heart of this beautiful new neighbor.

Pete's wooing of Angel wasn't going to be what was considered normal. He would conduct this pursuit exactly as if it were one of his assignments. Thorough research, methodical planning and precise execution would be the modus operandi. Of course, Pete couldn't account for chance or friction, but he would factor in personal genius. Within weeks of Pete first setting eyes on Angel, his mission was well underway. With the help of a source at the Sheriff's Department, he had – with dubious legality – run the license plate of Angel's car. He then passed the acquired DMV records over to his Boca Raton private eye who conducted a full and detailed background check on Angel and her entire family.

The dossier handed to Pete revealed that Angel was twenty-seven, unmarried and more importantly, never married. You'd be surprised how many Florida women in their mid-twenties had ex-husbands or, even worse, husbands who had been dumped but still remained legally attached. Angel might well have baggage, but at least it wasn't binding in law. Her personal finances were golden, with a lofty FICO score and no student loans. Angel's salary was high and came with a gold plated pension. Angel and her entire clan had no criminal records. This was a must, because if things were to get serious, as Pete hoped they would, he didn't want the prospect of bailing anyone out of jail. Pete had once dated a girl working at the *Globe* who turned out to be running a Lake Worth pill mill in her spare time. When her side business was busted, he got the call to make her bail. It was at the most inconvenient time, as he was hiding up a tree waiting for Cameron Diaz to hit the beach.

Health and well-being, especially mental-health well-being, in the magnet of crazy that South Florida is, required a high level of special due diligence. In the old days Pete had easy access to private medical records. As well as being totally illegal, this was now almost impossible following the arrest and imprisonment of a nurse who had been caught peddling celebrity details. The next best thing to official records was the piecing together of clues and evidence obtained from the primeval hack tradition of dumpster diving. Pete had learnt this skill set on his first week of tabloid training. The results of this dark art gave an excellent indication of the health, habits, comings, goings and personal diet of an individual. Discarded credit-card bills, airline tickets and info-filled notepads showed shopping practices and travel plans. From tossed food containers you could efficiently work out a dietary blueprint and general eating habits. Evidence of prescription drug use and medical conditions could be obtained from thrown out RX bottles. Booze empties, beer cans, half-smoked joints, drug paraphernalia and discarded condoms would establish an accurate level of hard living.

In order to avoid a nasty critter infestation in Florida's tropical climate, it's essential to take your trash out daily. This Angel did each morning, throwing her garbage in the building's dumpster in the brief time period between leaving her apartment and driving to work. As soon as she had driven a block from The Beach House, which Pete could see from his window, he would sneak down to the bins and retrieve her discards. As it was such an early occurrence each day, and The Beach House residents were heavy drinkers, sound sleepers and late risers, there was slim chance of these clandestine actions being compromised. After analyzing a week's worth of Angel's trash, the results were exactly what he'd hoped for. From the food wrappings and banana skins he gathered she liked to shop healthy and eat well. Angel's credit-card bills showed she didn't have any compulsive shopping habits. There was no evidence of hard partying or drug use, but most promising was her dumped reading material. The well-thumbed-over advice columns in *Cosmopolitan* could only be a positive indicator of adventurous potential between the sheets.

Surveillance, much like stalking (a word that Pete detested), is a case study in learning patterns and habits. Angel's particular patterns, Pete had quickly observed, were obsessively regular in their nature and simple to follow. Her early exit for work each day was signaled by the distinct creaking noise her weather-beaten front door made as it stubbornly opened. The unique chirp of her aftermarket car alarm when turned on or off indicated the imminent departure or arrival of her vehicle. Pete used these audible signals to track her comings and goings in a logbook that was usually reserved for celebrity movements.

The next piece of research for Pete's dossier on Angel was straightforward. Trawling through her social media, he deemed her to be straight and looking for a serious, meaningful relationship. He found that her taste in music, books and films was near enough to his so that with some minor bluff they had commonality. Angel was a big fan of country music, especially the early albums of Taylor Swift before she went pop and sold out. Pete had plenty of real-life stories about his personal encounters with Ms. Swift that he could entertain her with. He found out that Angel was a big Robert Frost and Beat-era poetry buff, and so would Pete be once he studied up on these '60s legends. He would then insert this newfound knowledge into his developing game plan. After a few clicks of the mouse Pete had a selection of mutual interest books, CDs and magazines shipped to him. He made sure he had plenty of props readily available so that if Angel ever ventured into Apartment #4, her instant awareness of their like-minded interests would propel the conversation in a "Wow! We have so much in common," direction.

The most important nugget of knowledge and a possible deal breaker for a romantic proposition is: "How does the mother look?" It's essential to establish this before too much time is wasted, as it's well known that eventually all daughters, for better or worse, end up looking exactly like their mothers. This vital reveal was confirmed to Pete on a Sunday stakeout at the Mancini's Hallandale Beach home. Pete easily tailed the family to church. Hiding in a park opposite the service, armed with his telephoto lens, he obtained the photo evidence he needed. It was good news – Mrs. Mancini had a great figure and looked absolutely stunning for a woman of her years. Angel had obviously inherited fabulous genes.

The final stage in the pursuit of Angel was going to be a little more difficult than tracking down a celebrity target, hiding in a car or behind a sand dune, and then clicking the shutter. As brave as Pete was on daily jobs, he was far slicker at taking out targets from a distance than making new acquaintances up-close. This was possibly his greatest flaw, and asking Angel on a date would require an element of human interaction that on a typical day he went out of his way to avoid. As with an exclusive story there was also some pressure to work quickly. Angel was beautiful and single, and in his experience (mostly celebrity related) ladies like that don't sit around in this status for long. This was a mission he didn't want to be scooped on.

Pete needed to ask Angel out in a casual, friendly, neighborly manner so that if she declined, he wouldn't have to go out of his way to avoid her at The Beach House. That wasn't as hard as you would think, as he had a lock-down on her schedule and daily movements, but it was a level of grief he was eager to steer clear of. One day Pete tailed Angel discreetly to Publix with the plan of nonchalantly bumping into her at the salad bar and striking up conversation. However, he aborted the mission at the last minute on the grounds that it was a little close to being lifted from the playbook of a serial killer. The perfectly orchestrated encounter needed to come across as totally random. He wanted to catch her distracted, on the fly and with limited time at her disposal. Pete needed just enough space to move the narrative forward and set up a date without too much time on the clock to allow for a crash and burn. In essence, he wanted a tabloid teaser line that sucks your attention and reels you in to buy the magazine as you're curious and want more. He wanted some banter, an introduction, and a suggestion they should meet up again when they both had a window and were less busy. Dinner, perhaps, he would casually put out there. Once he had her alone on a date, he knew he could charm her. Actually, he didn't know for sure, but he had a sporting chance and was up for the challenge.

Pete's amended plan was to catch Angel alone in her comfort zone of The Beach House and make his pitch. That wasn't so easy, though, as the rare times Angel was around she rapidly attracted attention. He'd observed her on the front patio reading a book and within minutes Gabriel, under the guise of going out to check his mail, was standing beside her making small talk. On one occasion Angel popped down to the pool and, like magic, Bodie had plunked himself down on a lounger next to her with obvious intentions. It wasn't that Pete couldn't hold his own with his fellow residents – it was just that he didn't need them trying to muscle their way in and becoming competitive rivals. That would be like a paparazzi scrum at the Federal Court House. In order to get a good shot you had to fight and use elbows and sometimes bite, and these were situations Pete believed in this particular situation were best avoided.

"The laundry room!" Pete said out aloud amidst a beer-fueled brainstorming session in the confines of the mission headquarters of Apartment #4. Those coin-operated rust buckets would be a great enabler of casual small talk. The problem, though, according to Pete's notes, was that Angel didn't have any particular pattern of doing laundry. He suspected she might do most of it at her parent's house. Possibly she'd been told by Rebecca to watch out for her washing being rifled through. There had been some alleged panty rustling last year from the laundry room. Randy Showers of Apartment #12 had been a little too quick to point the finger at some mysterious kids he had seen running from behind the building at around the same time as the theft. On the other hand, Rebecca not only relished attention, but also had a fertile imagination, so it was hard to pin down the truth.

It would have been way too old-school romantic and time-consuming for Pete to sit in his apartment, looking through a cracked blind and waiting for Angel to exit her door, dirty laundry in hand. Pete had a more sophisticated modern set-up to solve this issue efficiently. In his kit bag he kept a discreet wireless surveillance video camera that could be placed anywhere to provide a live feed. He used it regularly on intense stakeouts where you couldn't risk being seen waiting in a vehicle or the story would be blown, such as Brad Pitt, Justin Timberlake, Monaco royalty or other paranoid celebs who needed or thought they needed bodyguards and protection. Pete would put the tiny camera looking out in the direction he wanted to watch and then lay down flat in the back of his vehicle and view the feed remotely via his iPad. All an inquisitive celebrity or security detail would see was an empty car. Pete placed the camera above the entrance of The Beach House laundry room next to the exterior light. He added to it a motion detector trip that would start the feed as soon as someone entered or left the room. Each time this happened, Pete received a notification and would check to see who had triggered the camera.

It wasn't until late in the evening on the third day of this operation that finally his monitor showed Angel venturing into the laundry room. Pete sprung into action and grabbed his ready-to-go prop hamper, and after giving himself a precisely calculated buffer headed out to make the intercept. His aim was to avoid walking in on her while she was loading in lingerie or anything else that might destabilize the equilibrium. He had timed it so that he was approaching the back of the building clutching his own hamper as Angel was exiting the laundry room's door.

Pete's timing was spot on; as he approached the back of the building he saw Angel exiting. She was beautifully dressed in a pink tank top and denim Daisy Dukes. Her hair tied back in a tight ponytail. Pete himself was purposely over dressed for performing regular errands.

"Sorry, I just put some wash in," Angel said apologetically in her Jersey twang as their paths finally crossed.

"No worries. It's late and I'm in no hurry," he said before adding, "I'm Pete. I don't believe we've formally met!"

"Angel, Apartment #2," she replied while holding out a soft hand for the shaking.

Pete could smell her sweet perfume in the crisp evening air.

"You might be my new best potential source at the Coroner's Office from what some of the neighbors are telling me," Pete said immediately and mistakenly as he deviated from the over-rehearsed script.

"And you might be the neighbor I need to avoid being seen talking to again if I want to keep my job," Angel replied as she passed by him heading towards the front of the building. Angel then looked back towards Pete and said, "I know what you do!"

"Dirty jobs, both of us!" Pete replied in a shouting voice as she moved further away from his position.

Angel expelled a sigh, "Mine is a noble profession and at the end of the work day, I can assure you there's no blood on my hands."

"You're a tough cookie!" replied Pete as he sensed he had already struck out.

Angel turned her head back towards him and shouted: "You should see me with the bone-cutting pulsating power saw on fast mode!"

Trying to keep her attention he responded, "I can almost feel it slicing down my back."

Angel walked around the building to her apartment door. Pete wasn't far behind and caught up arriving at his own door as she was fumbling with her keys. Pete was sweating a little too heavily for a cool evening and had Angel noticed she would have seen the damp patches under his arms.

They both inserted their keys at the same time. Pete looked over to where she was standing. That one studio apartment that separated them felt to him the distance of two junctions on I-95.

"Good night Pete," she said, idly.

Seizing the now or never moment, he went for the deal clincher before his chance expired. "What are you doing tomorrow night? I thought we could have dinner." Pete was now on script, although his concentration distracted by the mental visual of Angel standing naked in the morgue holding her bone-cutting pulsating power saw. He followed up with a quick verbal insert, "I'm interested in hearing about your work, what you do. We both have unconventional jobs."

"I'm always happy to have dinner with a new neighbor."

"Tomorrow night work for you?" he asked a little too excitedly.

After a pause with a follow up that Pete felt could go either way, she said, "Knock on my door at seven."

Emily from Apartment #11 could be seen watching Angel and Pete's interaction from the window of her second floor unit. It was hard to get away with anything at The Beach House.

Angel and Pete both entered their apartments at the exact same time and closed their doors in synchronization.

Pete viewed the "knock-on-the-door" request as a positive omen. The formality of banging directly on the apartment door of another resident at The Beach House was a pleasantry that never occurred without a proper invite. The usual manner of inter-apartment communicating was shouting across the courtyard, or directly at doors, often at ones that were closed. For the more advanced community members a few had recently adopted text messaging. The unofficial Beach House rulebook with its "If the trailer is rockin' don't come a-knockin'!" etiquette interrupted the specific summons by Angel with its time and day request to be a sign of an official date.

Angel was quick to lock the dead bolt as soon as she closed the door to her apartment. She had purposely not given Pete her telephone number. It was more than just the concern he might hack into her voicemail, as she knew that's what shady journalists did, but a real fear was that he might pass it around to others at The Beach House. She had gone out of her way to keep her number private. Angel sat down on her sofa and contemplated the encounter with her neighbor. Angel's mind quickly wandered to what might be waiting for her at work the next day before her train of thought switched back to the dinner with Pete she'd just agreed to. It wouldn't be so bad; he looked and seemed harmless and at least would wear a shirt. Angel thought that Boston's would work for a venue. If it was a real date she would've picked somewhere fancy and romantic, but this was just a friendly meal with a new neighbor. Halo the cat jumped on her lap and licked her hand.

It was midnight when Pete's phone rang; the caller ID display showed London's *The Sun* newspaper. He accepted the call.

"We've Geronimo coming 4 p.m. tomorrow at the expected location," said a gruff Cockney accented man in a hushed voice.

Pete hung up the phone. He knew exactly what this meant, and had been waiting for this assignment for over a year. Kate Middleton, the Duchess of Cambridge, the next Queen of England (taking into consideration the bypassing of Camilla) was on her way to the tropical retreat of Mustique Island. Pete had a standing arrangement with *The Sun* editor that if they got information this was "going down", he would get the lucrative job. Princess Kate in a bikini was the biggest prize of them all in the celebrity picture world. This could potentially be a massive payday and major bragging rights amongst his paparazzo frenemies. Pete switched on his computer and booked himself out a series of flights the next day that would eventually get him to this most private of private islands in the Caribbean.

Angel left for work the next morning in a quixotic mood and for the first time she admitted to herself that her neighbor Pete was intriguing in numerous ways. She had always thought he was kind of cute, in a non-conventional, average dorky way, and with his line of trade might at least have interesting stories to share. Over lunch she found herself thinking a little harder about the choice of outfit she'd wear that night than she usually would for a casual dinner with a friend. She also thought a less crowded venue might be more appropriate, only so she could better hear those celebrity stories of his. That afternoon at work Angel had an extra bounce in her step, a feeling that she'd not recently felt. Angel found herself racing home along I-95 a little quicker than her cautious usual self did on a regular day, wanting the extra minutes gained to fully prepare for the evening. As Angel excitedly arrived at her apartment door she saw a hand-written note taped to it.

HOLD THAT DINNER. BEEN SENT ON SECRET SQUIRREL ASSIGNMENT. WILL TAP ON YOUR DOOR WHEN I AM BACK IN A FEW DAYS.

As Angel read the note, she found herself being a little more disappointed than she thought she would have, considering this wasn't really ever a proper date that had just been postponed.

Pete's big-earning assignment, anticipated to last a few days, didn't go down quite as he had hoped. He arrived at this little jewel of the Grenadines well in time to capture Her Royal Highness landing at the airport. However, the Duchess was a no-show. The information was "a little off," said the newspaper in London. They insisted that she would arrive any day and ordered Pete to stay put. That was fine with him, as he wanted to "nail the big one." Unfortunately, a day turned into a week, and when she did arrive his big exclusive tip had turned into a media feeding frenzy. Half of Fleet Street must've been on that plane with her. So much for that intelligence the paper had promised was coming from "a deep Palace insider." The way Pete thought he would be working this blue chip tip was stealth like shooting through the porthole of a hired fishing boat. The Princess would have no idea he was even there documenting her every bikini-clad move. The clumsy royal hacks who arrived en masse immediately alerted island police to their presence and it became totally impossible to sneak unnoticed near the hotel where the Princess was staying.

The following day an armada of a dozen boats arrived outside Kate's beachfront villa, each crowded with long-lens-wielding press photographers and their accompanying sun-baked blunts. In an arranged deal, Pete, along with everyone else, got pictures, but they were the shots Buckingham Palace wanted released and not the ones he needed. Not happening was the "cottage-cheese legs" snaps, the "gotcha nip-slips" and those "shaking the sand out of your bikini bottoms" frames – or in fact anything else that the tabloids relished. In place were carefully orchestrated photo ops. The Princess would be documented picking up trash on the beach with dusty natives and strolling on the island formally dressed with Prince George. All great Buckingham Palace fluff, but sadly no paparazzi payday.

Pete was on assignment in Mustique for two long weeks. He detested this type of "pack-job," with everyone sharing and lapping up each nugget of flack-fueled press management. Never again, he told himself, would he work a royal story. He was bored of the banal banter the British press herd thrived on. It usually consisted of new and ingenious ways of hustling their employers out of bogus expense claims and the continued quest for the most effective remedies for hangovers and sunburn. Pete was relieved when the Duchess finally left the islands and headed back to England so she could, as the news release stated, "Get back to work." As far as Pete knew, Princesses didn't really do much work; they produced heirs and spares and perfected the skill of waving.

Angel, as suddenly as she thought about what might have been the result of that perspective dinner date, that wasn't really a dinner date, engrossed herself back into the sanctuary of her career. It was a traditionally busy time of year with plenty of overtime to pick up. Angel constantly wondered if it was a seasonal change that made people die in ever weird and crazy circumstances at this time of year, as the frequency of deaths related to objects and substances inserted into the anus always spiked.

As hard as Angel worked she continuously found time to play, with an abundance of girlfriends with gossip to spill and secrets to share. It was on one of these slightly tipsy dressed-up nights on Atlantic Avenue that Angel believed she'd finally met her dream man. This was quite by chance as she was headed home after dinner, but at the last moment she and her old school friends decided to stop for one last drink at The Blue Anchor. The girls were hit on by what they initially thought to be a group of very over-confident men. One of them, by the name of Simon Godfrey, was twenty-eight years old, tall, blond, blue eyed and handsome. He was the son of a Palm Beach banker, a graduate of Duke and currently working as a Broward county high-school teacher. He told her that in the fall he intended to start a JD degree at University of Florida's Levin Law School. For Angel, it was love at first sight.

August 16th 2017, from the New York Daily News

FLORIDA MAN SHOOTS GUN OFF DURING STRIP CLUB SELFIE

A Florida man's gun selfie at a St. Petersburg strip club badly backfired. Police said a Tampa resident went to the bathroom at Club Lust to take a picture of himself posing with a gun. Somehow the gun discharged and the bullet went through to the women's restroom next door. Luckily no one was injured. The police arrested the fleeing man shortly after the incident. Officers said a gun, ammunition, Xanax and marijuana were found in his possession. The Florida man told authorities, "I was just trying to take a selfie."

Apartment #5 The Wolf's Lair

In the regular ebb and flow of friendships at The Beach House, most residents had, at one time or another, been inside every other apartment in the building. It could be for a casual dinner, to smoke a spliff, borrow a screwdriver or, more often than not, to collect on a loan. On a multitude of occasions these cultural inter-apartment exchanges had ended in the spilling of blood or swapping of bodily fluids. However, there was an exception to conventional Beach House warmth – over the years not one other resident had ever set foot inside the domain of Apartment #5. This dearth of neighborly spirit was at the sole discretion of its owner-occupiers, Bessie and Gabriel Garlech.

At first glance, Bessie and Gabriel, with their sturdy Germanic build and homely cracked smiles, seemed pleasant enough. Upon further investigation, though, it was evident that they were quite possibly as mad as the Hatter in *Alice's Adventures in Wonderland*. Yet madness wasn't the exclusive reason to avoid the Garlech's home space. Another deterrent was the vile stench that oozed from their door whenever it was opened; a toxic blend of sweat, cigarette smoke and over-recycled stale air. This lack of hospitality offered from Apartment #5 never became an issue for the greater community, and neither was it taken as a snub. It was merely noted as the natural order of life around The Beach House. The Garlechs cherished the status quo, and not only had no interest in anyone ever stepping inside their near four-hundred-square-foot homestead, but also lived in constant fear of this event ever coming to fruition.

Bessie and Gabriel were on a perpetual war footing, currently dedicating their full efforts and resources to a long-running feud with The Beach House Homeowners' Association. Initially, it focused on protecting the territorial virtue of Apartment #5's white front door. In the broader construct, this "Doorframe Defense," as they labeled this phase of their campaign, was the opening salvo of a counterattack that the Garlechs hoped would bring a victorious conclusion to their multi-year quarrel. With their toxic agenda and constant litigation, Bessie and Gabriel had alienated themselves from most of the building's residents, and communication with other owners only occurred via legal letters. The battle they started might have seemed like a good idea when initiated, but mission creep, stubborn foes and unpaid legal bills had them now looking for a way to exit a war that was slowly bleeding them dry.

Bessie and Gabriel hailed from Paraguay's barren hinterland. Their blond hair, blue eyes and Teutonic build were inherited from seldom talked about 1940s German ancestors. The South American upheaval of the '80s pushed the pair to seek a better life in the United States. And with *Flipper* and *Gentle Ben* reruns being the mainstay of Paraguayan TV, Florida became an obvious destination.

The United States of America doesn't make life easy for those newly arrived. Lady Liberty obliges the "Huddled Masses" for one reason only – to create a pool of cheap labor ripe for exploitation. When Bessie and Gabriel arrived in the "Land of the Free," they found themselves stuck in a revolving door of entry-level jobs with low pay without benefits. Paycheck-to-paycheck and trailer-park-to-trailer-park described the first decade of their American Dream.

An Unleash the Businessman Within convention in West Palm Beach would provide their ticket to the land of the middle classes. The Garlechs, self-empowered after discovering their latent business acumen, but not being able to afford a Subway store or Laundromat, handed over their savings for the next best thing. They purchased the franchise rights to sell high-end American-designed monogrammed toilet seats in the just-about-to-explode Indonesian market. The self-anointed captains of industry, with help from a stack of DVDs, a suitcase of product samples and a crate of catalogs, set themselves to work. Bessie and Gabriel took care of marketing and sales in their territory, while the production and shipping was handled by the Peruvian sweatshop and distribution center operated by the franchisee. The Garlechs were classic middlemen who, with the assistance of the new-fangled World Wide Web and by keeping unsocial nocturnal hours, were able to ply their trade in the East Indies from Florida.

Business grew slowly but steadily as the good people of Indonesia upgraded their toilet hardware with American-motif seats. Their best-selling item during the first year of business was a non-authorized *Baywatch*-inspired toilet lid and seat set. Numerous Indonesians of the 1990s started their days by placing their butt cheeks on the smiling faces of C.J. Parker and Mitch Buchannon before dropping their wolf bait. By 1995 the Garlechs, with newfound financial stability, left the trailer park behind and purchased a slice of The Beach House. What they hadn't realized, as they signed the escrow papers, was that The Beach House of this era was more *Road House* than the "sedate living by the sea" the realtor proclaimed. The Garlechs' new neighbors were a mixture of a fresh-out-of-jail, and a soon-to-be-back-in-jail, basket of Floridian deplorables. Bessie and Gabriel, with their Germanic DNA, relished the chance to bring order and stability to their newly acquired lebensraum. The Garlechs called an emergency meeting of condo homeowners and made an impassioned pitch to take over the reins of leadership. Bessie and Gabriel were unanimously voted in as Chairwoman and Chairman of the Board, with the building's slumlords being only too happy to pass over their obligations.

So, armed with a mandate and a copy of The Beach House Handbook, the Garlechs began a program of systematic, no-prisoners-taken, implementation of the rules. A tip-off to local bounty hunters relieved the building of its most troublesome tenants. Litter pickup, parking enforcement, new gardening detail and noise ordinance all made The Beach House instantly more livable. The "Abandoned Towel Theory," adapted from social scientists Wilson and Kelling, would be the foundation of combating anti-social behavior. If a beach towel was left unattended at the poolside for more than two hours, a warning letter was sent to the offender. A second violation and the towel was promptly deposited in the dumpster and a fine issued to the culprit. From his front-door perch of power, Gabriel and his hawk-eyed attention to detail became the enforcer who brought back middle-class stability to what had become a de facto seaside project. With the raising of living standards at The Beach House came the ability to attract a better class of resident. Within a brief period of time property values improved and apartments began changing hands at double the price Bessie and Gabriel had paid. The majority of the new buyers were investors and speculators, whose primary concerns were rental yields and profit margins. This new crop of owners had no inclination of how the Garlechs had transformed The Beach House from a mini ghetto back to borderline respectability.

The Beach House in general may have become a more cordial place, but within the walls of Apartment #5 the cozy harmony of married life could not defy the drag of gravity. Two individuals living, working, eating, shitting, chain smoking and possibly, on occasion, copulating, in a space that, according to the County Assessor's office, wasn't big enough to park two Ford pickups in, was enough to make anyone go crazy. A counter argument could be lodged, though, claiming that you had to be crazy in the first place to freely volunteer for this type of living arrangement. When the monogrammed toilet-seat trade was booming, the Garlechs were industrially preoccupied throughout the night and slept all day. However, a changing business environment, due to competition from Chinese imitators and altering Indonesian tastes, led to a slowdown in commerce.

Bessie and Gabriel now found themselves with free time throughout their previously busy nights. Gabriel invested these acquired hours researching and obsessing over outlandish conspiracy theories. His particular favorite belief was that a group of Jews, under the direction of Queen Elizabeth II and financially backed by the Rothschilds, was working together with the sole aim of destabilizing Western liberal democracy. Their plotting was allegedly conducted from a secret underground command center in the Yukon that would leave any foe of James Bond envious. Gabriel assured himself that this cabal was behind the 9/11 terror attacks and the banking crisis of 2008. He proclaimed that they currently planning a new "Big One." The deeper Gabriel delved, the more riddled with paranoia he became. He was certain that this scheming clandestine group was now onto him and tracking his every move. To become invisible from the "New World Order of Jewry," he let his driving license and passport expire, and removed his name from the deed of title to

Apartment #5. Gabriel needed to be undetectable to the world in the event he had to bug out when the shit hit the fan.

It was during this period of Gabriel's obsessive and freaky behavior that shirts and shoes became redundant and his day-to-day wardrobe was downsized to just one pair of swimming shorts. It also became apparent that regular bathing with soap was eliminated from his life. A distinct musk, noticeable to anyone within a fifteen-foot radius of him, developed. As he paced around the grounds of The Beach House, Gabriel could be heard saying to himself, "I smell like a real man and not some cock-sucking Jewish queer."

To take his mind off the impending revolution, Gabriel devoted larger portions of his expanding downtime to step up the enforcement of rules at The Beach House. These efforts became more apparent when an attractive female tenant or guest appeared in any of the building's common areas. Although Bessie sympathized with her husband's conspiratorial views, she dedicated her newfound hours to studying online law courses. Engrossed in this, she became less and less willing to leave her apartment, only departing in order to pick up cigarettes from 7-Eleven or to do a shopping run at the local Winn-Dixie supermarket. However, with Gabriel stepping up the Gestapo-style patrols around the building's pool and patio areas, Bessie developed a jealous streak, as she believed every woman in The Beach House had the goal of seducing her husband. Eventually, it got to a point where Bessie wouldn't let Gabriel leave the building's grounds alone, being scared that, left to his own devices, he might be corrupted. As long as Gabriel was on The Beach House grounds, Bessie could keep an eye on him and make sure the building's "loose women" didn't entice him. With Gabriel's mental state fueled by ever-more far-fetched conspiracy theories learnt from dark places on the Internet, and Bessie's demons stoked by jealousy, there was an accelerating decline in cordial marital relations.

To distract them from their crumbling marriage, Mr. and Mrs. Garlech diverted their energies into expanding and enforcing ever-more extreme rules at The Beach House. With her new freshly acquired dime-store legal knowledge, Bessie would craft the dictums and Gabriel, sans shirt, would carry out enforcement. Unilaterally, the pair upped their unchecked powers to include the ability to evict residents and fine apartment owners for tenants' indiscretions. They also beefed up an ever-expanding rulebook. A twenty-four-hour parking limit for visitors and new restrictions on communal grill hours were added. The leaving of clothes hanging on the washing line overnight had also become an infraction, which, if repeated on numerous occasions, would lead to fines and ultimately the threat of eviction. Too much noise or the smell of weed being smoked quickly escalated to Police call-outs.

Yet the new rule that truly ruffled feathers was the registration of "overnight visitors." This decree proclaimed that any night-time guest who stayed for even a mere dirty stopover had to be officially signed in by Gabriel and Bessie as a visitor. Failure to do this would lead to severe consequences. As upmarket as The Beach House had tried to become, it was still at its heart an old converted motel in a lawless South Florida. The expectation of residents was that a little "no fucks given" latitude should be tolerated. To park a car in an open spot, grill when they wanted, party when they wanted, smoke when and what they wanted, bring home whomever they wanted, and do with them whatever they wanted, were viewed as rights and not privileges up for revoke. Florida (North of Dade County) was, after all, still America. Beach-towel removal seemed like old-school policing from a bygone era, as a harsh totalitarian regime became the new way of life at The Beach House.

A residents' revolt, headed by Ethan Thomas from Apartment #6, started shortly after implementation of the guest-registry statute. Owners were called and verbally hassled by tenants and en masse rent checks were withheld. Ownership had become a business for the majority, and having tenants complaining and refusing to pay rent was unneeded grief. The disruption and outrage were so powerful that an emergency homeowners' meeting was called. The owners ousted Bessie and Gabriel from the positions that had by now become their raison d'être. The new board, unanimously elected by an eleven to one vote, comprised a Stanford graduate with a minor Palm Beach County property portfolio and a Corvette car salesman from Jupiter. Their first order of business was to strike any reference to rules regarding the leaving out of beach towels on the patio from the regulations. From here on, they unwound the Garlechs' perceived tyranny.

The Garlechs, humbled by their blitzkrieg ousting from power, retreated inside the four walls of their apartment to digest the unexpected events. Gabriel, who had seen the primary threats in life coming from Jews, bankers and the Queen of England, hadn't seen this coup coming. A blindsided Bessie, who had by now studied volumes of case law and had watched countless reruns of *Ally McBeal* and *LA Law*, knew there must be some form of legal recourse if, for no other reason, than that "going legal" was "The American Way."

The following day Gabriel, with a shirt reclaimed from the bottom of a seldom-opened draw, and Bessie, who had squeezed into her finest black Lycra leggings, made the decision to lawyer up. They drove south to the Boca Raton law offices of Dr. T Bagge & Partners. Mr. Bagge wasn't quite sure what they hoped to achieve, but a fat retainer made him sympathetic to their plight. Luckily for the Garlechs, he handed their case over to an eager intern who was being billed at $125 an hour and paid a stipend of $250 a week. And this studious lawman of the future found them a brilliant angle to exploit.

Florida is lawless in all aspects except one area – condominium law. Condominium regulations are governed by the Florida State Condo Oversight Committee, a powerful Byzantium bureaucracy of vicious civil servants housed in what is the tallest building on the Tallahassee skyline. As Florida was being torn up and developed by greedy businessman in the 1960s, some bright spark in the State Legislature drafted a report titled, "The Floriapocalypse to

Come." It prophesied that unless strong oversight by the State was set up, the Florida landscape by the year 2001 would descend into decaying, underfunded cesspits of anarchic condo complexes and gated communities. This would turn the State of Florida into a Third World wasteland with only geriatric slum dwellers and alligators remaining.

The response to this report was the setting up of the Florida State Condo Oversight Committee. This quickly evolved into a heavy-handed governmental department with an IRS-sized rulebook and some of the strongest powers in the land. The department enforced strict rules for condo associations, and if they didn't abide by these, fines and penalties could be handed out. In extreme situations they had the power to take over the running of an association or sell individual units. It became the one governmental body in Florida that couldn't be bought off and you didn't want to get on the wrong side of. And the law found to be firmly on the side of the Garlechs. The law-office intern discovered that the homeowners' meeting that had ousted them had been organized with just seven days' notice. The State mandated that all meetings had to be publicly announced by a minimum of thirty days. Thus, the meeting in which Bessie and Gabriel were booted from their positions was technically illegal and whatever happened during that meeting wasn't binding and thus void. Dr. T Bagge & Partners promptly served a lawsuit on The Beach House Homeowners' Association on behalf of Mr. and Mrs. Garlech. The association was forced to respond via hired counsel. As State law dictated, they set a new meeting with a thirty-day notice period. At that meeting they made the same vote, only this time legally replacing the Garlechs. However, what they really had done was started a war.

United in rage and fueled by their victorious first salvo, Bessie and Gabriel bunkered down into full-blown guerilla-warfare mode. Running their campaign from the operations room of Apartment #5, with logistical support from their retained lawyers, they prepared themselves for a long fight. The Garlechs' hotshot law intern studied several years of homeowner accounts and association minutes. After going through these documents, he found that numerous compliance mistakes had been made by the all-volunteer board of The Beach House. These minor technicalities were passed on to the Florida State Condo Oversight Committee.

The reply from the State was no-nonsense wordy violations and fines. Out-of-date licenses and incomplete paperwork submitted caused large penalties. A hefty fee for expired fire extinguishers was followed by a mandate requiring the installation of an updated smoke alarm system at the cost of $16,000. The swimming pool was closed because the pump was not up to code. There were so many complaints being issued that the State put The Beach House on formal probation. One more misstep and they would take full control of the running of The Beach House – and charge an extortionate amount for the privilege of doing so. Monthly association fees for all owners were raised to keep pace with legal bills and mounting fines. Rent increases on tenants couldn't even keep up with these exploding costs. The new board became bogged down with onerous paperwork and was forced to run the smallest things past their own lawyers for fear of making further mistakes. The Garlechs' two-pronged strategy included bringing their fight directly to fellow residents. The prior citizen enforcement of The Beach House rules turned into permanent harassment of residents for the most petty of reasons. The asymmetric war the Garlechs launched on the owners quickly achieved its goals. It made being an owner expensive, miserable and a burden.

More lawsuits against The Beach House arrived courtesy of the Garlechs. They requested financial compensation for their dismissal from the board and back pay for the unpaid hours they'd worked doing association tasks. They now demanded a verified audit of financial accounts going back seven years. If any issues were unearthed during this audit, the State would likely step in and take over The Beach House. With legal issues swirling, and property prices sinking it had now become difficult for anyone to sell their apartments. Most mortgage lenders refused to underwrite what was now deemed a risky concern. The owner of Apartment #2, not able to keep renters in place due to the harassment by the Garlechs, let their property fall into foreclosure.

Deferred building maintenance became the next issue at The Beach House. It was precipitated by a diversion of funds set aside for repairs now being gobbled up by legal fees, while an exasperated group of homeowners not wanting to invest further cash into their money pits only inflamed the problem. Paintwork was peeling, railings began to rust and the roof was springing leaks. The landscaping team quit due to continued aggravation from Bessie and Gabriel. Unable to find new gardeners willing to work in what was whispered around town to be a "nightmare building" resulted in uncut grass and weeds reclaiming the patio. The Garlechs, through their aggressive campaign, were effectively and surely destroying the building. It was unclear to the other owners what their endgame would be. It wasn't even possible to ask them in person, as they had served restraining orders, and cease and desist notices, on their fellow owners. The Beach House had hit the skids, and was once again blighting the neighborhood.

Pete Alexander purchased Apartment #4 of The Beach House from a motivated seller for cash. Years of dealing with tabloid editors had given him the gift of being able to sense and exploit fear, and the crisis he witnessed at The Beach House was reflected in the sale price. At the subsequent homeowners' meeting Pete galvanized the dejected group of fellow owners, minus Bessie and Gabriel who were boycotting it, into taking a line of tough action. What was needed, he said, was capital investment injected into The Beach House and a big-gun bulldog lawyer to launch a counterstrike against Bessie and Gabriel. The local small-town attorney they had on retainer wasn't up to the job, being more suited to setting up trusts than dealing with quasi-radicalized terrorists. Pete said the Garlechs needed to be played at their own tough game and grinded into the ground with no mercy. In his line of business, this was a regular mode of operating.

In a unanimous vote of those in attendance, the condo association agreed to go ahead with this devised plan. The building would be repainted, the roof repaired and new gardeners hired. A special assessment was approved to pay for this work and to retain new legal representation that specialized in real-estate law. All the homeowners viewed this as the last chance of bringing the building back up to scratch and stopping the Garlechs' onslaught.

The expensively hired team of specialist attorneys from Naples went straight to work. Within a day of being put on the job, they filed a harassment suit against Mr. and Mrs. Garlech. They sought punitive damages, legal expenses and court costs for the Garlechs' "Pattern of Erroneous Hostilities" and "Frivolous Nuisance Suits." This, at least, halted the flow of incoming while Bessie and Gabriel grappled with the twist in events. The Beach House lawyers presented a solid case in court to have the verified accounts request dismissed. A crew of no-nonsense Honduran gardeners from the wrong side of Highway 441, enticed with hazard pay, sorted out the grounds and ongoing upkeep. A painter was contracted to start work on revitalizing the building's exterior. Word got out that Dr. T Bagge & Partners had dropped the Garlechs for non-payment. There was a feeling among The Beach House owners that the wrecking crew of Bessie and Gabriel were on the ropes, although this wasn't always apparent to the general observer as Gabriel continued to parade smugly around the property as if he were lord of the manor. If anyone dared to ask about the current developments he would tell them, "You wait. This is just the beginning."

The Naples lawyers efficiently put out all the remaining legal fires. Fines were paid for mistakes that had been made, and the other claims by the Garlechs were dismissed without merit. With the threat of Florida State Condo Oversight Committee takeover behind them, the audit passed, the building half-painted, and the Garlechs lawyer-less and muzzled, it looked like the worst was over. As the painters put the finishing touches to the final coat and were working on the building's trim, a new and unexpected lawsuit was slapped on The Beach House. This one came via the law office of Bessie Garlech Esq. The Garlechs no longer needed outside counsel, as Bessie was a qualified member of the Florida State Bar.

Bessie had managed to dig deep for her latest layer of litigation. The new claims made were that the assessment for painting was illegal because it wasn't on the meeting agenda within a required period of notice. It had been added spontaneously on the night as part of Pete's improvised call to arms. Furthermore, the color, a slightly darker shade of green, and the trim, a bright flamingo pink and not the original white, were in violation of local ordinances. Legally, they needed not only a homeowner's vote to change the color, but also approval from the local Planning and Zoning Department. The Garlechs demanded that the building be entirely repainted in the original color scheme at no cost to them. They also asked to be reimbursed for any legal costs associated with these violations. Additionally, the Garlechs had a court order drafted declaring their front door to be their own property and not part of the community, and thus it would be illegal to paint it flamingo pink against their will.

The following day a letter arrived from the City of Delray and a hearing was set to discuss all these code violations. A week later a notice from Tallahassee was couriered to The Beach House. This latest legal crunch had been the final straw and it was the State's intention to take over The Beach House because of a "clear and present dysfunctional homeowners association with little likelihood of change."

The Beach House lawyers took the position that in all their years of representing condominium associations, they had never seen anything like this! They wholeheartedly said the motto, "A person who represents themselves has a fool for a client," was relevant in this saga. However, they concluded that as much of a fool Bessie was in the client department, she was "fantastic counsel and knew her law." After asking The Beach House for a larger retainer to carry on representation, their first piece of advice upon cashing the check was, "Under no circumstances paint the door of Apartment #5."

There had been no movement in the stand-off between the Garlechs and The Beach House owners in several months. The Door of Apartment #5 remained a dirty shade of white and an eyesore to all. Residents had transitioned in and out of the building, including Angel who had purchased Apartment #2, and Tim Flanders who left for the great tennis court in the sky. With business for the Garlechs moribund, the residents of Apartment #5 had more time on their hands than ever before. Bessie cooped herself up in what residents tagged "The Wolf's Lair" and continued to expand her knowledge of real-estate law. Gabriel spent his days strutting around The Beach House as if he were Donald Trump roaming the greenways of Mar-a-Lago looking for new friends. The attorneys representing The Beach House found the law offices of Bessie Garlech expensive and irritating to deal with. She certainly enjoyed writing long-winded letters that required hours of billable time for an adequate response. The Beach House legal eagles made a request to the City and State for more time while they prepared their case and a full retort.

* * *

Pete's return journey from Mustique was a seasoned traveler's worst nightmare. The inter-island boat was delayed by a storm so he didn't make the turbo-prop plane scheduled to take him out of St Vincent. That delay caused him to miss the connecting flights from Bridgetown to Miami. One day of expected traveling turned into two very long days of unexpected airport lounge living. To rub salt into the wounds of what had been a disastrous trip already, Pete didn't get his preferred choice of meal on the first-class flight from Barbados to Miami. He arrived home to The Beach House late at night, tired and extremely peeved that his quick payday had turned into a mammoth non-exclusive mission that financially hadn't been worth his time.

The next day, after a long-needed sleep, Pete left a scribbled note on Angel's door. It said he was back in town, and at her first availability he would like to reschedule their planned dinner. He would've knocked, but his prior invite to do so had been very specific in terms of time and day, and so to tap on her door now would be a case of familiarity that hadn't been extended to him at this stage of their relationship. For another thing, he knew she wasn't home, as her car wasn't in its regular spot. On the note, Pete left his telephone number and an open extension for her to bang on his front door any time she wished. The knock on the door or the communication by phone that Pete expected never happened.

After their spontaneous Blue Anchor introduction, Angel and Simon Godfrey hit it off. By the end of an evening that went by far too quickly, Angel had fallen hard for Simon. They exchanged telephone numbers and arranged to meet for dinner the following day. On this second more formal rendezvous at Delray's fancy Sundy House restaurant, Angel was more certain than the night before that she was in love. As well as being great looking, Simon dressed stylishly, had perfect manners, said all the right things and made all the right moves. He didn't have any qualms about her unconventional career, and in contrast to most men she went on dates with, seemed genuinely interested to hear about it. He also had solid life goals – a trait not found in most Floridian men. Simon's family background was pure Palm Beach aristocracy, and although he wasn't a prince, she thought her mother would surely approve.

Things moved speedily along between Simon and Angel. Emotionally, Angel knew she had found Mr. Right and within a few weeks was already looking to cash in frequent flyer miles for a subscription to *Brides* magazine. Simon had a condo in Deerfield Beach and they split their time between his place and hers. He was a little suspicious of The Beach House crowd, and didn't feel comfortable associating in that blue-collar scene. Simon's long-term intentions were to be a criminal defense attorney and eventually run for office, and he felt The Beach House pack was a little too close to mixing with future clients. He could tell the feeling was mutual, sensing the "no shirt and shoes" residents were hostile towards his preppy Lilly Pulitzer dress style and patrician ways. Angel felt she had finally found her dream man. Those Shania Twain and Taylor Swift songs she sang along to in the car all seemed to make sense now. Angel felt blessed, fulfilled and full of life.

It didn't take long for Pete to realize that Angel was no longer single. Her skin was glowing and the brief walk from Apartment #2 to her car had extra bounce and purpose. There were also nights when he knew she hadn't returned home. Pete did a thorough background check on Simon Godfrey, just to see if this "too good to be true" guy was really "too good to be true." Of course, it turned out that he really was Mr. Perfect. Simon was squeaky clean and there wasn't a spec of dirt to be found. His family must have been the lone one in the Palm Beaches that got rich without screwing anyone over, taking bribes or inheriting wealth derived from slavery. Certainly, he could easily make District Attorney, and maybe someday President of the United States. Pete felt personally deflated after reading through the dossier of information he had collected on Simon, and his inner Richard Nixon inferiority complex told him he'd missed his window of opportunity.

* * *

On a cool breezy night, with a full moon eerily illuminating the flamingo statue on the patio of The Beach House, a member of the Homeowners' Association slipped onto the property unseen. The document he pinned on the laundry-room notice board, with its thirty days of warning, would prove a shocking revelation to every resident at The Beach House.

March 5th 2014, from the New York Daily News

FLORIDA MAN ARRESTED FOR HAVING SEX WITH PIT BULL IN FRONT YARD AS TERRIFIED NEIGHBORS YELL AT HIM TO STOP

A Florida man was arrested for allegedly having sex with a dog. When officers arrived on scene, they were greeted by a small crowd of residents who were disturbed by their neighbor's activity with the dog. Police searched the Tampa area home, where they found a gun, ammunition and eight pit bulls. The man faces charges of sex with animals, cruelty to animals and illegal gun possession. He was released on $17,500 bond.

Apartment #6 Mayor of The Beach House

Ethan Thomas was the unofficial Mayor of The Beach House, partly by longevity and partly by popularity. So it was only right that he was the first person to read the unexpected notice posted on the laundry-room wall.

Ethan, born and raised in Miami, was now in his sixth decade of life. Over four-and-a-half of those decades he'd been a heavy drinker, and five of those decades a heavy smoker. For all of those decades he had consciously abstained from using sunblock. He kept himself thriving on a diet of Southern comfort food, preferably home-cooked on the grill, and loose women, preferably picked up at the two-for-one happy hour at his local, The Hurricane Bar. Ethan liked to keep things casual with women, and he abided by just two rules. First, they needed to be out the door by the crack of dawn, and second, on no circumstances were any fingers ever to be inserted into his butt.

Ethan had a quintessential white middle-class 1950s Floridian upbringing. The Miami of his childhood was sleepier, swampier and whiter than the "suburb of Bogota" that, in his opinion, Dade County had now transformed into. As a boy, he would stand in his back yard and look into the sky watching the Saturn V rockets head to the moon. Those beasts, like the America of then, were big, powerful and clearly felt from far away. That fire in the sky was visible a good inch wide from Miami, with a trail streak stretching over the entire horizon. But the rockets kept getting smaller, with the Space Shuttle barely even visible south of Vero Beach and a speck in the sky at most from Miami. Now there wasn't even a Space Shuttle and no way for Americans to get into orbit without embarrassingly asking for assistance from Russia. Ethan swore that it all started going downhill once Jimmy Carter gave away the Panama Canal. This was pure national weakness and he could see no obvious way back. Ronald Reagan was the last President he had voted for. Since then, no one had made you feel good about your country or proud to be an American.

Upon graduation from High School, Ethan headed north to study at the University of Florida. After four years of hard partying he graduated with a soft diploma in Liberal Arts. His first job out of college was as a travel rep for the burgeoning European package-holiday industry that had recently touched down in the United States. Ethan, with his good looks, perfect teeth and "local knowledge," made a quintessential "Have-a-Nice-Day" guide. Telephone numbers and room keys – especially from English women, who Ethan thought were the easiest – became appreciated gratuities from a continent that didn't fully understand the concept of tipping.

In the early '80s he took a job as an air steward with Eastern. Ethan, being a straight male, working in an industry dominated by women and gays in an era where aircrew turnaround at exotic destinations was days and not hours, had the time of his life. A bust airline and panic over a frightening disease with no cure finally grounded the copious amount of partying he enjoyed around the world. In the late '80s, Ethan, who had always been good with tools, took an entry-level job as a cabinetmaker. He worked his way up from apprentice to foreman, before opening his own woodwork shop in an industrial part of Miami.

Twenty years on and Ethan's all-American looks were a harsh shadow of their prime, his thin hair spliced onto a face with a beaten complexion from years of tropical sun. Exercise that was limited to walking from his car to the front door of the bar had transformed a once athletic physique. Filterless cigarettes had left his voice raspy and with a throat in need of constant clearing. The inside of his lungs and the state of his liver were of the quality to get you a golden ticket to Angel Mancini's refrigerated room. Medically, Ethan was a ticking time bomb with a fuse that was receding faster than available building land in Palm Beach County. He was aware of his situation, but wasn't going to make changes to his routine, and was happy to live hard and deal with the consequences when they came. He thought about death and told himself he never wanted to be one of those Florida old-timers eking out a long life in some retirement complex, living healthily, regularly visiting doctors and going easy on chasing skirt. Ethan wanted to solider on as long as possible. If he could plan his own death, he would die horizontally, a cold drink in his hand, a cigarette dangling from his mouth and a woman sexually gratifying him in the most twisted of manners.

Ethan's life, in essence, was simple. He worked just enough to provide a living for his crew of six and to pay his way in the world. His pace was inefficient but thorough, and he took pride in completion of projects. Ethan treated his staff well and for that he was respected and not taken advantage of. His daily eighty-mile commute to Miami and back was on one of the most dangerous stretches of road in America. You would never see regular accidents on I-95, only spectacular pile-ups that looked like scenes from a *Mad Max* movie. He timed his commute to avoid the worst of the traffic and so increase his odds of staying alive. Coming home late afternoon not only avoided the traffic crush, but was also a good time to start the process of unwinding and hitting a happy hour.

Ethan moved into The Beach House because it was easy. He was seeing a gal who worked in Delray and the location was congenial. He was happy to rent, as he viewed home ownership as an unneeded complication of a life that he wanted to stay simple. His mellow disposition and friendly mannerisms made him popular with all the other residents.

He was seen as the go-to guy for issues with landlords and general self-help, and he was the key tenant who led The Beach House revolt against Bessie and Gabriel's guest registry. Ethan hosted regular cook-ups on the grill, and all were welcome. He had lived long at The Beach House and had witnessed several of its evolutionary boom-and-bust cycles, although he was scratching his head at the latest happenings.

Being the unofficial Mayor of The Beach House had awarded Ethan just one perk. On Thursday evenings, he had exclusive use of the building's washing and drying machines. And around this weekly mission he had built a well-subscribed poker and BBQ night on the outside patio that had become a fixture of Beach House life. He played steadily throughout the evening, only opting out of a round when a load of laundry finished, drying needed to be folded, steaks had to be cooked or he had to take a leak. Tonight, on a pleasant evening, he was wagering quarters with Colleen Bromefield from Apartment #7 and Jacob Smith from Apartment #10. As always, new players would come and go as the evening progressed. Rodney from Apartment #3 had already been wiped out of loose change. The empty beer cans stacked around the table were all Ethan's doing, as the other two remaining players were currently on the wagon.

Jacob was one of those random inserted-in-country neighbors who arrived at his fully furnished rental in the dead of night with two physical bags and a dump truck of personal baggage. It would usually take a few days of dodging and ducking to extract exactly why a said person was in town, or at least a version of their story that they wanted to share, but Jacob was one of the more open cases and quick to lay bare his predicament to anyone who would listen. He was an educator from Missouri who was in Delray on a court-mandated stint in rehab.

From his middle-aged Midwestern kooky looks and JC Penney dress style, you wouldn't guess or necessarily believe that Jacob had been caught buying crack from one of his students. He looked honest and straight, the sort of man you trust your kids with or buy insurance from, but if you were sat next to him on a plane you wouldn't necessarily strike up a conversation in case he bored you to death. Jacob's reason for coming to Delray was simple – he had to dry out or go to jail. Even if he completed a successful stint in detox, and taking into account his first-time offender status, getting his license to teach returned was not guaranteed. Jacob had been staying at The Beach House for several months. He had a wife waiting for him in St Louis, but he didn't seem in any hurry to get home. His excuse was that he wanted to take a year out from the brutal Missouri winter, but Ethan sensed there was more to it. Jacob was a nice guy but a shit poker player; fortunately, he had brought with him a bucket load of quarters to lose.

Ethan dealt a round of cards to Colleen and Jacob while sucking on a cigarette and hacking up the phlegm in his throat. Behind him a fox scavenged for fruit under the mango tree that was swaying in the delicate evening wind. At this time of night the screaming and shouting from inside Apartment #9 was largely ignored and considered background noise, along with the chirping crickets. Ethan looked over at Colleen as she was analyzing her cards and tried to read her poker face. He had never been able to figure out quite what was going on in her pretty little head. Like Jacob, Colleen was a middle-of-the-night, two-bag implant at The Beach House. He had deduced that the two bags were full of tiny bikinis and skimpy lightweight see-through outfits, but he hadn't managed to decipher her story or why she was really in Florida.

Colleen was born and raised in the West Indies, with some kind of ancestral British mother-country origins. Ethan didn't even know there were white people in the Caribbean, let alone beautiful ones with classy posh accents and perfect teeth. When he was a guide in Miami, he could barely understand the thick brogue of the British girls he used to hook up with, and was scared to look directly at their open mouths for the horrors within. Colleen was in her late twenties or early thirties. Whatever her age, she was the wrong side of the "half your age plus seven years" formula – although that hadn't stopped him trying. Colleen was slender, had great bone structure and straight blonde hair. If she was a couple of inches taller, she could've been a model. She was always exquisitely dressed in ritzy outfits and designer swimwear. Tonight, she was wearing a white, translucent, linen shirt over a clearly visible lacy, black bra that kept in place her rocking breasts. To Ethan, she smelt of undiluted feminine Florida money, a dash of expensive perfume blended with a whiff of rich cocoa butter. Peach-colored short-shorts and bare feet with painted pink toenails finished off her look.

Each day, Colleen would get into a rented Mercedes car and drive off. Where and what she was doing no one knew and she wouldn't tell. It was a big mystery and, when asked, she never failed to sidestep the question.

The door of Apartment #2 opened. Angel Mancini exited with her boyfriend Simon Godfrey. They were dressed up for a dinner date.

"You two want to sit in for a hand," Ethan shouted in their direction, after taking the cigarette from his mouth.

"Not tonight. We've a reservation at City Oyster," Angel replied cheerfully, as the couple walked towards the street.

While Colleen was studying her cards, Jacob gave Ethan that man-to-man look and they both acknowledged to each other that Angel was cute, they had tried and, if given the chance, they would've instantly jumped in the sack with her. It hadn't gone unnoticed to Ethan that Simon hadn't even looked over or acknowledged his polite invitation. Ethan liked Angel, and thought she was a good kid with a solid head on her shoulders. He didn't have much time for her boyfriend, though. Simon Godfrey treated everyone at The Beach House like he was too good to share the same air.

From the corner of his eye, Ethan noticed the blinds move at Pete Alexander's apartment. Now there was a guy, with his tabloid sleuthing powers, who could figure out exactly how Colleen filled her secretive days. Ethan had asked, but Pete, who was possibly the only man in the building who hadn't had a crack at trying to seduce Colleen, seemed distracted and said he was too busy with work to do any digging.

"Angel and Simon are a beautiful couple," Colleen threw out as small talk to the guys on the table without enticing a reply.

All three players studied their cards and placed their bets. Ethan took a drag on his Marlboro. Colleen reached and took a single cigarette from Ethan's packet of smokes. She proceeded to light up the cigarette. Both Ethan and Jacob watched her take a drag. It was mesmerizing for the guys just how hot she looked while smoking.

Ethan decided to give it another go with his latest flirtatious overture. "What do you have on tomorrow afternoon?" he asked Colleen, as he laid down his winning hand and collected a stack of quarters from the middle of the table.

"I have an appointment in Coral Gables," she shot back in that posh English twang as she seductively took another drag from her cigarette.

"What exactly do you do all day?" said Jacob, punting out the million-dollar question.

"It's private and I don't want to talk about it," Colleen replied with a dismissive chill.

Ethan dealt out another hand of cards. He had a couple of steaks he needed to start grilling. He had enticed Colleen out of her apartment with the lure of food, so now he had to fulfill that part of the bargain.

The door of Apartment #8 opened and Bodie poked his head out for a breath of fresh air.

Ethan shouted: "Bodie! Can you sit in on a round? I need to put some meat on the fire and sort out my drying."

Even though he risked being late for work, Bodie would not miss an opportunity to share some of Colleen's sweet air. He walked over from his front door and filled Ethan's spot at the table.

Ethan strolled over to the communal grill that was placed next to the swimming pool. He fired it up and threw on steaks for himself, Colleen and Jacob. He cracked open another beer and took a gulp. Then, checking that he wasn't visible to anyone, he cleared his throat, undid his pants zipper, aimed at one of the floral bushes and took a piss. He had a bloated bladder, so it took a little time at his age to empty out. He could no longer hear Shane and Rebecca yelling and screaming, which meant one of three scenarios: they were passed out drunk; they were in the middle of crazy monkey love; or they were both lying dead in a pool of blood. The lights were on at Bessie and Gabriel's apartment, and he dreaded to think what they were currently plotting and scheming. Ethan was formerly a friend with Gabriel, but there was only so much paranoia and stupid rule making he could take. Ethan often had some of his happiest thoughts while enjoying a casual open-air number one. In this moment of peace and joy, he was thankful for a good life.

With a cigarette in his mouth, Ethan shook off and zipped up. He looked at his watch and realized his washing would now be finished and ready for the dryer. He strolled around the back of the building following the path past the clothes line and into the laundry room that was attached to the back of The Beach House. The Club Room, as it was cheerfully referred to, also housed the hurricane shutters and the building's hot-water heater. The entire room was in need of a good clean, and without doubt the washing and drying machines were ready for an upgrade. Ethan made a note-to-self to write to the board and request new equipment. That was the sort of thing he did as part of his unofficial Mayoral duties. He transferred his washing into the dryer, and as he made his exit from the room he glanced at the notice board that had been almost unused since Bessie and Gabriel were removed from power. During their reign of dread it had been dedicated to displaying newly implemented rules and regulations. It was while scanning the board and lighting up another cigarette that he saw an official posting on behalf of The Beach House Board. It read: "Thirty Days Notice of Special Board Meeting to Discuss Termination of The Beach House Condominium and Sale of property to Surf Way Developments."

Ethan examined the full memo again and could not believe what he read. He was no lawyer, but he understood the Queen's English and what he was viewing was boilerplate language discussing the imminent end of The Beach House. Ethan recognized the name of the building company. They had been responsible for the "gentrification" of large swathes of Delray Beach. On their watch, many of the old apartment buildings and houses around town had been bulldozed and replaced by cookie-cutter condos and McMansions built to the extremes of their lots. A stunned Ethan headed back to the poker table and shared the news. There was shock and bewilderment. For Colleen and Jacob The Beach House was nothing more than a temporary abode, but for Ethan and many other residents, this was their home. The poker night ended early on a depressing note.

Ethan would often say to people he had just met, in his folksy southern style, "I'll tell you this for nothing my new friend, the two greatest wonders of the world are these: the sound of a bunch of negroes singing in perfect harmony; and the sight of a beautiful woman pleasuring herself." Combine the two together and Ethan was in his personal Nirvana. With the power of the Internet, and in the comfort of your own home, with the blinds drawn and the lights dimmed, it was possible to while away the evenings looking for examples of what Ethan had pinned to be marvels of human evolution. This was exactly how Ethan concluded many a night after stumbling home from a happy hour without short-term company. With a cigarette in his mouth and Johnson in hand, he thought surfing the web looking for case studies was not a shabby way to close out the day.

Ethan had never set foot in a Black Church, as that wasn't his place, but he had often driven past them during a Sunday service and pulled over, listening and taking it all in. The clapping, hollering and "Praise be the Lord" chants were just an interlude for the beautiful singing. Ethan reflected that this sound of the South, the black voice in synchronization, belting out soul and passion, must have been the only thing that kept their people together during slavery. He could sit for hours listening to this music, which he said was "Manna from Heaven." For the audio element of his recreational hobby, Ethan subscribed to various YouTube channels run by large Baptist churches. He would stack up those gospel choirs on auto play and let them rip.

Through High School, Ethan recalled that the girls were way too prudish to masturbate in front of you. In college, if you got them drunk or stoned, you might be in luck, but it wasn't part of any repertoire for most females of that era. He clearly remembered the first time he saw a woman diddling herself. It was spring break in Biloxi and she was an Okie from Tulsa, Brittany being her name. It was magic and a vision he would never forget. From the 1990s onwards, girls were more open to solo performing with an audience, and with the casual screws Ethan picked up on Atlantic Avenue he always made this a priority request.

Ethan had been a partaker in porn since reel films were imported from Amsterdam and bought at seedy North Miami XXX stores. VHS cassettes had done for a dark enterprise what Cervantes and the novel had for the spreading of literature. The Internet, and every female armed with a video camera, had today flooded demand with a Sodom and Gomorrah end-of-days deluge of pornography. Self-filming amateurs had replaced big-budget porn stars. Although Ethan appreciated that he didn't have to pay for skin flicks, he did miss the quantity of big-titted blondes that was the mainstay of classic San Fernando Valley porn. These modern girls came in all shapes and sizes, and with varying degrees of skill and form.

Ethan's bachelor apartment was basic, and evidently a woman's touch could uplift the spirit. The fridge was full of beer and steaks, and the furnishings comfy but aesthetically dated and dull. The only item hanging on any wall was a sixty-inch plasma TV. Tonight, Ethan was distracted by the unnerving turn of events at The Beach House. It wasn't every day that you found your home was slated for demolition. With a soundtrack of the Mississippi Mass Choir singing *I Love To Praise*, he had taken his mind off events by busying himself in his passion of cruising for porn. He was digging deep and dragging out events in order not to think about the chore of finding a new home. It was while he was delving into a newly found user-uploaded amateur porn site called Blue Meth that he randomly stumbled upon his second unexpected shock of the day.

As he guiltily got his rocks off, Ethan would often think to himself that each of these girls had to be someone's daughter – although he speedily conquered this remorse by being relieved that he was not himself a parent. Over a lifetime of partaking in a massive consumption of porn, one thing had never happened – he had never recognized anyone he knew in a film or video. So on this occasion, he didn't believe it at first. The hair looked similar and the bikini body too, but surely it couldn't be. It was the voice that really made him take notice. It was slurred and stuttering under a heavy haze of booze, but that distinct accent – it had to be her. The clip was what he would politely describe as being "experimental" and "adventurous," and taken a few years ago. Ethan could tell that this video wasn't made with any notion that it would ever become public, and judging by the crazy antics she might not have been totally aware of it being filmed at all. He turned off the gospel music and poured himself a fresh beer. With his simplistic needs of watching a woman enjoy herself, Ethan didn't usually get into amateur stuff that included scrotums. Male ass and cock were not his thing, but today he made an exception. Ethan watched the full fifteen minutes of roughly edited, mostly raw video, several times over. He needed to make sure that it really was who he thought it was.

Ethan went to bed that evening with a head full of worry and bewilderment. Being the unofficial Mayor of The Beach House had suddenly become a heavy burden. While he wasn't exactly sure what would happen to The Beach House and where he might end up living in the future, he was certain that it was indeed his neighbor who was involved in a sordid and dirty, but highly enjoyable to watch, sexual tryst with two men. Ethan had always thought that under that reserved shell she might have a kinky dark side, and now he knew he was one hundred percent correct in that assumption.

September 17th 2015, from the New York Daily News

COPS REMOVE 3,714 BLADED WEAPONS FROM FLORIDA WOMAN'S MOBILE HOME

Police found more than 3,700 knives, swords and blades cluttered inside a freaky Florida woman's doublewide trailer. She appeared to have "booby-trapped" some of her floors, blankets and parts of her yard with knives. Officers received "minor injuries" while clearing the space. The dwelling was a true house of horrors – besides the colossal cutters collection, police found chicken bones, rubber body parts and other paraphernalia associated with satanic worship. Police originally came to the home to serve an arrest warrant for felony probation violation and carrying a concealed weapon.

Apartment #7 The Barbados Triangle

Since her sudden arrival from Barbados, Colleen Bromefield had thrown the social balance of The Beach House's delicate ecosystem totally off-kilter. Colleen was the last heir to an 18th century Barbadian sugar-plantation fortune and had been raised in a world of privilege, courtesy of what her great-great-grandfather's father had called "White Gold". In 1750, Reginald Bromefield, the second son of a Liverpool slave-trading family, arrived in the New World with the intention of making his fortune – and that is exactly what he did. Assisted by a shipload of "African help", Reginald started Barbados's first sugar plantation, and the Caribbean branch of the Bromefields had survived off the back of the riches from this agriculture estate for two centuries. Then, post-independence

Barbadian domestic politics and bad business investments by Colleen's family burnt through the bulk of the family estate. The last remnants of old money had been wisely invested by sending Colleen to a British boarding school. For Colleen, this formal education was like a stretch in prison, with cold showers, beatings and lashings of tough love. Upon graduation, she entered the outside world with a broad range of newly learnt hustles and tricks.

Colleen, now without family or fortune, was forced to live off her wits and a beautiful face that would let her get her way with almost anything. Her slender tanned and toned body, classical goddess bone structure and sophisticated British classiness were wonderfully complemented by a theatrical aura of "deer-in-headlights" innocence. This siren mishmash made her irresistible and a danger to anyone she encountered possessing an XY chromosome. What business Colleen had in Florida, how she filled her long hours away from The Beach House, and the method by which she supported her lifestyle remained a mystery to everyone. In fact, investigative questions of substance had seldom been directed at Colleen during her near three decades on this planet, which was a terrific perk of being deemed an object of desire. What wasn't in doubt to the red-blooded males who called this double lot on Andrews Avenue home was that while the entrance of Colleen Bromefield into their micro world had been the West Indies' loss, it was their gain.

Colleen played the attention angle well at The Beach House, and soon after arriving had the single males in the building at her beck and call. With The Beach House men folk in permanent rutting-season mode, constantly attempting to one-up each other in an effort to impress with bravado big-talk, Colleen never lacked company for a chat or to share a "fag", the British term she used to call a cigarette. When Colleen graced the pool or patio areas in the itsy-bitsy bikinis that made up the bulk of her daytime wardrobe, there wasn't a spare seat to be had on any piece of community furniture. It hadn't gone unnoticed by fellow residents that Ethan and Bodie were on synchronized swimming and tanning schedules with Colleen. She was gracious, remaining just enough of a tease to keep them interested, without them realizing they were being completely played.

Pete attempted to join in on the game, via stealth, from a concealed perch in his apartment, by setting up a camera in the exact same method he would in order to shoot a celebrity target. He had taken hundreds of pictures of Colleen sunbathing. He'd even managed a snatched nipple shot while she readjusted her swimsuit. Pete justified this neighborly act of voyeurism as a way of keeping his camera settings and color balance in standby mode, so at quick notice his gear was ready for lucrative celebrity action. If Colleen had ever found out what Pete had been doing, she wouldn't only have been flattered, but also would have found some way to use this perceived attention in an advantageous manner.

On any given day, the building's spoken-for males could be routinely viewed at the least ogling Colleen, and more often than not conducting full-on flirtatious deeds. Gabriel Garlech had a prime view of the beauty in her natural sun-lounger environment from his window. He mentally stored the visuals as a marital aid for assistance in the functional call of duty with his homely significant other. Gabriel had been repeatedly spotted lurking around the laundry area while Colleen's delicates were on full spin. His intentions were obvious, although he was never caught or compromised. Avuncular Jacob from Apartment #10, with his apparent middle-aged harmlessness, was adept at carrying out conversations with Colleen from the deep end of the pool as she laid out catching rays. With this awesome angle he had a prime position to talk directly at her cleavage without her knowing what he was doing. At least that is what he thought, as Colleen was well used to dealing with lecherous old men and had been manipulating them in order to get exactly what she wanted since the age of fifteen.

The "ladies" of The Beach House, both full-time residents and camp followers, knew the exact threat a woman like Colleen posed to their relationship status. In the spirit of Michael Corleone's "Keep your friends close and your enemies closer," they warily retained Colleen on solid frenemy terms. Rebecca Gravois, Colleen's next-door-but-one neighbor, made an immediate effort to befriend her. They went on walks together, making small talk, sharing beauty tips and passing pooled judgment on issues like how to wear white bikini bottoms while preserving modesty. They would occasionally talk sex, but Rebecca never believed that Colleen was as shy and inexperienced as she would have you believe. Rebecca, who was always thinking that Shane was going to be stolen by another woman, was especially cautious that she might make a play for her very own alpha male. She had decided that Shane was too quick to pop over to Colleen's when the call to change a light bulb, hang a painting, fix her waste-disposal unit or any other mundane task that she cried for help with in "faux distressed damsel" mode. The women of The Beach House knew all too well the weakness of their men, and could see exactly how Colleen had them all bent around her little Barbadian finger.

It was evident what Colleen was doing while she was at The Beach House, but what she did away from the building was another matter. Dressed like a television news anchor, with the reek of a first-class air hostess, she would slip away from the building in her rented Mercedes at various times of the day and night. Her only response to fielded soft enquiries by neighbors was a broad and convincing story about having job interviews in Miami. Once a month she would fly back to Barbados attending to what she said were "family matters." It was assumed that Colleen, with her aristocratic accent and perfect posture, was independently wealthy, and the renting of an apartment at The Beach House was a fluke. She should really be in Palm Beach or Naples or some other affluent enclave, and not this shabby building.

Colleen gave the impression that she was loaded and was never without money, new expensive outfits or flash pieces of jewelry. Little did anyone at The Beach House know that the family fortune was long gone, and that the cheap rent, flexible month-to-month lease and the anonymity of living among blue-collar neighbors had lured Colleen to her current home. Her little triangle of mystery was pivoted around Apartment #7 of The Beach House, unknown meetings somewhere in Miami and declared family visits to the Caribbean. The general Beach House community never found out exactly why this sweet little cookie dipped in arsenic had temporarily brought herself to South Florida, and if they had they would've wished they hadn't.

At some point in the middle of the night Ethan had given up trying to sleep. There were just too many crazy things running through a mind that was conditioned for simplicity. For sure, he was going to give the woodwork shop a pass today. It was nearing first light, so he sat on The Beach House patio with a coffee on the table and a nearly empty packet of cigarettes resting against an overfilled ashtray. A cotton-candied sunrise was emerging from the east, casting long shadows behind the pink flamingo statue that dominated the building's forecourt. For a solid ten minutes the natural light looked like it had been created by the giant filter that all television shows set in Miami are filmed with.

The door of Apartment #7 opened to greet the day and Ethan focused his glance in that direction. His first thought was that he wished the video he had stumbled upon last night featured Colleen. That would certainly be something for the ages. Then again, he reflected that a girl that hot was no doubt a total stiff in the sack and it would've ultimately been disappointing. Ethan observed Colleen locking her front door. She was wearing a black business suit with a white blouse, fifties-era oversized shades, a pearl necklace with a smart briefcase in hand. As always, she was dressed to impress and looked a notch past ten on the fantastic scale.

"Top of the morning," Ethan croaked across the patio as he stubbed out a cigarette.

"Hello, Ethan. Good morning to you," she replied, sounding to the woodworker exactly like one of the Earl's hot daughters in *Downton Abbey*. Ethan beckoned her to his table with the offer of a cigarette. "I have time for a quick fag," replied Colleen. She then sat down, sexily crossing her long legs as she lit up. Ethan sucked in her personal air. Colleen's perfume, mixed with the early morning dew, smelt heavenly.

"You look good today; going somewhere important?" he asked.

"Interview in Doral!" she said without elaboration.

Colleen leaned her appointments towards the afternoon, so Ethan was surprised she was out so early but knew when not to poke a bear.

"Take a look at this," he said as he passed his phone to Colleen.

"Oh golly!" came the fast retort. The image on the phone was a text message from the head of the Homeowners' Association confirming the authenticity of the laundry-room announcement. "Deary me! Looks like I will have to find a new home," said Colleen, now sounding more like a rich glamour girl in a *Benny Hill* skit than the Earl of Grantham's daughter.

Ethan mentally noted that, as usual, she didn't show concern for anyone but herself.

"Yes," said Ethan. "This has been keeping me up all night, among other things. I am going to call a residents' meeting. See what we can do. Coalition of the willing and all that!"

Ethan lit up the last smoke of the packet. Colleen sighed. She offered no immediate insight, but evidently took delight in the ball of fire ascending in the sky.

"Sun looks so much friendlier in Florida than Barbados," were Colleen's finishing words as she flicked the butt of the cigarette into the tray and effortlessly glided on high heels to her parked car.

The door of Apartment #8 opened. A disheveled Bodie dressed in boxer shorts and not much else stretched his arms out as he squinted towards the rising Sun.

"You look like you was rode hard and put away wet!" shouted Ethan in the direction of his woken neighbor.

"Heavy session, man. After I closed the Anchor, I finished the night off at The Ugly Mug."

The Ugly Mug was the late-hours bar up on Military and Atlantic in Delray's hinterland. It was notorious for a rough crowd and was the go-to place for service-industry workers who had just finished their shifts. The "Mug" didn't get hopping until 2 a.m. It was a notorious pick-up joint and if you so desired a take-home date was always an option.

"Come over here. I have something you will want to see," said Ethan.

Bodie popped back into Apartment #8 and re-emerged wearing a dressing gown Hugh Hefner would've been proud of when he was a younger, poorer man. He sat down in the seat freshly vacated by Colleen and sucked in the still fragrant air.

"That's the smell of some quality pussy I would like to become on friendlier terms with," were Bodie's first words after a long satisfying inhale.

For the second time that morning, Ethan passed his phone to a resident of The Beach House and showed them something unexpected.

"Wow, wow and fucking WOW!" exclaimed Bodie, after viewing what was on the phone.

"Those were exactly my thoughts," Ethan agreed.

Ethan had showed him the video he had chanced upon late last night. If Bodie were to bet on a woman that called The Beach House home finding herself on a porn site, he would've put his money on Apartment #9's Rebecca Gravois. She was a known goer and prone to lost hours or weekends while partying hard. During Rebecca's residency at the building, she'd been on carnal terms with several fellow dwellers, including him. Luckily for Bodie and the others, Shane, her long-time and very short-tempered boyfriend, hadn't been made aware of these indiscretions. To stumble upon Angel Mancini, the most professional and perceived normal woman who had ever lived at The Beach House, partaking in a bizarre drunken sex tape, was an unexpected turn of events, to say the least.

Bodie and Ethan viewed the video together for a second time. Ethan didn't usually watch pornography with other men for obvious red-blooded heterosexual reasons. However, due to the localized and unprecedented circumstances, he had made an exception. Blue Meth, the site Angel popped up on, was one of a multitude of amateur porn websites that had recently sprouted from nowhere and were currently all the rage in anything-goes millennial circles. The primary function of this site was to provide an outlet for aspiring Don Juans to share videos of romantic conquests and self-promote their swordsmanship. Through a "likes" tab and a ratings function, videos were ranked and, if popular enough, were featured on the site's "Sidebar of Shame." This enabled anyone possessing a smartphone, basic editing ability and a willing, or in some cases unwilling, compadre, the chance to become an Internet porn sensation. The legality of such sites was on shaky ground in the wild-west world of the Internet, but that hadn't stopped their explosive growth. The roughly edited video was, in terms of acrobatics and general willingness, high on the adventurous scale. It looked to have been shot in the cabin of a cruise ship. Angel was somewhat aware of the camera, being a willing partaker in the shenanigans and relishing the fun, although at times the two guys she frolicked with seemed to be more interested in each other.

"Up-vote that to top rating," said Bodie, in a down-to-business manner after viewing the video for at least the fourth time.

"The tits definitely look real," chimed in Ethan. This had always been a topic of banal small talk between the men at The Beach House, who had suspicions that Angel's defying of gravity came via surgical enhancement. The two men then sat there having the time of their life making gags about Angel being a natural with "stiffs" and "hard bones" and a general flow of morgue-related innuendo followed.

"Bodie! Where are you?" a husky female voice clearly audible out in the patio area shouted from within Apartment #8.

In a slightly embarrassed voice, Bodie whispered back to Ethan, "I'm entertaining. Better get back to my houseguest."

"Anyone I know?" Ethan asked.

"I don't even know her, and am scared what daylight might reveal!" Bodie then jumped up from the table and entered his apartment.

As an afterthought Ethan shouted, "Other small issue of the day, brother. The Beach House is about to be sold and razed to the ground, so we'll all need to find new digs."

Angel Mancini's frisky video segment quickly went viral among The Beach House community. For the men it seemed like Christmas had come early, with none showing disappointment with their gift. The usual technique for neighborly voyeurism at The Beach House was a cheeky peek through an improperly closed blind or listening with the aid of a glass on the wall to the guttural noises of someone in the moment. A sex tape of the cute girl next door, texted to your personal mobile device, was certainly an appreciated innovation to the 21st century world of love-thy-neighbor prying.

Pete, who was somewhat numbed by the occupational hazard of viewing celebrity sex tapes, was not fazed when the video link was passed onto him. At least there were no animals or children harmed in the making of this video, which was more than could be said for some of the sordid Hollywood clips he had witnessed throughout his tabloid career. He did feel for Angel though, because when she was made aware of the video's circulation she would obviously be mortified. For the women of The Beach House it gave them a theatrical topic to gossip over, laugh about and generally throw bitchy jealous shade in Angel's direction. As the video was shared, spread around and up-voted, it soon topped Blue Meth's "Sidebar of Shame."

Angel started her day with the grim task of dealing with the charred remains of a family from Cleveland who had been burnt beyond recognition in a fiery smash with a big rig. This stomach-churning identification by dental records would prove an easy lift compared with the double tragedy Angel was about to face. Arriving back at The Beach House with an armload of groceries, Angel found two notes posted on the front door of her apartment. The first was a printed message about the termination of the condominium and the intended sale to developers of The Beach House. This letter had been circulated by Ethan and was aimed at organizing an opposition fight against this shocking announcement. How had this happened? Angel asked herself. This looked unbelievable. As an owner she was in the dark and hadn't recalled any correspondence regarding the building's intended sale. Surely there would've been a homeowners' meeting to discuss this? The Beach House had finally begun to feel like home, so she didn't want to see the building razed to the ground and she certainly didn't relish looking for a new place to live.

The second note was anonymous and was nothing more than a printed URL link on a blank piece of paper. Angel put away her shopping and fed her hungry cat. She then turned on a laptop computer and entered the web-page link. Her expectations were some documentation in relation to The Beach House news, and not what appeared before her startled eyes. Her heart immediately sunk. For a split second she wished she could place herself in a cold locker at the morgue and vanish from the world. She knew exactly when and where this video had been taken – five years ago at a friend's bachelorette cruise around the Bahamas. That night, Jägerbombs hadn't been her best friend. The weekend was all a bit of a blur and a total one-off break from her rigid world of clean and sensible living. How would she explain this to Simon? Angel shut down the computer, curled up on her sofa and began to cry.

The Beach House condominium association was made up of twelve individual units. With each unit came an equal vote. Pete, Angel and the Garlechs were the only owners who resided in the apartments they owned. The other nine condos, via speculative punts, attempts at building mini real-estate empires and unexpected inheritance, were in the hands of just four absentee owners.

Brian Moriarty, the chairman of the Homeowners' Association, was a Stanford graduate, whose main business was commercial air-conditioning unit distribution. His wife Candace, looking for projects to fill her empty nest days, bought Apartments #5 and #10 at the height of the frothy 2004 real-estate market. Soon tiring of crazy tenants and the landlady business in general, she handed over the administration of these apartments to her husband and looked for other ways to find meaning in life. Scrapbook classes with fellow unfulfilled housewives would be her latest specialism. Brian had been dealing ever since with the hot mess that her now underwater Beach House investments had become. To keep the Moriarty marriage from going south, The Beach House was never mentioned at the dinner table. In fact, they never discussed it at all.

Kyle Bokeman, a middle-aged mullet-wielding Corvette salesman from Jupiter, looking to divest profits reaped from helping midlife-crisis males "find new roads," poured his cash into real estate. He owned Apartments #8 and #11, as well as other properties scattered around Palm Beach County. These holdings, when not rented out, also doubled as handy boltholes to facilitate the long-running affair he conducted with his busty head of sales. Kyle was the vice-chairman of the Homeowners' Association.

Felicia Blanc, a Parisian heiress who never failed to mention she was related to Napoleon in every single conversation, had acquired Apartments #1, #3, #7 and #12 in a fit of absent-minded empire building. She was mightily proud that she controlled three of the four corner units and a majority of the building. Felicia additionally operated a boutique on Atlantic Avenue and possessed a palatial villa in Corsica. Susan Hockman, a retired psychiatrist from West Palm Beach, was an accidental owner. Susan, who insisted on being called "Suze" by people she had met more than twice, had inherited Apartment #9 along with its associated problems from a previously unknown second aunt. In her opinion, the small profit she made from renting the apartment wasn't worth the paperwork and aggravation.

These owners had one thing in common – they all wanted an escape from the headache and burden that The Beach House had become.

This cabal of four held three-quarters of The Beach House voting stock, and with it – if they acted in unity – they had a majority position and were able to make binding decisions on behalf of the entire building. The back-door offloading of The Beach House, spearheaded by Kyle Bokeman, had full backing from the frustrated group of absentee owners who were fatigued by the long legal war with the Garlechs. In strategic terms, this end game was a mutually assured destructive move that would take the conflict with Bessie and Gabriel nuclear. The upside for the owners from concluding a sale was that the building wouldn't need repainting, there wouldn't be a dysfunctional Homeowners' Association for the State to take over, there would be no more city fines and the costly litigation would end. Selling the building to a spec builder was a scenario that gave the owners a way out, a cash return on their investment and a final move that left the Garlechs at checkmate. The only possible moral victory that Bessie and Gabriel could claim was that they could keep their door white until the very end. Knowing those two, this would be when the Sheriff's department banged on the door with a notice of eviction. This play by the Homeowners' Association was on solid legal ground and had been signed off by their expensively retained legal counsel. The other residents of The Beach House would be unfortunate collateral damage.

May 1ˢᵗ 2013, from the Miami New Times

FLORIDA MAN CALLS 911 EIGHTY TIMES TO DEMAND KOOL-AID, HAMBURGERS AND WEED

A Tampa man did not have a good reason for calling 911 eighty times last week. The thirty-four-year-old wanted Kool-Aid, hamburgers and weed, and he wanted Police to deliver the items. The Florida man kept 911 operators busy by blitzing them all day with his requests. When Sheriff's deputies showed up at the man's house, he was honest about his demands. Instead of delicious snacks, the officers gave the man a pair of handcuffs and took him to jail.

Apartment #8 The Intersections of Florida Life

Due to the constraints of The Beach House's architecture and cultural microclimate, the condo's residents were never the type that social anthropologists would generalize as middle-class, suburbanite, soccer mom/dad or other variations of ordinary. That legion of model citizenry, content with progressing through standard cycles of life, regular nine-to-five work, raising children, abiding by the law and causing a minimal amount of disruption to those around them, gave this slither of Delray a wide berth.

There were three categories of residents living at The Beach House. These classifications, if presented in a Venn diagram, perfectly reflected the elements of the Florida population that were in the process of either an upwardly mobile or tragic downwardly disabling journey through life. There were the aspirational inhabitants on the ascent, using their occupancy as a base and stepping stone to greater and better things. This breed of tenant came with a preset plan and brought an aura of hope and buzzed with a personal vision of tremendous things to come. They possessed the pirate's map of life, only needing to adjust the key, make sense of the scale and decipher that last code to find the treasure. Then there were those residents on the downward trajectory. By the time they found refuge at The Beach House, they were often in rapid free-fall, using the place as a branch of varying strength to hold, climb back onto, pause, regroup and take a needed time out. These beaten and battered souls had lost their treasure and would do anything to find a new map, with a new bounty, another path and an opportunity to find a slice of what they once had. For them, The Beach House was the last gallant resting stop on a possible plunge into the abyss.

At the intersection of these two groups were those happy to go either way, or remain as they were in limbo. They used The Beach House as a purgatory with purpose and a tool of assistance on the unknown road ahead. These inbetweeners always had a scam, a hustle and, just in case it all went south, a speedy escape route planned. They weren't in need of any treasure maps and even if they found one they would throw it away or dismiss it as fake. This class of Beach House resident would make their own magic, big or small, and by one method or another, even if this might be through plunder, pillage and borderline criminality. This kind of resident wasn't in a hurry. They were just happy to tread water and make do, and felt no pressure to jump on the up-down escalator of life.

Sitting outside the Venn diagram, and missing among the localized Beach House population, were the fringe subsets that were essential contributors in the fabric that kept Florida strange and extraordinary – the rugged, sun-weathered, *Soldier of Fortune*-subscribing, armed-to-the-teeth, off–the-grid, swamp-dwelling, redneck Florida man. This staple of Sunshine State fiction was placed at the bottom end of the food chain by the standards of modern corporate cultured decency. At the other end of the Florida loci sat the "robber baron" residents of Palm Beach and their evil redheaded cousins, the South American "drug barons" of Miami. Ironically, for reasons of gruesome business or sporting pleasure, *Solider of Fortune* was also this subset's reading material of choice. Dictated by geography, privacy and sanity, none of these two peripheral classifications of Florida natives would be anything but accidental tourists within The Beach House's peculiar ecosystem.

Bodie Miller, the current occupant of Apartment #8, was a strange individual who flirted with all the different types of the non-normal population that call Florida home, even down to the subscription of *Soldier of Fortune*, of which he had been an avid reader since a kid. Bodie's life was a perpetual roller-coaster ride of constant ups and downs, with the general course in recent years making it more of a downward-themed trip. His position in that great Venn diagram of Beach House residents was in a constant state of flux, never staying for long in any one set and always in danger of leaving the circles entirely. Bodie's pirate map had blown away long ago and a new one had yet to be found. He was entering the middle of middle aged and, like many native Floridians, was a big guy in every way. He was genetically tall and, from good living and a sedentary management of exercise, a little larger in some areas than he ought to be. Like numerous men of his age he was making the best of what hair he had left. As a package, though, he had a friendly face and calm mannerisms that instantly won him friends and lovers.

Bodie's short-term station was working bartender shifts at The Blue Anchor. His medium-term situation was a longer-than-expected residency with no end in sight at The Beach House. Bodie was not only neighbors with Shane Dolman and Rebecca Gravois, who lived directly above him, but they were also old friends from High School days. It was Shane who had given Bodie the heads-up when Apartment #8 had become available. Bodie had on occasion crossed the line of friendship with Rebecca, as his broad, readily available shoulders to cry on were an easy stepping-stone to mutually agreeable seduction. It was, however, their dirty little secret.

The studio apartment Bodie inhabited was kitted out exclusively by his cheapskate landlady, being at best Spartan and at worse tragically depressing. The furnishings were old, well used and came with an odor that a Costco sized crate of air freshener couldn't eradicate. Paint peeled from the ceilings and rust corroded kitchen fixtures. The only useful thing about the underpowered air-conditioning unit was that it muffled the constant humming noise of a decrepit refrigerator and helped in the task of defusing the ambient soundtrack of Beach House living. It certainly failed in its primary function of keeping that little studio cool in the sweltering summer months. The constant fucking and fighting from Apartment #9 directly above could often be heard through the building's poor sound proofing. This was a known nuisance when Bodie moved in so he didn't complain, and as he possessed first-hand knowledge of Shane's legendary temper this was a prudent course of action.

From a glance around Bodie's apartment the only indicator of a previous better existence was a single black-and-white photograph resting on a makeshift bedside table. Taken during the spring of 2007, it showed a suited-and-booted Bodie on his wedding day to his former wife. Bodie met Nani, a radiant Hawaiian transplant in her early thirties, during a bar crawl in Pompano. Tall, slender, with a dark complexion and long flowing black hair, she was naturally beautiful and could've come straight from Central Casting's big book of "Dusty, Seductive Island Girls." The sex was awesome to the point that Bodie's only problem was finding enough stamina to satisfy her insatiable lust.

Nani had none of the usual emotional baggage Bodie found in Florida girls of her age, such as ex-husbands, kids, drug dependencies, regrettable tattoos, criminal records, the need for rehab or a crazy disposition. He put that down to what he decided was Polynesian sensibility with a cultural pride that emphasized putting the man first. In addition to her beauty and level headedness, Nani had a well-paid job at a swanky Boca Raton hotel's concierge desk. And aside from her demanding sexual appetite, she was self-sufficient and not needy. Having found perfection and not wanting to give her an opportunity to escape, Bodie married her as quickly as possible. A brief romance was followed by a speedy engagement, and within a few months of meeting they wed at the same Hard Rock Hotel made infamous as the death place of Anna Nicole Smith. Shane was best man and Rebecca was Maid of "Honor." This wedding, seven years ago, and frozen in time in a single picture sitting next to Bodie's bed, was the zenith of his life. That year was going to be when everything finally came together for him. For a brief moment everything looked picture perfect and Bodie was living a quintessential American Dream.

Bodie grew up in Delray Beach, graduating from the old High School before it was relocated inland. In that early 1970s era, the city was known as "Dullray." Being from a "good ol' boy" family, Bodie knew which side of the Atlantic Avenue tracks was his part of town. His father, Bob, was a high-octane salesman at the Ford dealership on Federal Highway. His mother, Janice, filled her days raising kids, socializing with other moms and a little light work in retail if she needed pin money. It was a suburban Florida middle-class upbringing with all the reassuring expectations of a comfortable life delivered and backed by the tail end of American exceptionalism. Bodie flunked out of Florida State in his sophomore year. His intended Major, Business Studies, had ended up as a minor distraction to his real area of concentration, partying. He headed back to Delray with odd jobs in construction, bar tending and hotel management keeping him liquid through his twenties and thirties. He was the quintessential local barfly-drifter-dreamer who was always happy to sport a round, or loan a needy friend twenty bucks.

Halfway through the first decade of the twenty-first century, Bodie had a life-changing epiphany. In every direction he saw friends, family and freshly arrived carpetbaggers getting rich off the back of the great State of Florida. Within the span of a generation, he had seen Delray transform and become one of the hottest, most vibrant destinations in the State. Bodie now observed the same wealth, gentrification and progress spreading to Deerfield, Lake Worth, Lantana and all the little places in between. He thought that he deserved a slice of the pie and wanted in on the action.

Over a couple of "happy hour" pints at Boston's, he formulated a plan. Observing the busy valets at work, he concluded that those same people who were unable or couldn't be bothered to park their own cars, or walk the necessary two blocks for free parking, were a segment of the population ripe for further pickings. He assumed they also wouldn't or couldn't be bothered to clean their own cars and would happily pay for someone else to do it for them. In many cases, the skill of using soap and a hose, much like raking leaves, cleaning the pool and cooking, had not transcended the generations. Thus, a broad stratum of the American population was now dependent on hired hands. This segment of the public would be the market that Bodie intended to profit from.

In Bodie's brief stint at Florida State, the one business class he managed to pass with flying colors was "Creating and

Managing the Project." He would utilize his brief higher education and an ingrained Protestant work ethos to design, plan, build and operate a state-of-the-art car wash. After a day of reconnaissance he found the ideal location for this venture, a parcel of undeveloped land on the western fringes of Lake Worth adjacent to the latest emerging subdivisions. There were no car washes within a five-mile radius and new housing developments were mushrooming all around. Bodie knew he was onto a good thing after noticing the move-in cash-back promotions that came when closing on real estate in one of these freshly built housing tracts. Having assessed the personal psyche of the typical Floridian, Bodie figured that the owner of a spanking new home would also want a shiny new ride sitting on the drive. The cash-back offers that provided the deposit, along with effortless finance available, at every local car dealership made this easily obtainable for all. Most of Bodie's friends, even those with questionable credit, were driving around in new trucks and cars. With all the vehicles owned by this rapidly increasing South Florida population in need of waxing and washing, Bodie knew he was onto a winner.

Business finance was cheap and easy to obtain, with the local bank being only too happy to lend Bodie the bulk of the $1,500,000 he needed to lease land and build a fully functioning car wash. The only stipulation was that he was required to show a little "skin in the game," and come up with a down payment. The remaining balance would be at a low fixed interest rate for one year, before resetting to market rate. With some help from his father, Bodie worked the numbers and calculated that a year was all the time he needed to get the business up and running.. His father was delighted that Bodie had at last settled down and was finally utilizing the business brain that, until then, had been wasted, so he was more than happy to assist with the seed money. He withdrew the needed cash from his buoyant retirement account, which had in recent years been increasing in value at an extraordinary rate.

February 1st 2007 was opening day for the creatively named Bodie's Luxury Wash and Wax. It was truly a blessing that the typical Florida resident took great pride in having the biggest truck or SUV available. Those larger vehicles were charged four bucks a pop premium. Bodie was amazed how easy this business was to run and it quickly became little more than a license to print money. Now flush with cash, Bodie bought himself a fully loaded Ford Expedition and leased a Porsche Boxster for his wife. The purchasing of a $775,000, 4,000 square foot townhome at Delray's Pineapple Grove came next. This real-estate purchase was made easier with a bank providing a ninety-five percent loan. Of course, this large home needed furnishing. Even when firing on all fronts, Bodie was a little financially stretched, but this wasn't a problem as the new home fixtures were taken care of with the help of some freshly acquired credit cards. Due to the rapid success of the car-wash business and not being enough time in the day to spend the money generated, Nani quit her job and became a full-time housewife. Bodie and Nani began to talk seriously about starting a family.

In a short seven-month stretch, Bodie had completely rebooted his life. He had transformed from deadbeat drifter to happily married captain of industry, with a beautiful wife, established business, large but generously mortgaged home and a fleet of expensive rides. Sure, Bodie had a "little bit of debt," but that was the American Way. As Bodie signed the paperwork for a second car wash in a newly developing part of Deerfield Beach, he optimistically uttered the words, "If you don't speculate, you can't accumulate."

"What could go wrong?" Bodie often asked himself as he closed out each week's books. What could go wrong was the price of oil could dramatically change and with it, the world economy collapse. In the summer of 2007 oil was priced around $80 a barrel. By June 2008 oil was priced at $146 a barrel. Bodie did recall a little "supply and demand" economics from his brief college stint, and as a kid had a vague recollection of people lining up in the streets for gas. However, he naively presumed that as the modern world was post-industrial, post-race, post-gender, we must also be in a post-oil spike period of civilization. At first, when gas started going up, it was not a big deal. People grumbled and complained, but they still needed a clean car, even if it wasn't the Ultra Wax Special.

Spring 2008 saw the effects of a high oil price directly hitting the consumer pocket book. It started with small cuts and trims in family budgets. Business was still rolling along and Bodie thought that with a bit of luck, John McCain would win in the fall and this slight "blip" would be over thanks to "new blood" in Washington. Backing out of the lease on the Deerfield location cost Bodie his deposit, but at this time it was prudent to "halt organic growth" and focus on the "core business."

As the official 2008 hurricane season approached, Bodie realized he had his own personal Category 5 about to wreak havoc. A dirty car was the very least of Florida man and Florida woman's immediate concerns. The economy had begun to implode rapidly and people started to lose their jobs almost as fast as they lost a confidence to spend. Within months, Bodie's regular customers couldn't afford a car wash, and nor could they afford the gas that moved their cars, the monthly payments to keep ownership of their cars or the mortgage payments for the houses they parked their cars in. The national economy was tanking and it looked like the world was heading for the sort of depression that was studied in one of the university classes Bodie had skipped. By the time gas prices fell, banks were failing, stock markets had crashed and it was too little too late. Bodie knew he was finished when his best customers were the repo men coming to clean up their newly acquired rides.

By the summer of 2009 Bodie had lost his business and was late on payments for his own cars. His credit cards were frozen and his mortgage was delinquent. "Fucking Obama" was a phrase that Republican Floridians uttered when the aid and stimulus that they loathed and detested, and their congressional Representatives voted against, didn't make it their way. By the start of 2010 Bodie had lost his cars, and turned his townhouse keys over to the bank, that had taken over the bank, that had with great eagerness written him the original no-paperwork, no-document, little-money-down loan. Nani had pawned her engagement and weddings rings, and from what he could gather was back on the west side of Oahu living with her ohana. The Great Recession had transformed Bodie and he was no longer the kind, gentle, happy-go-lucky guy she had fallen in love with and married. Bodie was single, homeless, bankrupt, his life had hit rock bottom and all his dreams had been extinguished.

His old school friend Shane, who had moved into The Beach House a year before, gave the sofa-surfing Bodie a heads up that there was a vacancy in the building. It just so happened to be Apartment #8 located directly next to him. In a twist of unrealized irony, Shane had found the prior residents – an elderly Italian couple with a constant pattern of noisy screaming matches and audible muted make-up love – to be undesirable neighbors, and was glad when they left. He was unaware that the two Italians had moved out because they couldn't stand the constant noise of fucking and fighting coming from his apartment. Susan Hockman, the eccentric landlady of Apartment #8, was old school and didn't run credit reports or ask for any proof of income. As a retired psychologist who still had an aura of dime-store shrink, she judged a perspective tenant's ability to pay rent by the firmness and sweatiness of their handshake. Tight grip and dry palms was deemed desirable, but if they were loose and clammy they needed to find lodgings elsewhere. This was lucky for Bodie, as much like half of America's citizenry and possibly America itself, he had a credit rating verging in the realm of junk. If Susan or anyone else had run his FICO score there was no way any keys would be handed over. With a dry, firm, winning handshake, Bodie took possession of the little $750 a month residence. This was with great relief, as sleeping on his dad's couch – a man who had also lost his shirt in the car wash enterprise – wasn't fun.

Bodie was not bitter or angry and accepted what had happened to him as part of the game of life. This recession, which had robbed him of love, dignity and a bright future, was like a violent electrical storm and totally beyond his control. Although much like the final scene of *The Usual Suspects*, the signs, had he noticed, were obvious. Money was too easy, lending requirements for finance too loose, and greed uncontrolled and rampant. Had Bodie stepped back and thought about what was going on for just a minute, the outcome would have been obvious. For Bodie, The Beach House would be a way back to greater things. One way or another, he told himself, he would rebuild his life. He didn't know how, or when it would be possible, but this was still America and everyone got a second chance.

Workingmen's bars were one of the few sectors of the bruised economy that hadn't witnessed an economic collapse. Lucky employees in any industry who hadn't lost their precious jobs were worked even harder by their bosses and reminded daily how they could easily be fired and replaced. These over-worked and under-pressure citizens turned to cheap bars as a place to unwind and let off steam. The unlucky in life without a job, but with their extended stint on unemployment, needed an escape from the tedious full-time job of looking for a full-time job. These hopeful wage earners of the future would spend their dole money on beer and cheap food and wish for better days ahead. Bodie, always a hard grafter and well known around town, was appreciative for the offer of work at The Blue Anchor. It was a job that he liked, was good at, and the pub's British owners gave him respect. Importantly, it was walking distance from The Beach House as Bodie was without a car. From here he would start again and begin to work his way back to the place he was once at.

It was a busier evening than usual at The Blue Anchor, with Team USA soccer playing England and the game was broadcast live. Soccer, played by people of all sizes, genders and ages, was a game that united the American silent-majority. A fixture of this caliber was a rallying call for the reassuring factions that followed the nation's seventh most popular sport. In a show of comradery, in perhaps the only real peaceful international arena the United States participated in, Floridian fans extracted themselves from their comfortable air-conditioned living, and ventured out to absorb the atmosphere and energy of local bars. Suburban families paraded spawn, with safe names like Brad, Madison and Taylor, and took great pride in their cherub faces painted in patriotic red white and blue. The moms dressed in comfortable JC Penney stretch jeans, flat shoes and fulfilled with that satisfaction of having done their part in creating and raising a new crop of Americans. The men of the fan base, disproportionately named Todd and Brian, sporting SEC frat boy facial hair that was all the rage back in 1997, had one eye on the game and the other on a pretty waitress, someone else's wife or a friend's blossoming teenage daughter. The only sign that all might not be sedate within the clean-cut suburban families that supported their side was the chilling edge to the "USA! USA! USA!" chants that punctuated times of exciting play.

The fact that the England fans in Florida were greatly outnumbered by the locals was a familiar story for expat England fans the world over. Too much sun, too much booze and a distance from the "Old World" had made them more British than the British who still called Britain home. Some fans talked about the "spirit of sixty-six", winning it all again, but for most, disappointment and being on the losing side of a penalty shoot-out was all part of supporting their side.

Pete had used this game as an excuse to entertain a group of hacks from the Boca Raton-based *Globe*. After all, this was their local and they didn't need much of a reason to hit the pub. It was good business to put a couple of hundred bucks behind the bar and let the guys go for it, as it was easily paid back with tips sent his way. The men sitting at his table today were an eclectic bunch, but to the casual observer they looked more like a group of accountants in need of urgent detox, rather than the cut-throat tabloid newsmen they actually were. The score at half time was level, one goal to each side. The mood in the pub was jovial – on edge for a win, but all-in-all friendly.

Bodie was worked off his feet serving the packed house, but he appreciated the buzzing crowd and his overflowing tip jar.

Pete was placing a large order with Bodie at the bar when Angel Mancini and Simon Godfrey entered through the pub's main entrance. Angel was dressed elegantly in a granny-chic paisley-print dress and matching shoes. The "Team USA" scarf draped around the neck of preppy Simon looked out of place over his crested blazer. Pete waved towards their direction, noticing the uncomfortable body language the couple shared. Bodie poured the final pint of the order and gave Pete that man-to-man-look as if to say he knew exactly what the other was thinking. It had been a week since Angel's "performance" had made its way around The Beach House. Pete was surprised that the first person to make him aware of it was Gabriel Garlech. Pete couldn't figure who had flagged it up to Gabriel, as he wasn't exactly a popular neighbor and he couldn't imagine anyone going out of their way to share revelations with him. As Pete lived next door to Gabriel and Bessie he tried to keep on cordial terms, but saw The Beach House's immediate and pressing issues leading back to the havoc reaped by this crazy paranoid pair.

Angel and Simon settled into the far corner of the pub to watch the second half of the game. As the on-pitch action slowed for a substitution or an injury stoppage, Pete glanced over towards their table. From a career in observing couples interacting, he could easily tell that neither Simon nor Angel was having much fun. If he had pictures of their interaction the caption would lean towards the overused phrase, "Trouble in Paradise." As the final whistle blew and the game ended in a draw, Pete excused himself from his group of fellow journalists and made his way over to Angel and Simon's table.

They quickly stopped what they were saying, or possibly arguing about, and Angel motioned for him to take a seat.

"Not the most exciting game," Pete said, breaking the chilly air as he made himself comfortable.

"Soccer's not my thing – ball wrong size and shape," shot back Simon as he ripped up a beer mat in frustration. If anyone had asked, polo, rugby and College Football were his games.

"The match had its moments," Angel replied.

"How do you think USA will do at the World Cup this year?" Pete punted out as a safe on-topic question.

"No idea," said Simon, not caring and looking like he would rather be somewhere else before adding, "What do you think, Angel? You have good insight, a level head and always make solid judgment calls."

Pete noticed the edginess of Simon and the general unease of Angel. In an effort to move the conversation along he changed the subject, saying, "Angel, we've not had a chance to talk since..."

Simon launched straight into what was on his mind. "You saw Angel on all fours getting double-teamed,' he interrupted. "I know you were dying to mention this, embarrass me and have your one-up moment. Of course it was on your mind, so let's just get it out in the open. Sunlight is the best disinfectant and all that. I bet you and all your sad friends have been laughing your heads off while not busy jerking off to my fiancée. Over to you, Angel. Anything you'd like to say?"

The deadly silence was brief, but seemed much longer. Simon then resumed his rant with haste. "Maybe you don't want to say anything, Angel? Just simply pick up a couple of guys, get to know them for five minutes, take them home and let them do what they want to you. Why not video it as well? Just so you don't forget the special occasion. Of course, great idea!" At that point Simon stood up and made himself known to the entire bar. Pete sat there in silence assessing what might happen as Angel became redder, sadder and on the verge of tears.

"Listen everyone. May I have your attention?" Simon said in a bellowing voice before making a "Shhh" sound and bringing the entire pub to silence. "My future bride here, the beautiful Ms. Angel Mancini, likes to fuck random strangers, preferably in multiples!"

"Simon, please don't," said Angel, now in tears and trying to bring a halt to the verbal slow-motion manslaughter that was in brutal progress. Pete, not able to think quickly enough about how to act, took the road less travelled and did nothing. All eyes in the bar were focused on Simon and Angel.

"Darling, please. This is for you," Simon said, cutting her off in a posh Palm Beach tone before delivering the rest of his monologue. "So guys, maybe ladies, please come over and introduce yourself. Don't worry. She doesn't want to really know you, just screw you. Bring your video equipment as well.

She loves to be filmed blowing strangers." Simon's voice was now getting louder and angrier. "Yes, she will make you famous. Our Angel here is an Internet sensation. You might be familiar already with her. Blue Meth, girl-next-door of the week! My entire family knows exactly what type of lady she is and how and where she likes it put. Actually, I think most of South Florida knows her disgusting ways. Open calls start now... Please come on over and don't be shy. Fill your boots, guys, this lady is open for business!"

Simon put his crested blazer back on and with a flip of the wrist perfectly adjusted his Team USA scarf before storming out of the pub. Wholesome soccer moms looked aghast at what they had just witnessed. A toddler decked out in Stars and Stripes gear began to wail uncontrollably. An elderly England fan with a table full of empties broke the silence when he said a little too loudly to himself, "That lass, tasty. Where do I sign up?" A few of the men in attendance from their perplexed expressions were certainly interested in taking up the advertised offer.

In an effort to distract proceedings, a quick-thinking Bodie rang the counter bell and shouted, "Team USA Happy Hour Special NOW!" Everyone went back to what they were previously doing.

Angel was now fully engulfed in a cascade of tears. Pete was not quite sure what he was expected to do in this type of unusual situation, so he headed for safety and rewound the conversation to the moment before Simon had gone postal. "As I was about to say before your fiancée sidetracked us, we've not had a chance to talk since the building sale announcement. Do you have any ideas? I have a few…"

Angel snapped back in a low tone intermingled with sniffles, "Pete, do you think I could give a flying fuck about the building!" Angel then picked a Guinness-is-good-for-you slogan napkin and wiped the tears from her eyes before adding, "As a side note, Pete, you are beyond useless and did nothing to stop him! You're really a pathetic man."

"What exactly was I meant to do?" asked Pete. "Sit him down and say, 'Calm down, get a grip on yourself!' Did you want me to tackle him to the ground? Punch him? Knock his lights out?"

"All of the above or anything."

At that instant a drunk elderly man, with a face that looked like a bird, staggered over to their table. "Hello, Miss!" he said in an Irish accent. He took a sip of his pint before adding, "You're a fine filly and I want a ride."

Angel re-upped the tear flow, picked up her bag and ran out of the pub. Pete, like a flipper in a pinball machine, pushed the drunken little man in the opposite direction and he bounced away. Pete downed the rest of his pint and thought to himself that this entire scene had been messier than a Port-a-Jon in a twister. Bodie looked over from the bar at Pete and gave him a stern look. Pete shrugged his arms and shoulders in a "What do you want me to do?" way. Bodie pointed to the door and mouthed back, "Go after her!"

Pete jumped out of his seat, headed out the front door and scanned the street. Angel had not gone west into town and he couldn't see her east, but possibly she could be over the hump of the Intracoastal drawbridge. He walked speedily over the bridge and as he reached the top of the slight arch he could see Angel on the opposite side of Atlantic Avenue. He caught up with her just outside Kientzy the jewelers. The wind was blowing hard and warm from the south. A full moon gleamed high in the sky.

"Angel, hold on!" Pete shouted.

"Fuck you, Pete. I don't want to talk about any of it," she replied. They were now both halted outside the jewelers. "I know all you guys at The Beach House are laughing at me. 'Angel of Death, looking quite alive in that position!' You're all joking to each other. Watching the video, spreading it around to anyone and everyone you know."

"You know we call you Angel of Death?"

"Of course. Rebecca doesn't miss a chance to let everything slip just to piss me off and be a bitch."

"We mean well!" said Pete, before adding, "The video really wasn't that bad. Not ideal, but nobody's perfect." The tears were still rolling down her cheeks and she hadn't replied. "It was taken years ago anyway, you were young and dumb..." Pete added before being cut off.

"And full of cum! Isn't that how the expression ends."

"I was going to say, 'And it's history,' but yes, that is an expression that could be used in this particular situation." They began walking together down Atlantic. They took a left on Andrews Avenue heading in the direction of The Beach House. "Anyway, from what I recall, the two guys dealt with most of the spooge," Pete added.

"You have a keen eye for detail."

"Stuff happens," Pete replied before adding, "Yes we all saw the video. It wasn't so bad, and most had seen worse, but of course being a neighbor, a cute one at that, it does get people talking."

"I was devastated. I really hoped it would vanish, go away, but it didn't. I knew I was in trouble when my brother working with the Peace Corp in Samoa messaged me about it. I think my dad is aware, but he's in total denial."

"Awkward," said Pete as they carried on walking.

"It got worse. I showed Simon and it wasn't a big deal at first. He was sympathetic and understanding. 'We all have a little crazy in us,' were his words. Well, that was until someone in his family saw it. They were shocked, horrified and told him, 'You need to ditch this girl. You can do better. This will haunt you so end it now!'"

"This kind of stuff occurs all the time in Palm Beach. I have covered much worse on the island," Pete replied.

"I'm sure, but we are in an unforgivable everything-in-public-domain age," she said. Angel's phone rang. Caller ID alerted it was Simon. "I am not taking his call. I think we are done. His main concern was that this would destroy his future political career. He really didn't care about how this was hurting me."

Angel turned off the phone.

"He's a nice guy," said Pete.

"I believed he was Mr. Perfect, that I had won the jackpot – or so I thought."

"That engagement ring he gave you is a serious cash investment. Not far off the one Reese Witherspoon's husband mortgaged himself up to his neck for," Pete pointed out, trying to put a positive spin on the situation.

"He can have it back. You guys back at the building all think he is an arrogant prick, don't you?"

"If you're happy we're happy, but he does have a way about him," Pete said.

"My family adored him, my friends not so much."

"About the video. Don't worry. You are in Florida living in a building full of whack jobs and you cut up dead bodies for a living. In the scheme of life it's not a big deal, and we will all survive," Pete said trying hard to put polish on an obvious turd.

"Easy for you to say, but for me it was distressing and embarrassing," said Angel. "It's like one of those readers' letters in *Cosmopolitan* that I thought were made up. Sandwiched on the page between the 'His penis snapped in the middle of reverse cowboy' and, 'My Boss fifth-based me during the lunch break,' I could visualize it with the comparatively sedate headline, 'I found my sex tape on the Internet and wanted to die.'"

"Those letters in *Cosmopolitan* are made up," Pete responded. "I know that for a fact. I do business with that magazine."

"Based on a thread of truth I guess, but fleshed out," Angel said.

"In my book, everything you read is based on a slim version of the truth," Pete said with uncertain ambiguity before adding, "Although your little horror story is perfect, I will pitch it to *Glamour* magazine. Their readers' stories are all true."

Pete and Angel reached the front entrance of The Beach House and stopped. The building's Bauhaus-font sign was gently blowing in the wind. Gabriel could be seen standing next to the dirty white door of Apartment #5 observing them. Angel's tears had dried and the moonlight enhanced her beauty.

"We never had our dinner together, Pete," she said with maybe a tinge of regret.

"I gave you an open invite to knock on my door and you never did. I don't do that for everyone. Most need an appointment."

"I know, my bad," she replied. "You were gone for weeks. I had no idea where. I then met Simon. Work and life intervened, but I should have made time for a neighbor."

"Stay there and don't move," Pete said, before running over to his apartment. He exited with a six-pack of beer and came back to Angel. "It's a beautiful night – let's have a beer on the beach."

"That is a wonderful idea, my Sir."

For a brief moment, Pete looked to Angel a little less than the plain average man she had always viewed him as.

They walked together the short distance to the beach, passing on their journey the spot where Tim Flanders had ended his life. The night was warm and the waves were breaking short and hard. They were not alone on the beach. Dogs were being walked and loved-up couples took in the fresh air. Sitting themselves on the shoreline, they drank, talked and laughed. Before picking up the beer at his place, Pete had taken a look through his notes on Angel and knew exactly which subjects would keep the conversation flowing. Angel told Pete about the crazy things that happened at the morgue and Pete chronicled to her his celebrity encounters. As predicted, Angel was impressed with his Taylor Swift stories. They talked about the meeting Ethan was planning to try to stop The Beach House sale. From what Pete's research had concluded, the buyer had ties to the New England mob and was not a guy to mess with. They both knew that the Homeowners' Association was on solid ground and a traditional legal challenge, even if the two of them did a deal with the Devil by forming an alliance with Bessie and Gabriel, would fall flat. They found each other's company easy and the beer supply expired long before they ran out of conversation.

They walked back to The Beach House together, Pete careful to give her a respectful amount of personal space. As they arrived at the flamingo statue, the natural point where their paths would split and deviate before they entered their respective front doors, they both paused. The window of Apartment #3 was open and Elton John's *Rocket Man* was audible in the night air. Emily Scott, the tenant residing in Apartment #11, had just entered her doorway accompanied by her beau de jour.

"Thank you, Pete. I needed that," Angel said to her somewhat distracted neighbor. She then turned her phone back on. It pinged multiple times to indicate missed messages. They were all from Simon.

"Angel, I have an idea," said Pete.

"Ok!" she said with an air of expectation.

"Your tape..."

"I had almost forgotten," said Angel. "Please don't talk about it. The second part of the evening was going so well."

"No, I have an idea," Pete persisted. "Your tape, I think I can make it go away. Let me rephrase that. I cannot wipe it from existence, but I might be able to make it disappear. It would possibly solve the problem you have with Simon."

September 12th 2016, from the Orlando Sentinel

FLORIDA MAN KILLED TESTING BULLETPROOF VEST

A Florida man who wondered if a bulletproof vest "still worked" was fatally shot by his cousin. A Police report said the Tampa resident put on the bulletproof vest and "wondered aloud whether it still worked." His cousin pulled out a gun and responded, "Let's see." Officers found the victim outside with a gunshot wound in his chest. He later died at a hospital. The shooter was charged with manslaughter and felon in possession of a firearm.

Apartment #9 Mental as Anything

In Pete's murky world of tabloid sleuthing and celebrity hunting, he was sometimes required by choice or circumstances to cooperate with those who could be viewed in his game as the natural enemy. Often a celebrity would oblige and court the press when they wanted self-promotion. A little more exposure, extra visibility and a boost to their personal stock was the desired outcome. Occasionally, the A-lister reaching out to Pete wasn't always wearing a happy face and holding out open arms. They dreaded the shots Pete had captured, that were now held in his possession and could be unleashed with a mere click of a mouse. It could be unflattering swimsuit snaps showing too much "cottage cheese", or maybe a photograph revealing a compromising situation with someone they shouldn't be seen with. Pete's images could be used as leverage in a negotiated quid pro quo trade that might get him something in return for making an unwanted story or set of pictures go away.

Cooperation with a celebrity could also be for personal motives. Pete was amazed how vengeful the rich and famous were to their ex lovers. Much of his best work had been tip offs coming from dumped celebrities happy to dish dirt and destroy the reputation of their former wife, boyfriend or girlfriend. Hollywood really was one massive version of High School, with never-ending backstabbing and dissing rampant. Pete had no qualms about making money off the back of their pettiness, jealousy and stupidity.

The rich and famous are rarely the brightest and sharpest tools in the shed. They have an unfortunate tendency to put themselves on the wrong side of the law. It might have been an occupational hazard in this business for Sean Penn to throw a rock at you, or an over-zealous bodyguard to smash a camera, but these acts came with consequences. The standard method of getting charges dropped would be for the perpetrator to make a deal, and give the journalist something in return. Publically, everyone would play nice and the celebrity or his associates would get off free.

All these various arrangements, deals and schemes required clear and open lines of sensible communication. Back in the day, the method of parley between tabloid hacks and celebrities – was loose and casual. If you were lucky, a showbiz manager might reach out and punt an offer. If you were unlucky, there would be no effort of diplomacy and you could be on the receiving end of a celebrity's fist, a projectile launched in your direction or a seemingly random and menacing break-in at your home or office. The link between the chased and the chasers had yet to be monetized and made into a profitable enterprise.

Journalism, like many aspects of the modern world, had been subject to hostile takeover by beady-eyed lawyers. The go-to guy in the contemporary era for the glitterati, to be that link and bridge in making unwanted news, disappear or never happen at all, was Matthew Knight Esq. This Malibu-based legal Rottweiler was known cheerfully and appreciatively as "Mad Dog." Knight, a sharp-elbowed Mr. Cleanup, had made himself incredibly wealthy providing the strategy, logistics and legal firepower that enabled the misdeeds of the rich and famous (if they were his client) to largely go undocumented. All the more astonishing for a successful lawyer with a batting average second to none was that he had attended a third-tier law school and never once in an illustrious career personally appeared in a courtroom. For his style was not colorful cross-examination or skillful litigation, but brutal gunboat legal shakedowns enforced by nasty apocalyptical e-mail broadsides. These strikes, usually launched late on Friday evenings, gave a short window of compliance and a warning that, if not adhered to, would mean an immediate end to that world the unfortunate recipient held dear. Mr. Knight didn't let facts get in the way of his efforts, and often masked what could and could not be done with explosive language, vague extracts of largely irrelevant case law and dubious accusations of misdeeds. In reality, he was little more than a bully with a cheap law degree and an expensive taste in suits – although that was a familiar combination for those in Los Angeles who called law their profession.

Knight was feared and loathed by tabloid editors the world over, and if you were in his target scope you quickly acted in accordance with the requested demands. What wasn't commonly known by his basket of rich clients was the extent of the dealings Mr. Knight had with hacks when it suited his aims and he could convert a little collusion into lucre.

Matthew Knight Esq. was indebted to Pete, and had given him his personal cell number and with it the promise of a favor in the future if ever needed. This was part of the deal for making something nasty and humiliating disappear for one of his top clients. The gist of it was that a rich, famous, happily married father of four was caught in a compromising situation with a teenage boy, an eight ball of what looked like cocaine and a cage full of what were certainly clawless gerbils. The shocking photo-proof of this sordid tale had come into Pete's possession. Not having an immediate market in the family friendly periodicals he dealt with, Pete approached Mr. Knight to see if he would like it removed from the market. As a result of the arrangement between Pete and Knight, the evidence was safely buried in the vault of dark secrets maintained at the lawyer's practice. There it would remain as long as the client kept Knight on retainer. In the multi-facetted deal Pete had struck, he was delivered several bikini photo shoots with the said actor's very famous wife – and a level of appreciation from Mr. Knight that money couldn't buy.

It was while kicking back on the beach drinking beers with Angel that Pete had the idea of using Matthew Knight's skills and that banked favor as a solution to make her embarrassing problem disappear. One of this lawyer's sidelines was an industrial-scaled operation that involved making pictures and videos owned by celebrities that had found their way into the public realm evaporate into thin air. These could be videos hacked from computers, stolen photographic prints, imagery lifted from social media, or on occasion a sex tape that a disgruntled ex had made public. Armed with DMCA takedown notices and legal copyright ownership, Knight's minions would hunt down the public evidence of formerly private moments and make them private once again. Upon locating a perpetrator, Matthew Knight would scare the hell out of them with a "fuck-off-and-die" barrage of legal threats. It was rare that the defendant did not yield, kiss the ring and comply in short order. The services that Matthew Knight offered were not at all cheap and weren't available to his non-client base. Of course, if Pete were able to help Angel and make her raunchy video history, it would solidify his hero credentials.

Pete had put the call in to Knight's office at the crack of dawn West Coast time. This legal lion, like a cold war-era nuclear missile, was a fire-and-forget weapon with little doubt in capability. Pete was now sitting back waiting to hear the confirmation that Angel's problem had been dealt with, and he had already planned the next several moves in the pursuit of his beautiful neighbor. He intended to have the good news ready to deliver as Angel arrived home from work that day. Off the back of it he would suggest they had dinner together and celebrate what he had made happen. Seeing how well last night went and the "shining knight" feat he was on the verge of pulling off, she couldn't possibly decline his invite. From there, the seduction he anticipated would be plain sailing. Pete smugly patted himself on the back for creating such a cunning plan, although if he were to look in the mirror and self-analyze the way in which he operated it was little more evolved than Middle School romantic **fatalism** at its nerdiest.

Pete required some cover to stake out the patio area while waiting to catch Angel as she came home. For he couldn't just sit there in the shadows and pounce like a stalker as she opened her front door. What he needed was to be comfortably situated, nice and calm, having control of the dialog and holding the mental high ground. He had acquired this methodology in theoretical form from watching a box set of old John Cusack movies. He did wonder, though, how John Cusack's characters might have changed their play calls in the age of mobile cellular communications. Pete could send Angel a text, but he was sure that subtly organized theatrics gave his quest extra gravitas. Lloyd would never have won the heart of Diane with a barrage of text messages. What sealed the deal was physical effort, a display of imagination and Peter Gabriel's *In Your Eyes* blaring out at full blast.

For Pete's operating cover he suckered in Shane Dolman and Rebecca Gravois from Apartment #9. These two were the other crazy couple, aside from Bessie and Gabriel, who called The Beach House home. Apartment #9 had historically been a magnet for oddballs with an edge, and these two had not broken that tradition. Corralling them to the patio wasn't a hard feat. Shane and Rebecca seemingly had a lot of time on their hands and were easily tempted out of their dinky living space with an offer of a game of cards and complimentary beer.

Shane was what could be politely described as a "local's local." Growing up in Delray as a kid, the ice-cream vans still played Dixie and he had carried with him through life those same rough Southern edges. Shane's vocabulary was limited and not fit for your grandma, with every sentence containing one of his three favorite words: cunt, kike and cocksucker. In these days of gentrification, this type of person was a member of a dying breed. Contemporary life in Delray had socially evolved and the ice-cream vans now played a more progressive selection of tunes. In terms of physical appearance Shane was large, which was part derived from over-indulgence at his bar of choice, The Frog Lounge, part working hard doing manual labor and part Germanic DNA. He was middle-aged and possessed a large shaven head that, without assistance from any apparent neck structure, was firmly bolted onto a broad muscular body. He was raised in a then tough part of Delray and had never left the city for longer than a weekend fishing trip. After scraping through High School he worked odd jobs in construction, and when that was dry he did security and bouncer shifts around town. He had a long history of temperament issues that had led to regular run-ins with the law. His file at Delray Police HQ was thick, well thumbed and went back decades. Mostly there were violations for drunk and disorderly, DUI, bar brawls and a few charges of domestic abuse. He had a couple of thirty-day stints in County Jail to his credit, and if he broke probation again a minimum stretch of two years in prison awaited. As an all-round package, Shane Dolman was downright Neanderthal and it was prudent to give him a wide berth if you ever sensed he was angry.

The Nancy to Shane's Sid was his long-term on-off partner Rebecca Gravois. Although they had attended High School together, she had left upon graduation for better things. A degree in Communications from Georgia Tech directed her to a succession of jobs in Atlanta. As a young and attractive twenty-something, she worked her looks to the best of her ability and eventually landed a good paying job at CNN. Rebecca was nearly happily married to a low-level executive at Coca-Cola, but too much booze and a series of affairs with her newsroom bosses broke that up. A decade of hard living in downtown Atlanta finally caught up with her when she came to realize she was well past the wrong side of thirty and had a serious and deadly addiction to booze. Picked up by her parents and hauled back home, they paid her way through a Delray Beach rehab.

One day, while dining at The Green Owl, she bumped into her old prom date Shane. A quick catch-up on life over scrambled eggs and strong coffee rekindled the romance, although, as she recalled, their original dalliance was low on romance and high on sex in the back of a pickup truck parked out west in the swamp. They had been together on and off for several years now. The violent fights, loud screaming matches and toxic physiological mind games were made tolerable by the generous amounts of self-prescribed rough and dirty sex. The relationship was noxious, unhealthy and dangerous, but the two of them thrived on it and now knew no other way to survive. Rebecca was back to her drinking ways and would often stumble home drunk, barely able to make it through her front door. Many a time she would simply crash on the patio, waking up in the morning surrounded by a pool of vomit and piss. Rebecca and Shane were possibly soul mates with their destruction, jealousy and rage, but anyone who knew them was scared as hell what might happen when they finally went too far. For now, though, they were content being tortured prisoners of love.

Rebecca was playing the role of banker and dishing out the cards. Pete always felt sorry for the woman, but could not help getting a little enjoyment watching this train wreck in progress. It was similar to why readers of tabloids liked coverage of Miley Cyrus, Lindsay Lohan and anyone Kim Kardashian happened to marry. Rebecca was wearing large sunglasses that shielded possibly more than bleary hung-over eyes. She was aged beyond her years from burning the candle at both ends, but it was still possible to see that at one point she would have been beautiful. Had she taken a different path she would have enjoyed a good life, marriage, possibly children and might now be living in a nice little house with a heated pool and a fire pit purchased from Pier 1.

Bodie had joined the game and, so far, was winning. This was perhaps his longest winning streak at anything in years. If you looked under the table you could see Rebecca seductively playing footsie with Shane's best friend. Rebecca thrived on the potential danger element, and if Shane ever noticed it would get ugly – fast. Rebecca was telling everyone at the table about a no-risk way of making serious money trading stocks. She had a system that was "fail-safe". Pete couldn't help but wonder why, if it was so good, she was splitting the rent on a tiny studio apartment.

"Are you guys going to Ethan's meeting about the building?" asked Pete, as he put another losing hand on the table.

"If it was down to me," said Shane, pointing to the white door of Apartment #5, "the simplest way of settling this problem with them is to take those motherfuckers down to the woodshed and make 'em go away. That is what I would do to those cunts if I wasn't on probation."

"Yes, we will be there," said Rebecca, answering for her and Shane, "although I'm not exactly sure what we can do. As you're a homeowner, Pete, you should have rights and could stop it."

"I'm working on it, although I'm wondering exactly how."

"Pete, we have a business opportunity for you. Myself and Rebecca," said Shane.

"Stock picks?" Pete suggested with a look of panic.

"It's very easy, you don't have to do much and guaranteed returns," said Shane trying to reel Pete in.

Jacob from Apartment #10 exited his front door and walked down the steps that led from the building's upper level down to the patio.

"Joining us for poker, Jacob?" asked Rebecca.

"No, I have a date in town," said Jacob optimistically.

Pete looked up from another bad hand of cards, happy to be rescued from the get-rich-quick offer Shane was about to make, and noticed Jacob was dressed up more than usual.

"A date? You have a wife!" Pete fielded to the man he knew to be well and truly under the thumb.

"Ha, she's in Missouri and I'm in Florida. Man needs some space in troubled times."

"Balls deep by end of first date or move on!" were the uncouth words Shane offered up as serious advice. Rebecca, who was not looking thrilled with his suggestion, gave her partner a look of disgust.

Pete's phone rang. It was the call from California he was waiting for. Walking away from the group to the privacy of the front garden's mango tree, he answered Knight's call.

"All sorted, Matt?" Pete asked.

"This nut is a little tougher than usual, Pete," Matthew Knight answered in a rough Queen's accent.

"You're joking. You get the big bucks for cleaning up messes."

"I told you that Friday evenings were when I get optimal results. You being in a hurry for no good reason didn't help. Hit them on a Friday! Make them sweat over the weekend, and by Monday they cave in. That's the way I work. You know that! None of this Tuesday morning lark!" the exasperated lawyer rumbled down the phone.

"What happened?"

"Not sure even a Friday would have made any difference on this one," explained Knight. "The guy is slick and bases are all covered. He has his shit buried deeper than an Alabama tick."

"These porn guys are breed of their own," Pete tossed back in a token gesture of understanding.

"OK, so the Blue Meth owner is called Tandy Jenkins. Based in your neck of the woods, North Miami. Guy runs a slippery operation. Servers in Belarus, money flowing through Luxembourg and limited American-based wealth he has buried in his primary residence."

"And with Florida law being what it is it's impossible to make legal claims on property that is homesteaded," added Pete.

"Exactly. Tandy runs a bunch of porn sites. Some are amateur user-generated uploads like Blue Meth. Others rely on live action wannabe famous girls under contract with him. I had a gal in the office pretend she wanted to be one of his new stars. Guy is sleazy as hell, but aside from a name and an address he is a virtual ghost. No pictures, no social-media presence or any idea of what he looks like. I did get him in e-mail correspondence, but he wasn't at all intimidated. He sent me back a link to all the other lawsuits he has piled up. He has more incoming backed up than LAX on a rain day," said the rarely stumped Matthew Knight. "The guy wasn't bothered and told me to 'Bring it on!'"

"What about copyright violation? Can we get the site taken offline locally if we prove the video is stolen?"

"I tried that approach," said Knight. "Played nice, said we don't want money and just the one video deleted. No flies on Jenkins and he knew exactly the little shoot in question. He said the video was shot in international waters, GPS data to prove it. Due to location and the ship registered in Venezuela, property and jurisdiction don't recognize copyright laws or legal ownership claims. We cannot nail him that way."

"So you are telling me this North Miami jerk has defeated California's greatest, 'Mad Dog Matthew Knight?'" said Pete in an ironically stumped tone.

"I hate to say it, but yes, he has me snookered," came the reply. "Fucker has nothing visible that we can take from him and isn't at all scared. I ply my trade on fear, panic and the threat of taking your goodies. I have zero leverage on Tandy Jenkins."

"So, looking at the scenario we have here, it must be similar to dealing with the lawyer Gloria Allred. How do you settle stuff with her, make those messy accusations from all those distressed damsels go away?"

"If you cannot legally scare, the only choice you have is to give them something they want or need or cannot live without in exchange," said Knight.

"Everybody has their price."

"Yes, money is always the equalizer, but how much cash do you want to part with for this?" asked the lawyer. "Tandy Jenkins no doubt has plenty of dough sat offshore, and besides, he didn't make any noise that would indicate he wanted his beak wetted. Is this broad in the video your girlfriend or something? This is a lot of bother for nobody!"

"Not a girlfriend and certainly not a nobody, just a friend. A neighbor, actually."

"Pete, this is big-league grief for the girl next door," said Knight. "Your second option – and this is out of my field of expertise, especially as we are talking on a cell phone – is to threaten or have them physically shaken up. A little bit of forceful coercion, I have heard, is a way of oiling the wheels, making people change their outlook on life."

Pete looked towards the hulking mass of bare-chested, bare-footed Shane Dolman.

"Matt, you say this scumbag lives in North Miami. Send me over his details. I have an idea." Pete hung the phone up and went back over to the group of poker players.

"Shane, I need a bit of muscle down South. Can I hire you for the rest of the day?"

"$20 an hour and I bring the tunes for the ride," Shane said, as he jumped from his seat and headed back to his apartment to retrieve footwear and a stack of compact discs.

Pete had ridden shotgun once before with Shane, and on that occasion Shane had dictated the soundtrack. For a man who had never owned a passport, Shane had an eccentric taste in international music. For reasons unknown he would exclusively listen to Antipodean songs of the '80s, with Crowded House, Mental As Anything, Men at Work and Midnight Oil being the essential components to his limited music library. Pete could only think it was some kind of natural trait that went along with ownership of the quintessential Australian name.

The traffic going south on I-95 was rough. Even the Haitian racers didn't possess adequate space on the highway to participate in their favorite sport of lane weaving without using signals. The sky to the south was black and the outside air thick. Shane was, at best, a man of few words, but there was only so many times Pete could listen to *Live It Up* before he opted for the risk of what a conversation might bring.

Turning down the music system, Pete took a chance, saying, "Shane, the business opportunity you were going to offer?"

"Glad you finally asked, Sir. We, myself and Rebecca, are offering you, Pete Alexander, the opportunity to buy premarket shares in Brilliant USA Inc," said Shane with his salesman hat firmly in place.

"Shane, what exactly is Brilliant USA Inc?"

"Brilliant USA Inc is an investment vehicle that will give you a guaranteed yield of 12% per annum. This is over five times more than your main street bank offers and beats stock-market returns," Shane said, not deviating from message.

"How exactly are you and Rebecca making this happen? She works part-time at a boutique and you work odd-job construction. 12% per annum is Warren Buffet territory!" enquired Pete with an air of disbelief.

"That was the old us – we're now in business," said Shane. "We're not actually investing your money; you're investing in us, in our company. You would be buying equity in our operation."

"Your operation?"

"We have secured exclusive franchise rights with Brilliant, a British kitchen appliance maker, for the North American market. We then parcel out regional rights to the West Coast, Hawaii, Sunbelt, Canada, etc," said Shane, before pausing for air and adding further detail. "We need additional investment in place to expand our territory to South America."

"You live in a sub four-hundred-square-foot apartment, so where are you going to store all these appliances and run this business from?" asked Pete.

"The equipment never comes our way, so we don't have to get our hands dirty. We are what they call, 'Executive level,'" Shane proudly declared.

"So you pay this company in England a fee and then you have rights to sell their washing machines. You then break up your North American rights and sell them on?"

"Exactly. The regional distributors then sell the appliances to local dealerships," Shane said. "The money is all up front."

"How did you and Rebecca become involved in this amazing opportunity?" Pete asked, trying to delve deeper.

"Luck, my friend," smiled Shane. "Life is all about luck and we hit the mother lode of it some months back. We were at the Lion & Eagle Pub in Boca and by chance sat next to an English gentleman who was in Florida for a meeting. Actually, he was there to finalize the agreement to market his Brilliant appliance line in America. The fellow he was set to meet never showed up, and we got talking. To cut a long story very short, the other guy's loss was our gain. We shook on the deal that day. It was a real chance thing that we just happened to be sat next to the guy like that. A lot of business happens that way, you know."

"This guy you met in the pub, did he show you his products?"

"We saw pictures of all the washing machines and dishwashers," said Shane. "They are European style, small with low energy consumption, and will be the next big thing. They're real quality – the Range Rover of appliances is how we market them."

"You have paid him money to secure the rights?"

"Of course. He wanted cash up front and we pay him a monthly license fee. We have made it back and some from our investors. He told us exactly how to do it and we never used any of our own funds. At this point it's all profits, my friend!" said Shane in a way that might convince anyone who hadn't been privy to his criminal record.

"Who exactly are your investors?" Pete asked in a spirit of skepticism.

"I am not liking your tone, buddy," said Shane.

"Shane, you have your sales patter down smoothly, but I tell you why I smell a rat."

"This is legit," was Shane's quick interrupting defense.

"Shane, I have just listened to you give me the lowdown for five minutes and not once have you mentioned any curse words. You don't sound like yourself at all."

"Fuck you, man. This is a good business. We're already making money for our investors. Offering you an 'in' was a favor I now regret. I was going to give you a good deal, but I'm not liking your fucking 'tude," Shane angrily shouted as he rummaged through his pile of discs looking for his favorite Midnight Oil live in Perth bootleg.

"I have to say your business scheme seems dodgy as fuck," Pete continued. "You meet a random guy in the pub, hand over money and sign a distribution deal for kitchen appliances you have only seen pictures of. You take investor money, presumably from people you know…"

Shane cut in, "Only selected people, family, friends from The Frog Lounge and Rebecca's customers at the boutique."

"You promise 12% returns to these investors?"

"It's guaranteed," boasted Shane. "Our word is our bond and we are already paying out!"

"You then sell on regional rights?" continued Pete.

"Yes, and the regional guys pay us up front and then collect from their outlets," said Shane. "The product is amazing. It sells itself."

"Has your first shipment come in yet from England?"

"It's at the port waiting for some paperwork to clear," explained Shane. "Anyway, that's immaterial, as we are collecting fees already and paying our investors back."

"Shane I hate to say but this doesn't pass the smell test and reeks of being a Ponzi scheme," Pete said, finally cutting to the chase.

"What do you mean?"

"Bernie Madoff!" was all Pete said.

"That Jew shithead was selling stocks that didn't exist! We are selling washing machines. Real things people can touch and a product people need."

"Yes, but you haven't actually ever touched or seen any, and you're paying money to investors from money that has come from other investors. This is a classic pyramid scheme!" said Pete.

"No, this is all kosher. Rebecca is taking care of the paperwork and finance and she is one smart cock-sucking piece of cunny."

"Now you're sounding more like yourself, Shane," said Pete. "I think I prefer you when you're not giving me your beachside time-share salesman spiel."

"So, Pete, shall I put you down for $5,000 in Class A preferred stock?"

"I'll sleep on it, Shane. How about that?" Pete said as he quickly stuffed in a CD from Shane's pile of music without looking at the offerings. It happened to be *The Best of Men at Work*. Surprisingly, the track listing reached double digits. After listening to Shane's business plan Pete was not sure if his neighbor was doing the conning or being conned. Whatever was going down, he was going to stay well clear of Rebecca and Shane as their operation was in the realm of "iceberg right ahead." Pete had seen a lot of strange things go down at The Beach House, but an international Ponzi scheme run by the second craziest and possibly stupidest people in the building was something original.

Pete pulled off the highway at the N 125th exit and followed his navigation system along designated surface streets. The little mid-century tract homes typical of this area were in various states of upkeep and decay. North Miami had always been on the seedy side, but in recent years it had established itself as a poor man's Van Nuys with a flourishing sex industry of XXX shops, strip clubs and back-garden locations for low-budget porn. It was no surprise that Blue Meth was operating from this loosely regulated city in the notoriously law-light state of Florida. The only other times that Pete had been to this enclave of Dade County was to work the kiss-and-tell stories of local hookers. He would be happy to make this visit brief, as he viewed the entire city as a sticky cesspit and a place to avoid. Pete had explained to Shane the exact nature of their mission. Shane's response, after an unneeded graphic review of Angel's video, was to point out the heroic nature of this quest and in his opinion the deserved reward. His suggestion was that, at the very least, Angel should, "Suck him off and swallow his load." Pete politely said he would keep that in mind, but had no such expectations.

Pete pulled up across the street from his target destination on NE 131st street. The mint-green 1960s-style house was located at the end of a cul-de-sac and backed onto a busy freeway. It was an unlikely location for the headquarters of a pornography empire and perhaps for that very reason the perfect place to choose. Property records showed it to be a small, three-bedroom, two-bathroom house purchased at the bottom of the real-estate market. An ugly garden of dead grass and chain-link fencing provided the unwelcoming frontage to the street. It had a hot tub and small sunken pool in the back yard.

Pete and Shane got into the back of their vehicle and, from concealed positions behind tinted glass, observed the residence. Lights were on in the house and there were visible signs of life and movement coming from within. Occasionally, girls in their late teens could be seen smoking and chatting on cell phones in the patio area next to the pool. These kind of low-level adult video companies often relied on creating their own exclusive content. They would recruit naïve and vulnerable girls from the suburban Midwest with a one-way ticket to Miami, the lure of cash and the promise of making them famous. It was common for the girls to live in the same houses where the skin movies were shot. Often, the film's producers withheld the bulk of the money the women earned to pay for board and lodging. These girls' careers lasted, on average, a mere few months, but that celluloid record of the career could often haunt them for life. It was a dark underside of Florida that, like many in this tropical dreamscape, was unregulated, ignored and given little scrutiny.

The rain was now hammering down with a ferocity known only in the tropics. Thunder coming so soon after the forked lightning indicated the storm was overhead.

"Pete, the easy way to settle this is to get hold of this kike-faced cunt and punch his lights out. That's what I would do if I weren't on probation. Piece of shit, this cunt," said Shane, looking at his watch hoping he would make it home at the very latest for the evening happy hour at The Frog Lounge.

"Shane, have you ever thought that if you solved problems in a logical thoughtful manner, and not with your fists, you might not be on probation?" said Pete, now tiring of his one-trick-pony monolog of aims achieved by physical threats and force.

"Pete, why am I here?"

"As per the plan, please just do what I ask and that is all I need."

"Is that even legal? You know I'm on probation," the now agitated thug, sans neck, replied.

Pete and Shane walked quickly in the rain to the front door of Tandy Jenkins' pocket palace of porn. Pete carried a clipboard and pen in his hand. Shane's only prop was his muscle. Pete rang the door and pointed for Shane to stand just to the right and not be visible when it opened. A scantily clad, barefoot girl in her early twenties came to the door. The smell of marijuana and cheep perfume from inside was overwhelming.

"Can I help y'all? " she said, in an accent originating from Tulsa.

"Package for Tandy Jenkins. I need him to sign here," said Pete, confidently holding out his clipboard and pen in the beating rain. The delivery-guy ruse came in many incarnations and was an old-fashioned tabloid trick that gave the nosey hack a legitimacy and purpose. It was amazing just how far you could get and how many doors opened under this pretense. The young, possibly stoned girl left the door open and, saying nothing to Pete, did a 180-degree turn and walked back down the hallway. A visible snake tattoo crept up her ankle and didn't leave much open flesh between her thighs and the butt cheeks that bulged out of the denim short shorts she was squeezed into. Loud acid punk music vibrated around the household. A minute or so later, a puffy bearded head poked out around the corner of the hallway.

"Delivery for Mr. Jenkins," Pete said while waving an empty envelope. The cautious pornographer, who knew that if it was a lawsuit it would have instantly been thrown to the floor and accompanied by the words "You've been served," now relaxed. Taking further stock of the situation, assessing Pete to be average looking in every way and thus clearly nonthreatening, Tandy Jenkins thought nothing of venturing to the door and signing for the delivery. Pete could now clearly see his adversary of today. The man who stood in front of him was tall, white and morbidly obese. Tandy possessed a large head buried under a pile of hair coming from every possible pore in every possible direction. He was barefoot and wearing a dressing gown that Pete presumed was the extent of his outfit. Possibly, if he had not found his calling in porn, he would be the kind of freak who lived in his mother's basement and, for fun, hacked the Democratic Party computer networks. Surely, though, if Tandy were to expand his girth much further he would end up on the national news being extracted out of his house with help from the fire brigade.

As Tandy reached the door, Pete held out his pen and went to work. "Tandy Jenkins, I am here on behalf of the law offices of Matthew Knight and I want to talk!" said Pete. This was Shane's call sign to earn his wage. He jumped out of the shadows and did his sole required action of the entire plan. In one broad stroke, Shane put his size eleven and a half workman's boots directly between the door and its frame in an effort to hinder its ability to close. The foot-in-the-door trick was another old-fashioned tabloid trooper ploy that had been in effective use as a "compliance method" to extend face time with a subject since doors were invented. The theory was that so long as you maintained control of the airspace, even with just a slither of open door, you had a line of communication and with it a chance to sway a conversation, get in an extra question and enhance the ability to achieve journalistic goals. Pete saw Shane with his brawny muscular bulk and big feet as the perfect wingman to take with him on today's irregular assignment. Shane needed to keep that door open for as long as possible while Pete made his nuanced pitch. The deal Pete wanted to present couldn't be expressed without a certain length of quality time. What Pete had not inputted into the equation was the sheer mass of Tandy Jenkins – he was truly enormous. Tandy's reflex lunge, slamming the door on Pete, was with such brute force, and backed by so much weight, that when it made contact with Shane's Granger boots it was an exercise in futile physics. The door, which in its defense was not made of the highest-quality materials, shattered into multiple pieces upon impact with the iron-tipped shoe.

Tandy crash-rolled out of his house and landed in a heap on the concrete pathway. In the process, his dressing gown opened wide, proving Pete's assumption to be correct that under the robe he was ready for business. The scene was made less shocking by the fact that whatever jewels he possessed were lost in a mass of hair that replicated the forest on his face. Shane grabbed his foot to make sure it was still there. Miraculously, a scuffed shoe was the extent of the damage – not that surviving the incident without injury had made Shane any less angry. Pete looked at Shane's face and ascertained that his probation predicament was not currently deemed an issue. Tandy rolled over, covering his junk, and tried to take stock at what had just happened. Pete, who had managed to avoid the crashing pieces of door, assessed the situation before him. If there was one phrase that not only summed up what had just happened but also the looks on the two examples of unsavory Florida citizenry in close proximity, it was "mental as anything." The evolving scenario was made all the more dramatic by the heavy thunderous rain.

It was while Shane was double-checking for movement in his toes and Tandy was catching his breath that Pete laid out the terms of his extraordinary offer.

October 12th 2013, from the New York Daily News

FLORIDA MAN WINS LIVE-ROACH EATING CONTEST COLLAPSES AND MYSTERIOUSLY DIES

The winner of a South Florida roach-eating contest died shortly after downing dozens of live bugs. Broward County authorities said contestants ate the insects during a competition held at a Deerfield Beach reptile store. The West Palm Beach resident became ill shortly after the contest ended and collapsed in front of the store. He was taken to a local hospital where he was pronounced dead. Piles of bugs were found lodged in his windpipe. The grand prize was a ball python snake.

Apartment #10 Midwestern Sensibilities

It had all started quite by chance some six weeks ago. Within a small window of time, Jacob Smith had Celia's work schedules dialed in. On Tuesdays and Fridays starting at 4.30 p.m. she worked the early evening shift at the Starbucks on Federal Avenue. Saturday and Sunday nights Celia had a second job as a waitress at Delray's premiere eatery, City Oyster. He had yet to visit her at the restaurant, although he had watched her busily waitressing from across the street. He was always careful to hide in a secluded spot and never be seen. Jacob lived and planned out each week around those two nights Celia worked as a barista. In fact, those two evenings had become the highlight of his unplanned and much extended stay in South Florida. Today, though, he was going to take their relationship to the next level. He was going to declare his love, pull off the rescue, save the girl, plan out their lives and create the fairytale ending they both deserved.

Jacob and his fellow legion of rehabbers had colonized this Starbucks franchise and made it their ground zero in the daily battle they waged against their demons. They would hang out for hours, blending into days, doing nothing and anything to avoid the temptation of getting "that fix of junk" or downing "that bottle of Jack." These drying-out addicts came in all sizes, ages, races and social economic groups. The banal banter amongst them revolved around how long they had been "clean," what "step" they were at and who was paying for their costly treatment. Ironically, these tortured souls were never visible for long without a large coffee in hand or a cigarette between the lips – one addiction traded for another, albeit a de-escalation of vice.

It was late afternoon and the air was muggy as Jacob sat down on the outer patio area of Starbucks. As usual, he kept to himself and didn't court new friends. For entertainment today he was eavesdropping the adjacent table while vacantly watching the speeding traffic thundering down Highway 1. A virgin *Palm Beach Post* sat on his lap ready to be absorbed. This place, as always, was a scene shunned by regular Delray citizenry. The transient tweekers self-quarantined in this quasi-public space was a win-win situation for all. The rehabbers had a place they could call their own and regular folks knew exactly where to avoid. If the Delray locals needed coffee or a place to meet they would visit the town's second

Starbucks outpost three blocks to the west, or any of the half-dozen independent Java Joints dotted around town.

"I've been clean for six months," a pretty blond, not far removed from High School, volunteered to Jacob as she ferociously tapped a packet of Camels on the table. In her other sweaty palm a Texan-sized cup of coffee was held with a death grip. Sat beside her was the latest of her steady boyfriends. To be precise, he was the third incarnation of Mr. Perfect with no decompression time between break-ups since she had landed in Florida. Her frantic parents had shipped their little girl south from Connecticut in an effort to save her life. The family doctor, on a large referral fee, had assured them that this problem could only be tamed by professional treatment of the highest caliber. Her folks depleted their retirement accounts to pay for their angel to get the finest help possible. While she was now clean of crystal meth, this young girl filled her days as little more than a cum depository for a former heroin addict double her age. If only her parents knew they had traded in their future golden-years cruises so a low-life creep could spend his afternoons violating their snowflake in the most unnatural way. At least they could rest assured that she was clean of drugs – for now, anyway, as her stability was fragile and the smallest amount of emotional unbalance could trigger a relapse. Every one of these hollowed-out minds that floated around at this Starbucks had a similar story to tell if you dare ask them.

"Congratulations," Jacob wearily replied. "Clean six months myself." Jacob took a sip of his coffee and looked down at his newspaper to indicate that was all the conversation he was giving.

It was on a thundery afternoon six weeks ago that Celia first stumbled into his life. At first Jacob hadn't really noticed her, as she was just another pretty young face behind the counter wearing a green apron and a displaying a plastic smile. That day he was sat at this same seat, casually listening to the plotting and scheming of unknown halfway housers at the next table. Their plight was simple: if they could rustle up some seed money, with $3,000 the amount being thrown around, they could kick-start their venture. They had an idea, the next big thing, the next Snapchat or Twitter. It would be huge if they could secure the cash. It was a recurring discussion repeated day-in, day-out, on this particular patio.

"You're back, and in the same seat," were the words all those weeks ago that jolted Jacob from his daze as Celia emptied the overflowing ashtray from his table.

"Sorry?" replied Jacob.

"You sat in the same seat last time you came," the young woman said cheerfully.

"You're correct. You've a good memory," he replied, suspiciously, although to be fair her odds were good to have forecast this correctly. His Midwestern sensibility, or what non-Midwesterners call "boring predictability," directed him to sit in the same seat each time he revisited a specific location. This careful unoriginality was extended to other areas of Jacob's life. For example, at each restaurant there would be one particular dish he would order and he would never deviate or dare to venture for something untried or fresh. Every time he flew on a plane he would always have the same seat, 19F. His clothes were mail ordered and from companies that historically did not alter style. It was Midwesterners like Jacob who had been the force behind profiting off similarity and order, and creating chains like McDonald's that replicated comfort and the bland. Law and order, sameness and Victorian thrift were what Jacob believed had made the Midwest "God's Own Country!"

Jacob now attentively watched the woman who had struck up the most basic of conversations efficiently go about her work and clean up the other tables. She appeared to be in her mid-twenties and petite in stature. From what he could put together under that ugly corporate uniform, she had a slender, toned physique and a pert derriere of a dedicated yoga disciple. Her thick, lush, black hair tied in a bun revealed a glorious bone structure wrapped in smooth olive skin. Centered within her face were light-brown piercing eyes of a devious quality. Jacob saw a nametag pinned on her apron; it read Celia. With her trash bag filled and the surrounding tables clean, she waved him goodbye and entered the store. Her sweet perfume briefly wafted in the humid air before being overpowered by a cloud of cigarette fumes from the couple sitting at the next table. *Wow! How nice was that*, Jacob thought to himself. Jacob was an English teacher before he crept up the ranks into school administration. There was still a literary bug that had not been eaten alive by desk jockeying, and he could've easily penned five thousand flowery words detailing the vision of beauty that had momentarily entered his realm.

That night, back at Apartment #10 of The Beach House, Jacob was unable to shake Celia out of his head. He couldn't get over that it was Celia who had taken the initiative and struck up conversation with him, and not the other way round. Surely this had to mean something? Jacob's wife, on their daily call, had sensed trouble with her husband, possibly fearing the worst, thinking maybe he was using again. Jacob brushed it off as nothing more than being homesick, and he made assurances that he was one hundred percent clean. That night in bed, Jacob intensely knew what he would like to do with Celia. He lived that over and over again until he could no more. The next day, following recovery class, Jacob went back to Starbucks and sat in his regular seat. There was no sign of Celia. The day after that he did the same, but once again she wasn't there. He asked the manager what had happened to Celia. She was a little suspicious of the dogged questioning from an obvious pupil of the Twelve Step, but eventually informed him that she only worked Tuesday and Friday evenings.

On Friday he skipped his daily rehab appointment and spent the entire day preparing for what he now believed to be a second date. After a hard jog along the beach to Linton Avenue, he came back to his home from home and began to ready himself for the evening. He prepared to the same exacting standards as he had all those years ago when he began courting his wife. What he saw in the mirror was a slightly embellished version of his true self. He was not tall or short, but felt just right. For a fifty-five-year-old guy he was not fat and had more hair than most of his peers. The gray in his hair was "George Clooneyish" and the glasses he now had to wear only added to what he saw as a distinguished package.

For once in his life Jacob broke with his regular pattern of regularity and went to the Boca Mall and bought clothes that he had no prior familiarity with. For this "date" he would dress in what he viewed as South Florida chic with his regular schoolteacher garb left firmly in the closet. As he headed out of the door of Apartment #10, Jacob's self-image wasn't a disgraced, aging Middle School Principal from Missouri. What Jacob saw in his fertile Walter Mitty mind was Don Johnson in his *Miami Vice* prime – loafers, no socks, a white linen jacket and quite possibly a Ferrari waiting outside. Most importantly, for the first time since he had been off drugs, Jacob felt he had something to live for.

On that next "date", Jacob had sat patiently on the Starbucks patio drinking coffee while pretending to read a Robert Reich book on income equality. He knew Celia would be working her shift and he had his usual spot on the patio. He was hoping she would come out again to clear the tables. It was all set up perfectly and was now just a matter of waiting. Eventually, in what seemed to Jacob an eternity, she exited the coffee shop with an empty trash bag in her hand. After three long days Jacob thought she looked even more beautiful than he had remembered. Today, the long black hair wasn't tied back and it flowed freely in the light wind. The green apron was off, revealing shapely curves from the front and tantalizing straps from the back. A small gap between her black pants and shirt displayed an erotic slither of naked flesh. Jacob tingled with anticipation and expectations of what might happen. It was like being sixteen again on the bus to school, when at that time of his life each day he would meet the young girl who eventually became his wife.

"You're back again!" Celia said as she made a beeline for his table. Jacob once again smelt her distinct perfume as she welcomingly invaded his airspace to pick up a coffee cup that had fallen on the floor. As she rose to put the cup in the trash, Jacob snatched a cheeky glimpse of a white frilly bra that had been made visible with assistance from a loose shirt that could not defy gravity.

"I'm here often," he replied. "My name is Jacob. Nice to see you again, Celia."

She gave him a how-did-you-know-my-name look of surprise.

"I read your name tag!" he added after sensing her unease.

"Of course," she said before walking to the next table and empting the ashtray.

"You've a pretty name," he said with a smile. "Were you named after anyone in particular?"

"Celia Thaxter, a nineteenth century gardener."

"From New Hampshire," said Jacob knowingly, as he followed up with another question. "Is that where you're from?"

"No, not at all," she said. "I'm from California. McFarland in the Central Valley, to be exact. The same town as the Kevin Costner movie, McFarland USA."

"Are you here for school or work?" said Jacob, now feeling a sense of effortlessness and rhythm that he hadn't felt since his teenage seducing prime.

"I am at Florida Atlantic, studying dance."

With that nugget of intelligence Jacob could now explain her toned body, although he felt she was too old to be an undergraduate and there must a back-story. Before he could think of a follow-up question and find out what it was, Celia had darted back into the store. She waved promisingly in his direction as the door closed behind her. Her signature perfume dissipated into the thick humid air in the same sad way that bubble gum loses its flavor far too quickly.

After a calculated interval of time, Jacob went into the coffee shop to see if he could find Celia. He saw her standing behind the counter serving a long line of customers. With the store's busyness, even if he ordered another drink the amount of face time granted wouldn't be worth the price of admission. He was always a practical man at his core, although on the face of it he was partaking in a not-so-practical endeavor. Jacob went back to the patio hoping she would come out for a second time. As the sun set to the west and the crowds descended on Atlantic Avenue, Jacob headed home to The Beach House without talking to Celia again.

The following Tuesday, Jacob, with a little more knowledge of Celia's shift times, strategically arrived at the coffee shop a little after 6 p.m. As he entered the store he could see his muse was working the counter again. His heart pounded heavily with hope as he waited in the long line.

"What can I get you, Jacob?" Celia asked with perceived kindness as his turn came.

"Coffee, large," he requested. Jacob had evaluated that not only was this the most manly drink on the menu, but also that Celia would personally pour it for him on the spot. The fancy drinks were handled by the baristas out back and he wanted her personal assistance and as much one-on-one time as possible. Jacob was hypnotized watching Celia make the beverage before him. As he handed over his money, he brushed his skin against her soft hands. Jacob directly placed the change Celia handed back into the tip jar in an attempt to impress. He assured himself that Celia had smiled at him while making the drink. He thanked her and began to walk away. Just before he exited, Jacob looked over his shoulder in her direction. She was busy serving the next customer, a young-looking surfer dude. The attention Celia was giving this man made him jealous. Jacob sat at his regular seat on the patio mentally pacing while waiting for Celia to come out and clear up empties or even just come out and chat with him for no other reason than she wanted to. Celia evidently wasn't doing any clean-up duties that evening. In her place, a chubby disinterested man worked the patio and Jacob didn't see her again that night.

Like clockwork, the following Friday Jacob went back to Starbucks. Celia was not working the counter on this occasion. Jacob did his usual thing of sitting outside in his regular seat, listening to fellow rehabbers share their woes whilst watching cars speed by on the highway. There wasn't much of interest in the *Palm Beach Post* that day. Jacob liked to hunt the paper for those only-in-Florida stories that came across as crazy, extraordinary and not remotely able to occur in any other part of the world. For the first time since Jacob arrived in Florida, he started to feel a little homesick for St Louis. At this time of year the days were long and the weather just perfect. There was no need for air conditioning or heating. Jacob glanced up from his paper and saw Celia was back on patio clean-up detail. She smiled as soon as she saw him and went straight over to his table. It was from this precise moment on that Jacob assured himself that a flirtatious affair had begun, and it was his duty to nurture and grow it and take it all the way to its obvious conclusion.

Jacob learned from Celia that her last name was Rose and, eager to know more than he could find from Google, asked Pete as a favor to do a little journalistic digging for him. Once Pete was assured that Jacob was merely pursuing an understandable romantic indulgence and didn't have sinister intentions, he was glad to assist. For sure, a favor given by Pete wasn't forgotten. Missouri, after all, was Brad Pitt's birth state and the actor regularly flew there to visit family. Having a friend in those parts who owed you one was always a card to call in sometime in the future.

With just a full name and hometown given, Jacob couldn't believe the thickness of the dossier that Pete placed under the doormat of Apartment #10 on Celia Rose. By now Jacob knew her age (twenty-seven), her social security number, credit history, past places of residence and even more useful, her current address. He had learned from one of their chats that she lived in Boynton Beach, but now he had the precise location of her home. Pete had also included her telephone number, e-mail and Facebook account in the file. A brief biography described her family origins. Celia's parents had entered the country illegally. They worked on farms in California's Central Valley. Celia, however, was born on the lucky side of the border and was an American citizen. Like many hardworking first-generation immigrants, she had graduated from High School with first-class honors. She had spent two years at Chico State, making the Dean's List each semester. There were even some pictures in the file of her from a college dance performance.

Pete had detailed where Celia went for regular yoga sessions. Jacob once parked up opposite and, as Pete told him to do, hid behind a sunshield in the back of his car to avoid being seen. Jacob watched her arrive and leave the yoga studio. He thought she looked fantastic in those tight pants the girls these days wear, yoga mat in hand and perspiration coming from all the right places. For fear of being caught in this unexplainable act, he didn't do it a second time. At no point did it cross Jacob's mind that his pattern of behavior was strange or creepy. As Jacob became more obsessed with Celia, he became focused less on his recovery.

Jacob made sure he was at Starbucks every day Celia was working. On those days if Jacob didn't seek her out, Celia would come and find him. The conversations they shared, sometimes a few minutes, often longer if she could swing it, were in his opinion magical. On each encounter Jacob learnt something new about Celia and piece-by-piece she fleshed out her life story with additional parcels of color. Celia told him how she started working at the age of seventeen as a café waitress. At twenty-one she became a bar server. The money she made was handed straight over to the family. It paid the bills, it paid for her little sister's schooling, and more importantly, it paid the immigration lawyers that assisted her parents to legality. As a result of growing up in a poor household, she had never learned to drive or even ride a bicycle. Jacob found this innocence endearing and wanted to be the one to teach her these skills. He relished the little details of Celia's simple life and was fascinated by the minutia of an existence that was so far removed from his suburban Midwestern world.

Celia told Jacob that she had ended up in Florida after following a boy, Sergey Putin, a Ukrainian-Russian immigrant. They had first met in High School. Celia dropped out of college to follow him to Florida when he moved there to pursue a filmmaking career. In Pete's file there was a picture of this man – Russian pride tattoos on his arms, skinhead haircut, diamond earring and wife-beater vest. He looked like an extremely nasty-looking character. Jacob assumed he was the kind of guy who smoked too much, drank too much and shouted too much. What started as a promising job in editing for Sergey soon morphed into a sleazy position on the bottom rung of the adult-movie industry. Sergey was currently a talent scout for new girls trying to get acting roles in skin flicks. He lived in a cheap rental house in North Miami pimping out somebody's fresh-faced, barely legal daughter. He made a good living, drove a slick car and mostly didn't mix business with pleasure. Celia despised his current career and had told Jacob that this was a major cause of friction within their relationship. They didn't live together any more and often fought, broke up and then made up. It was a turbulent partnership at best. "What boyfriend?" she would often say to Jacob before adding, "Oh him! Nothing is going on with us." The relationship seemed to Jacob more off than on, but they always seemed to get back together. What did someone like Celia see in him? She could do much better. She will do much better! Jacob would make sure of this, he told himself.

The talk between Jacob and Celia flowed naturally. It was only constrained by the time they could snatch during her busy work schedule. Celia had shared her near-term aspirations with Jacob. She wanted to finish college, move back west, possibly somewhere with seasons. She hinted at Oregon, as it was affordable and had plenty of rain. Celia loved rain. She wanted a house with a garden and children – lots of them. She didn't really like Florida, as she despised bugs, humidity and non-existent public transportation. The racial tension reminded her of California's Central Valley. Celia had little fondness for the people in Florida, saying they were "meanies" and smoked too much, and their tattoos were not artistic but pointless. Celia rarely delved into Jacob's life. He put the lack of questioning down to her easy-going nature and the open-mindedness of her generation. Never did he contemplate it indicated a lack of interest on her part. Jacob himself was economical with the truth, implying to Celia that he was freshly divorced. Celia had figured early on that Jacob was in a rehab program; it was almost a condition of entry to that particular Starbucks. Celia didn't ask for specifics and he was happy not to offer them. Jacob concluded she was desperate to leave Florida, almost begging him to take her away. Celia just needed some help, a push and one extra good reason to go.

After six weeks of perceived mutual flirtations, Jacob thought it was time for action. The build up, pursuit, research and patience were all going to pay off today. Jacob hoped this would be the last time he ever had to come to this Starbucks and sit here with all these scummy junkies, rednecks and the dregs of Palm Beach County. He felt a different, more confident man than that first day he had met Celia all those weeks ago, with his mind fresh, his hair with a more youthful tint and a wardrobe updated for a task. He didn't think about drugs any more, as his thoughts and focus had shifted to Celia. She had filled a void in his life that had previously caused him so much trouble in St Louis.

Jacob was convinced that he would rescue this beautiful girl and together they would start a new life. Rural Oregon was the place she talked about. He would teach again, at a private school of course where they wouldn't dig into his past. He would support Celia as she finished college. That was important because she needed a degree. Then she could get a job at a community theater. There were many of those in Oregon. Jacob had decided that Oregon was possibly the community theater center of the world. Of course, there was the Shakespeare festival that would be the busy time of year for her. He thought Celia would make a great Lady Macbeth, as she could pull off that tragic look with ease. He would quickly start a family with her, so he could keep her close and she wouldn't stray. Barefoot and pregnant would be a great look for this young woman. It would be a shock to his now grown children, but they would get used to it someday.

Jacob's daydreaming about his new life with Celia was rudely interrupted by a commotion from the next table. The pretty young blond who had earlier volunteered her sobriety to him had just got into a blow-out argument. Jacob looked up from his paper to see exactly what was going on. Tears flowed, cigarette packs were launched as projectiles, clenched fists drawn and angry stares maintained. The girl jumped from her seat and ran across Federal highway narrowly missing being taken out by a Ford F-150. "Fuck you, slut!" shouted the rather unpleasant man she had been sharing her table and recent life with. It wasn't evident that she had heard him from the far side of the busy road. Jacob looked at his watch. It was 5.30 p.m. and he hadn't seen Celia today. He walked into the store and asked the manager where she was. He was told that she had called in sick. Jacob couldn't wait three more days to do what needed to be done. He would drive himself crazy spending even another hour without making his move. He would go to her home. Jacob thought it would all make perfect sense to Celia once he made his pitch. This was meant to be.

Jacob took the Old Dixie highway north for the five miles that separated him and Celia. He parked up across the street opposite her home. Until this moment, he had only ever viewed her place on Google Maps, as he was always too scared she might see him if he drove by. On a computer screen the building looked a pleasant picture of Florida living. Up close it was a dump situated on a street where parked cars were old, black teens loitered and dogs snarled rather than yapped. Jacob exited the car and walked to Celia's front door. It was cheap and in need of painting. The mailbox was stuffed with junk mailers. He peered into a window and saw a kitchen in need of a blitzkrieg with bleach and soap. Loud Metallica music seeped out of the building, easily drowning out the rattling air-conditioning unit. *This would be her last night in this hole*, Jacob thought to himself. He once again vowed to make a better life for Celia.

Jacob rang the door buzzer and waited. Sweat dripped from his forehead onto his spectacles. He mopped his brow with a shirtsleeve. He hoped the moist patches under his arms would be interpreted by Celia as a hazard of tropical living and not an indication of nerves. He had to look in control as he made his case for their future together. Nobody came to the door. Jacob was feeling uneasy, and as he looked over his shoulder he saw an aged Haitian woman in a unit across the courtyard staring at him. A flash of sheet lightning lit up the evening sky. A distant boom of thunder roared from the direction of Highway 41. The wind picked up its speed and jostled the street's palm trees. A storm was coming in from central Florida. Jacob rang the bell once again and this time followed up with a hard knock on the door. There was still no answer. A light-skinned black youth with a bushy head of dreadlocks came out from the adjacent apartment. He stood watching Jacob as he lit up a joint.

Feeling out of place at best and at worse being eyed as a repo man, bounty hunter, plain-clothed cop or some other pariah who frequents poor neighborhoods, Jacob decided it was best to leave before questions were asked. It was obvious that if Celia was home she couldn't hear anyone or anything under that racket of heavy-metal music. He started to have second thoughts about his plan. Although not happily married, Jacob was satisfactorily married and that was something he should respect. His teacher's union would make sure he secured another job back in Missouri when he was finished with his program. It may not be in Clayton or the County, but he could easily get a decent job in one of those crumbling St Louis schools. Even with his blemished record, a white former principal teaching in an inner-city school would be quite a coup for the system. What was he thinking? Could he really just check out of rehab and head west with a girl half his age? Did he really want to support her, become a father figure to her? What would they talk about? What would they have in common? Girls this age, especially from California were brainwashed. Recent history to them was to believe that Ronald Reagan was evil and out of control, destroying jobs, crushing the poor and setting loose on the streets the insane. Meanwhile, "God-like" Bill Clinton ran a budget surplus and his administration oversaw unchallenged prosperity. Jacob lived through all these times, and what coastal Liberals miss is how close the United States was to nuclear oblivion – that is, before Ronnie outspent those Commies. As for that Bill Clinton, the "Goldilocks" economy was the result of a bubble. People forget that while he was fooling around with the interns the terrorists were attending flight school right here in Boynton. Trying to make Celia a more educated citizen would be their pillow talk. Yes, Jacob thought, it might just work. Their relationship would be high-octane passion followed by informative instruction. His job would be to educate her, teach her to drive, teach her to ride a bicycle, teach her to be a lover, to be a wife, to be a mother. He would be supportive and nurturing and caring. And for Celia, her job was simple – she needed to make him happy. How could she not make him happy with that smile, that laughter, that innocence? If he was patient and listened and understood, he could protect her, let her flourish. It was destiny and he knew from the day he met her that they had a connection. He had to make it happen but obviously, as she was not coming to the door, it wouldn't be today, but maybe tomorrow or possibly next week.

Jacob made a retreat for his car. He turned the ignition key and started up the engine. The frigid air conditioning instantly fogged up his glasses. He took a cloth and cleaned off the condensation. As he placed the clean spectacles back on his face he looked out of his windshield and saw Celia through her kitchen window. Jacob could only see her from the waist up at this angle. Her hair was wet and tied up above her head like a tiny pineapple. She wore a white tank top, evidently with no bra underneath. Celia was revealing more skin than he had ever witnessed on their informal encounters. Like a vision of beauty before him, she stood clearly visible through the window. On his car radio a Roy Orbison classic played. His heart skipped a beat and he shuddered as she altered her direction and stared straight towards him. Celia's piercing eyes locked onto Jacob's. Could she really see him in the dark? She smiled, that same smile she always gave Jacob, the one that hit all the right notes and kept him captivated and always wanting more. Jacob thought she must have seen him. Celia had to have been in the shower when he banged on her front door. He had no choice but to make his move and tell her his feelings and explain his plan for their future life together.

Jacob slowly exited the car as he kept his eyes fixed on Celia, who was still on the other side of the kitchen window looking in his direction. Suddenly, a man came into the room with Celia. He was a rough-looking shirtless individual covered in tattoos. It was Sergey, her boyfriend. Was this really the man that she kept going back to? How could this be? He wasn't worthy of Celia or anyone else. Sergey reached his arms around Celia and kissed her neck – not tenderly, as Jacob dreamt he would, but in a physical, boorish, even violent way. Celia's eyes closed in the manner of a woman who was enjoying the roughness of the clinch. It was finally obvious to Jacob what was going on. A post-coital seventh-inning stretch to the kitchen for snacks before the two of them went upstairs to partake in the rest of the game. When Jacob was banging on the door earlier, they were in bed together. Sergey held her tight and kissed her all over. He then sunk to his knees, out of sight but from the pleasure in Celia's face Jacob knew what was occurring.

Jacob was angry. Celia would never reach her potential if he let this relationship carry on. The sight of this low-rent thug pawing over her was too much for his vulnerability. Jacob had a baseball bat in the trunk of his car; this was always a good option for venting rage. The plan in his head was that he could go into Celia's home and mess up this prick. Possibly kill him. Once the deed was done, he was sure they could dispose of the body in the Everglades. Nobody would miss him. Nobody would care. Jacob could carefully construct a trail that, upon any investigation by local authorities, would tag rival pornography pimps as prime suspects. Celia would initially need convincing of his plan, but would thank him in the long run. It was all very Carl Hiaasen, complete with the good honest guy getting the girl and eventual justice being served by a pack of hungry gators.

The kitchen light went off and he could no longer see Celia and the Russian. Jacob's heart sunk to a deep place that he had not known since arriving in Florida. He had a good idea what Celia and her boyfriend would be doing now. A mentally deflated Jacob slowly drove out of the apartment complex towards the junction that fed onto Federal Highway. His turn signals flashed right until at the last moment when he pulled a hard left and headed further north. He drove through deteriorating neighborhoods until he was in the center of one the region's seediest. Middle-aged white guys cruising in this part of town were only after two things – hookers or drugs. What Jacob wanted quickly found him, and more frightening was just how effortlessly he found it.

Jacob drove over the long Intracoastal Bridge that separated the modern *A Tale of Two Cities*. On one side was West Palm Beach – a worker-bee conurbation with some thoroughly rotten neighborhoods. On the other was the City of Palm Beach, which was one of the richest municipalities in the entire world, and quite possibly the only city in the United States that made Beverly Hills look shabby. These two towns leached off each other in the brutal symbiotic way that keeps the American Dream always out of reach for the majority and maintains the one percent firmly on top. Jacob cruised through the opulent downtown and pulled up to a parking space on the intersection of S. Ocean Blvd and Jungle. He had no idea that he was sat across the street from Ivana Trump's mansion. He rolled down the car window taking in the sounds and smell of the Atlantic Ocean. The storm that earlier looked to be coming this way had moved south.

En route, Jacob had picked up the additional items he needed at the Winn-Dixie supermarket on Okeechobee Boulevard. A disposable plastic lighter and a roll of tin foil would suffice. It was more than obvious to the nervous cashier what his customer's intentions were. Tonight this store worker was lucky, as Jacob had the decency to pay for the goods – many in his situation wouldn't. In the car glove box he retrieved a Bic pen. This he disassembled, throwing the nib and ink cartridge onto the floor of the passenger seat. With elementary origami skills he made a depositary from a square of tin foil. Jacob filled this with the hard rock resin that he had acquired from a "corner boy" of about the same age as one of his former pupils. Jacob contemplated that the reason for the chase he had started all those weeks ago was for this inevitable outcome. Could he be that weak and in need of such a rambling exposition to validate the want? Although did he really need an excuse for abuse? He never had one previously. At the very least, if he did it should be a good one – something that he could explain to his wife and family, something they would possibly comprehend.

Smoking crack discreetly in a confined space was a multi-dexterous process that required skill. Once learnt, it was something never really forgotten. In his left hand Jacob held the tin-foil reservoir and filled it with the entire contents of his "dime bag". In his right hand he held the lighter and set it on a high continuous flame. Jacob inserted the empty barrel of the pen into his mouth. He then heated up the foil until the crack boiled and hissed. The odor, a distinct sweet burnt plastic-like smell, rose into the air. Jacob desperately sucked up, with the aid of the pen barrel, as much of these fumes as his mouth could hold. Once the smoke was in his mouth he was careful not to exhale or inhale, simply to hold, contain and let the crack do its work.

After the fumes had been given the needed time to absorb into the brain through the mouth's saliva glands he blew them out of the car window. The foul air was caught in the tropical slipstream and diffused into the evening wind. Jacob quickly reached the euphoric high he desired. He put the tin-foil wrap down on the passenger-seat floor and dropped the hot lighter onto his lap. He lowered the car seat to horizontal. He closed his eyes and was taken back to a place that seemed like only yesterday he had just left. After many months, he finally felt like he was home.

June 15th 2015, from the New York Daily News

FLORIDA WOMAN TOOK SELFIES DURING SEX WITH DOG INSIDE GRANDMA'S HOUSE

A Bradenton woman admitted to taking selfies as she had sex with her dog. She was charged by police with two counts of sexual activities involving animals after investigators found graphic photos on her cell phone. The 18-year-old told police that she coaxed her dog into licking her vagina between 30 and 40 times over several years. Each time she wanted to have sex with the dog, she'd lock herself in a bedroom, take off her pants and call the pet over. In her defense, the teen said the pup would "put her snout into her vagina on her own". The woman then snapped photos of the pup licking her vagina. Police said the dog showed no signs of injury when a vet checked it out.

Apartment #11 Fifty Shades of Delray

Sally Purdue wasn't the first and certainly wouldn't be the last resident of The Beach House living a secret double life. In fact, she was living at The Beach House under an alias and so far no one had figured out who she really was. Ms. Purdue had moved into the building eight months ago and, unusually for the screwball bunch that called this ramshackle complex home, rarely socialized with other residents.

By night Sally was a barmaid at Boston's on the Beach, the legendary local hotspot half a mile south on the A1A. By very late night, as seen by the "strange" of both sexes who accompanied her home and the unashamed guttural night chorus broadcast from her apartment, she was a lady who enjoyed rich amounts of nocturnal pleasures. During daylight hours Sally didn't often venture out from the confines of Apartment #11. It was what Sally did during these days, presumed by most sleeping off the previous evening's exertions, that was the secret portion of her strange twisted double life.

Sally had recently eased into her thirties and possessed a beautiful girl-next-door look that camouflaged a troubled edge. Fortunately, she was blessed with a genetically toned physique that didn't require effort or regimented exercise. A set of slender pins and a brace of solid B-cup breasts that a Boca housewife would trade her second Range Rover for were her most noticeable assets. Complementing this stellar body was porcelain skin, bright-blue eyes, thick brown hair and pencil lips artistically placed on a petite Scandinavian face. As an all-round deal, she was the kind of woman that heads never failed to turn for. Sally was well aware of her sexuality, and the power that came with it, and intended to utilize what God had given her for as long as possible.

Sally was raised in a hippy commune in Bolinas, California. She had only vague recollections of her father, who had bolted for a life of less commitment sometime before her third birthday. She was aware of her mother, but this woman was far from hands-on and outsourced the bulk of parental responsibility. As the saying goes, "It takes a village to raise a child." Replace the village with a group of hippies and, for better or worse, that was who was responsible for the raising of Ms. Sally Purdue. At this commune clothing was optional, drug use abundant and love either free or deemed for the taking. All the conditions needed to create an untraditional upbringing were firmly in place. A man who had masqueraded as her "uncle" for the first twelve years of Sally's life stole her innocence, and from there things only got worse. Sally was sixteen when the State finally broke up the commune and took all her "uncles" to trial on charges that were variations of abuse, rape and sodomy.

The other children she had been raised with, knowing only filthy living conditions, unchecked drug use, sexual exploitation and organic food, bolted for anything but this cocktail of what had been drilled into their heads as "normal." Relatives took in the luckier ones. Sally's best friend went to a nunnery and took her vows. A few of the older kids displayed rebellion towards their wild upbringing by enrolling in religious Midwestern Colleges. They were hastily conformed to societal norms by Bible-thumping priests who worked overtime to eradicate free love and sin from their souls. Once weaned off their prior healthy diets, they quickly got fat on junk food and blended in with their local host communities. Wherever these kids ended up, the common dominator was a sense of no longer feeling like a recurring character in a Joan Didion essay. Sally, unlike her fellow teenage peers, doubled down on what she had known and took it to the next level.

Possibly the only useful thing they did have at the Bolinas commune was a fantastic system of first-rate homeschooling. If you were willing and wanted to learn, a devoted pool of volunteers was available to provide a level of education that suburban schools with funding and good intentions couldn't match. Sally had taken full advantage of this, and upon the disbanding of her way of life applied to study English at the University of California. Being a white person, even perfect grades are never enough on their own to get admitted to the jewel-in-the-crown of American Public Universities. For at Berkeley it's essential to have an "X factor" or some other dispensation, with being a former child soldier, illegal alien, skilled inflated pigskin thrower or having a parent in San Quentin being amongst the most obvious ways to receive a thick letter from Admissions. Sally's personal statement, padded with recollections of sexual abuse and a horrific unconventional way of life, made her exactly the kind of "diverse person" the University wanted. Sally enrolled as a mature-for-her-years sixteen-year-old freshman in the class of 2001.

Berkeley was really nothing more than the Bolinas hippy commune on an industrial scale. Sally moved into Casa Zimbabwe, an unclean co-op in a leafy neighborhood north of campus. Her fellow housemates were as filthy and drug riddled as any of the "family" from her former life. During freshman week, Sally turned the clock back and became a self-anointed "born-again virgin." With her mask of innocence she started the year by participating in casual hook-ups with real virgins. The sex, which was kept somewhat legal by Romeo and Juliet laws, was indulged in escalating amounts as the months went by. At the end of the first semester Sally was sexually experimenting as much as a seven-day-a-week, twenty-four-hour day would allow. By the conclusion of her sophomore year she had conducted affairs with married professors and had serviced, or been serviced by, depending on your perspective, most of that year's Championship Rugby team.

For her junior year Sally upped her game and became an official pillar of the Cal community. With her eloquent English skills and deep carnal knowledge she was an obvious choice to be the *Daily California* newspaper's "Sex on Tuesday" columnist. The campus community thought the racy writings of her predecessor Emily Chung were raw and uncouth, but Sally's sexploits were at a level that her cohort wasn't expecting. Back-door-love, orgies, anilingus and written accounts of whoring for money were just the start of a sadistically brilliant series of columns that won regional notoriety and national scorn. The liberal-leaning campus was in complete outrage and there was even a move by the Chancellor to take over editorial control of the paper. A mini riot on Telegraph Avenue by Free Speech Advocates put a stop to that. The student community was split between people who spat and slut-shamed her and volunteers of all sexes who wanted to participate in her voracious life. If Sally had a dollar for every Psychology PhD student or Woman's Studies professor who wanted to study her, she'd call a house in the hills, and not the dirtiest, cheapest living space on offer at Cal, her home. With Professors' spouses worried about their husbands' fidelity, the football coach concerned about his players' focus and the campus medical department disturbed about its skyrocketing antibiotics budget, many people were happy to see Sally finally do a walk with no shame at graduation. With an Honors Degree in English under her well-notched belt, she was ready to take her show on the road.

Sally purchased a beaten-up Volkswagen Bug, packed up her few belongings and headed east. She stopped first at Bakersfield before hitting Las Vegas and ultimately linking up with historical Route 66. Over the next six months Sally would take odd jobs and work her way the entire two thousand miles of the "Mother Road." The mini romances, dirty sexcapades and menial jobs undertaken were all chronicled and became the basis for her debut book *Sally Does Route 66*. This published travel diary, heavy on frisk-and-fucking, was banned by Walmart, but given much love from Oprah. With all the publicity generated, the first edition sold out quickly and a larger second print run was rushed through. Suddenly, and unexpectedly, Sally was financially comfortable with a fat advance for a second book.

A newly minted Sally purchased a starter castle in Santa Fe and then bizarrely hid herself from the world. The surprise success, literary infamy and minor celebrity status were just too much for this disturbed girl to handle. Sally thought she might have creatively peaked too soon, and self-doubts and depression set in. Her sequel efforts went flaccid and a decade or so of sexless writer's block would ensue. Finally, after pressure from her agent and a depleted bank balance, Sally set to work on her long-overdue sequel. Scared of her fame, she used the fictional name Emily Scott, created a back-story for cover, dyed her hair and donned Clark Kent glasses. Sally's alias was that of a freshly divorced woman who had fled an abusive husband and general disenchantment with the "Land of Enchantment."

Sally had never been to Florida and only decided upon it as a potential destination after stumbling upon a cable rerun of the '80s flick *Body Heat*. This film's depiction of a steamy climate, rough men and unbounded raunch portrayed it as the perfect place to get her creative juices flowing. She packed her car with enough props to support her constructed origins tale and hit the road. She had promised her publisher that the finished work would be in the style of her first book, with lots of sex, a little travel literature, a dash of Floridian culture all rounded off with lots more sex. It would be written in the same sardonic and perverted style that Sally Purdue had shifted thousands of books to her loyal audience of those not-fucked-as-much-as-they-needed-to-be, fly-over-state soccer moms. The working title she picked out was *Sally Does The Sunshine State*.

Sally knew she had made a good choice of destination when, shortly after crossing the Alabama-Florida State line, she managed to lure back to her motel room a pair of "Top Gun" cadets from Pensacola. They "may nearly have been officers but they certainly weren't gentleman," she scribbled in her notes. A few days later in Jacksonville, an uneventful early morning "quickie" with a Waffle House cook on the hood of her car turned out not to be quite as "all-star" as the breakfast he had just made her. By the second week of her journey she had stopped in the old world town of St Augustine and had a memorable dalliance with a woman's volleyball player from

Croatia. The violent afternoon thunderstorms, the thick night air and the pounding waves reinvigorated her lust for life, her desire to write and the yearning to tell a story. With Florida as her self-prescribed Viagra, Sally was once again in full stride.

Sally slowly travelled down Federal Highway stopping in many quintessential Florida beach towns. Daytona, Titusville, Merritt Island and Vero Beach were all checked off her list. Three weeks into the trip she had made it as far as Palm Beach and by now had a fully perfected working system in place. Sally would rise late, always alone after ditching the previous night's partner. She would then go for a swim in the ocean. Over a late lunch and a cocktail she would start writing up her notes from the previous day and transform them into colorful prose. She would then see how the afternoon played out. Being an attractive woman who exuded sex appeal, Sally knew how to get attention from both genders. She could pick and choose, and if the quality and quantity available weren't quite what she was looking for, she wasn't afraid to do a bit of hunting herself. Her fail-safe backstop as a pick-up joint was the lumber department of The Home Depot. There she would never fail to find buff men or lesbian gals who weren't shy roaming the plywood and paneling aisle. After each evening's trysts she would make an escape and head to the next town where she would repeat the process all over again. Sally modeled her style on Paul Theroux's proven travel-writing techniques, although she recalled that unlike her, he was always far too eager to make his excuses and run from the slightest dalliance on offer.

Sally's plan was to keep going south until she reached Miami. There she would stop for a few weeks and catch up with her writing and hopefully experience some of the Latino love-machines that she had heard called that part of the world home. From Miami she would send an early draft of her work to the publishers in New York. Then she would continue south to the Keys before taking a sprint back up the Gulf coast. She had planned stops at Venice, Sarasota, Tampa and Crystal River before ending where she started in the Panhandle. All was going well until the unfortunate combination of a vaginal wart outbreak (she suspected the Greek hotel concierge from Jupiter) and a late-season Category 5 hurricane brought her trip to a sudden halt. Holed up in the Delray Beach Colony Hotel, waiting for the storm to pass and the STD clinic to reopen, Sally was held captive by circumstances beyond her control. Not able to fuck anyone for forty-eight hours gave her some clarity in life, and as quickly as she usually fell in lust with people, she fell in love with the sleepy town that had taken her prisoner. Sally decided to stay a little longer and at the very least catch up with her notes.

Enamored by her host city and following the storm's passing and her treatment for warts, Sally set about looking for short-term accommodation in Delray. After a quick drive around zip 33483 she stumbled upon a "For Lease" sign at The Beach House. This place, with its proximity to the sand and the town's nightlife, was the perfect set-up for an extended stay in Florida. The décor inside, although a little battered, was tastefully done in an old plantation style. As Sally wanted to blend in like a typical freshly arrived transient, she took an advertised bar job. Her amended plan was to hunker down in this apartment, finish the book and satisfy her publisher's demands. The sex she would let come to her and working as a barmaid there wouldn't be a dearth of opportunity. Delray Beach was an easy drive to the rest of Florida and she would get the color needed to finish off her book by taking day trips. Sally realized that the product wouldn't be quite as genuine as she liked, but in reality her "comfortable-pants-wearing" readership were more interested in the gritty sex than the scenic local commentary.

Sally had managed to hide under her alias as Emily Scott and carry on her work undetected for many more months than she had intended. Her one rule was not "shitting in the stream" by screwing anyone who lived at The Beach House. The way she avoided this was to keep herself to herself and maintain interactions with other residents at a bare minimum. Sally had a packed schedule trying to juggle her job and writing, but was now close to finishing the book. If asked, she would be the first to admit that she was currently at the happiest point ever in her life. Her only worry was what to do next once she had fulfilled her writing obligations. This was one of the reasons she had stayed in Delray Beach longer than expected and why she was loath to complete the final chapter.

As Sally left for her evening job she noticed that three signs promoting various interrelated Beach House developments had appeared on the premises sometime between last night when she came home with the Italian waiter and now. A large "For Rent" sign had been attached to the door of Apartment

#10. In smaller writing underneath it specified "Short Term Only." Jacob Smith had hastily bolted Florida the previous week in the middle of the night. Sally had passed pleasantries with her neighbor on several occasions and thought he was handsome and polite in a folksy, charming way. Had they not been neighbors, he might possibly have been invited to help with her research. However, the sudden demise of Jacob hadn't been totally unforeseen, as in her experience the quiet ones were usually the most dangerous. Even so, it was quite an unfortunate set of circumstances that had led this mild-mannered educator to make such a spectacular headline-grabbing departure.

Jacob had managed to go full Ted Kennedy and plough his car into a Boca Raton drainage canal. Evidently he was high as a kite on crack and had been driving his car on back roads trying to get from Palm Beach to Delray whilst avoiding the customary heavy police presence on A1A. In his drug-induced state Jacob not only managed to overshoot his final destination by a city, but he also over-steered his car off the road. Jacob careened into a waterway at the intersection of Glades and Butts Avenues. As Boca's finest yanked him out of the vehicle, it was clear that he was close to becoming a late night snack for two mammoth gators that were circling his half-submerged sedan. The retrieved car contained drug apparatus and the police toxicology report indicated high levels of some very poorly made junk. The medical office commented that he was lucky the drugs didn't kill him outright. On multiple fronts he had become very close to booking a morning appointment with Angel Mancini.

Jacob was booted out of the zero-tolerance rehab program and, as per contract, no refund on any of the prepaid fees was given. His probation in St Louis was broken and in short order his wife hauled him back to M-i-s-e-r-y as people in Missouri affectionately label their State. Once on home turf he was thrown into prison. It was highly doubtful he would ever be given a license to teach again. Jacob was a well-liked guy at The Beach House, often to be found bobbing in the pool and chatting away with others in that affable Midwestern way. All the residents, with the possible exception of Pete, couldn't understand what had set him so off-kilter. To everyone else it looked like his rehab treatment had been going so well.

The second sign that had sprung up was so big it could almost be seen from space. A massive wooden billboard had been erected on the southwest corner of the building's grounds. Above an artist's impression of what was to come, a large swirly font read "Surf Way Developments – New Luxury Living." In smaller writing underneath was detailed an e-mail address that prompted interested parties to sign up for further details. Sally thought the artist's concept of the new building looked cool and it was possibly the kind of place she would buy if her agent managed to sell the film rights to her next book. The final placard was related to the second. A simple homemade sign was hung from the neck of the large plastic flamingo that sat in the center of The Beach House grounds. It economically stated in pink wordage that matched eleven of the twelve front doors, "Save Your Home! Meeting Monday 8 p.m."

Sally was aware of the building's unfolding dramas, but as she was really just passing through town she hadn't shown much interest. She put the time and date of this meeting into her phone and thought perhaps she would attend as a friendly token of solidarity. As Sally left for work there was the usual gaggle of residents sat on the courtyard shooting the breeze. She waved as she passed by, but as always did not stop or get sucked into their world. In the other direction Pete from Apartment #4, who she had never formally met, was walking onto the grounds. He smiled as their paths briefly crossed.

The offer that Pete had made with Tandy Jenkins was luckily accepted within seconds, as otherwise it was hard to predict how the scene between the pornographer and Shane would've played out. Pete had figured his only avenue of approach to strike a deal was to give Tandy something he wanted and couldn't get anywhere else. Pete had just such a shiny, unique curio that was ideal to broker that deal. When Pete was first a freelance photographer all those years ago in Malibu, he happened to be in the position to shoot a celebrity sex tape. It was not just any celebrity, but the hottest star of the day – Baywatch babe Pamela Anderson and her husband Tommy Lee. The situation that led to this occurrence was a combination of intelligence, surveillance, technical skill and, of course, being in the right place at the right time. Pete had received a tip that Pam and Tommy were moving house. He staked out their home and followed the removal vans to a new hillside mansion. Pete took a vantage point on a small hill facing the garden and watched the house with the aid of a very long lens. The hope was that he would get an exclusive set of pictures of the couple moving in their belongings. What he hadn't expected, but possibly should have prepared for, was that the first item they moved into the home was a king-sized bed. Seconds after the plastic bubble rap was shed, Tommy bent Pam over this bed and christened the new mansion. Had any curtains been installed they would've possibly drawn them. Instinctively, Pete pulled out his video camera and hit record. It was a quick affair, but it did provide evidence of the legendary size of Tommy's manhood.

Pete, who was shit-scared he would be busted as a voyeur, then packed up his equipment and headed for safety. When played back the video was grainy and murky, but definitely showed the celebrity couple of the day doing the deed. Unfortunately, while the tape was red hot, high-flying Pam was under the legal umbrella of one Matthew Knight Esq.

These were the days before deals could be worked out with celebrities and their agents. The sex tape was without a possible marketplace and thus buried in Pete's safe without ever being broadcast or sold. A year or so later it was made even more obsolete by a second sex tape coming into existence, this one homemade, stolen from their house and then marketed allegedly with their compliance. Fast-forward a decade and the celebrity tabloid industry was on a different level. As Pam Anderson's career was not quite what it was, and being a little behind with the California taxman, she could no longer afford high-powered legal protection. The celebrity tabloid marketplace had also changed. What was seen as a grubby tape, of a private moment, and not marketable when shot, was now an "Exclusive Celebrity Sex Tape" that could reel in web views. Pete thought Pammy, in private, of course, would be happy for a personal publicity boost. Who knows? They might even give her a slot in the new *Baywatch* movie on the back of the exposure this tape would bring.

Tandy accepted the deal offered. Pete would hand over his exclusive tape and in return Tandy would relinquish rights to Angel's video and have it withdrawn from the Internet. Although the deal was quick to make, the legal logistics to finalize it were long and drawn out. It had taken Knight a week of legalese to iron out the agreement. Who knew that obese porn kings paid such attention to the small print?

Pete had just arrived back to The Beach House after exchanging tapes with Tandy. He wanted to give Angel the good news and didn't think an appointment was necessary in light of the feat he had just pulled off on her behalf.

"Pete! Sit down and join us. We need your wisdom. We're planning for the meeting next week," shouted Ethan as Pete walked onto the building's grounds. Ethan was sat with Rebecca, Shane and Apartment #1 tenant Long Island Iced Tea Bob. Their patio table was groaning under the weight of empty beer cans.

"Little busy, not now," said Pete, as he passed by the group on the way to Angel's apartment. As Pete tapped on the front door of Apartment #2 a shirtless Gabriel exited from his own doorway and stood in front of his window. Gabriel totally ignored Pete and was focused on trying to overhear what Ethan and the others were talking about.

Pete banged on the door again. Finally, it creaked open as far as the security chain would allow.

"Hi Pete. Did I forget you were coming over?" said Angel who was wearing a paisley silk dressing gown.

"Uh, no. Sorry about just knocking like this, but I've something important to tell you," Pete said with eagerness in his tone.

"Hold on," she said. The door closed to allow the security chain to be unattached. Angel then reopened the door and slid her body out of Apartment #2. She was dressed for bed. Early night, Pete assumed.

"What's going on, Pete?" said Angel, feeling maybe something terrible had brought this unprompted visit.

It was now obvious to both of them that Gabriel was watching. "Can I come in?" Pete asked.

Halo came to the door and meowed. Angel bent down to stop the feline from running outside and picked up the cat. Angel's front door now opened wider and revealed a large bunch of roses on top of her bedside table.

"It's not really a good time, Pete. How about tomorrow? We can fix an appointment. Would seven work?" she said in a hushed voice trying not to be overheard by Gabriel.

A gust of wind then blew the door open wider. Angel tried to stop its momentum, but it proved impossible as her hands were clutching the cat.

Pete could now see Simon Godfrey sat on Angel's sofa. "Hello, Simon," Pete shouted. Simon waved back.

Angel stepped out of her apartment and closed the door behind her. "We're working things out," she said sounding slightly embarrassed.

"After the way he treated you!" said Pete loud enough for everyone at Ethan's table to look in his direction, and for Gabriel to be shamed back into his own apartment – albeit leaving the door ajar so he could carry on listening to whatever Pete and Angel might be discussing.

"I know," she said. "But I really want it to work. We're good together."

"That's great," said Pete sarcastically. "Well, don't you two thank me all at once but your kinky little video has gone away. Don't ask me exactly how I did it, but I have had to cash in a lifetime's worth of get-out-of-jail-free cards and all my buried treasure."

"You mean you really were able to have it wiped from the web?" said Angel. "I thought that was something you said to…"

"To what?" Pete impatiently asked.

"Impress me."

"I am a man of action," shouted Pete. "I don't mess around and I certainly don't need to impress anyone!"

"I cannot believe you did that for me," said Angel, as she dropped the cat and embraced Pete before kissing him on the cheek.

When the small crowd on the patio saw the kiss they erupted in cheers and started chanting in drunken unison, "We want tongue! We want tongue! We want tongue!"

On hearing the chants, Angel pulled away from Pete and beckoned Halo to come back to her. Pete felt the kiss was similar to the one Luke Skywalker received from Princess Leia after he rescued her from the Death Star. It wasn't quite the reward he had hoped for, and presumably Luke also had grander expectations, although in Luke's situation it all worked out for the best. However, Pete doubted Angel would turn out to be a long lost sister separated at birth.

Pete couldn't understand why she would get back with Simon – these women were beyond belief! Angel thanked Pete again and said she owed him an expensive dinner. As Pete walked back to his apartment, Ethan and the gang were loudly and far from discreetly discussing Angel and Pete's chances of getting together. Not good was their verdict as they all agreed Simon was quite hot and fabulously wealthy. Pete shuffled the two doors home feeling he had most likely put himself through a tremendous amount of ball ache for absolutely nothing.

February 17ᵗʰ 2015, from the Orlando Sentinel

NAKED MASTURBATING FLORIDA WOMAN STOPS TRAFFIC

A naked Florida woman ran into a residential Orlando street and began pleasuring herself in front of a car. The trapped driver had no choice but to watch as the naked woman then leapt onto the hood of his vehicle and started a jumping, stomping frenzy, which caused $1,500 worth of damage. The police report described the woman as being in an "altered mental state, displaying extremely irrational and volatile behavior". She was charged with criminal mischief and exposure of sexual organs.

Apartment #12 Walking on Lake Okeechobee

Randy Showers stood outside the front door of Apartment #12, drinking his morning coffee. He drank only one hundred percent Hawaiian from the Ka'u region of the Big Island. He never added milk or sugar. Any "junk" put into what he said was the finest coffee in the world was, in his opinion, sacrilege.

Randy was well versed in sacrilege; after all, he was a collared Man of God who often told his flock that he personally channeled Jesus. From his elevated second-floor corner position, Randy had a good view of the hive of activity around The Beach House. Palm trees were bending in the force of strong, warm winds that were blowing from the direction of the Everglades. A team of surveyors was measuring up the property parcel with an array of fancy gadgets. A slow-moving and confused-looking man from FPL was tagging and flagging the route of the gas lines between the building and the street. A crew from Surf Way Developments could be seen busily cleaning vulgar graffiti that had appeared on the billboard advertising its new planned development – a large penis and balls in flamingo-pink spray paint wasn't exactly exuding the dream of luxury that would soon be on offer in this locale. The swimming pool had already been drained and cordoned off to save the Homeowners' Association spending money on cleaning services for the remainder of the building's existence. All these events and commotions only added to the general glumness and end-of-days feel circulating around The Beach House.

All the tenants had been served a thirty-days notice to vacate. Pete and Angel, with their inside knowledge as owners, said it was almost certain that nothing could be done to halt the sale, as it had been a binding majority of title holders who had pushed through the deal. Paperwork had been processed, permits pulled, and the City and State had all signed off on the condominium termination and the replacement project. The city of Delray had been overzealous in accommodating this development – no doubt seeing all the extra dollars that increased assessment on the new building would bring to their coffers. The State was also unexpectedly helpful. They hadn't relished the impending takeover of this dysfunctional Homeowners' Association, as it would have been real work for some happily underworked Tallahassee civil servants. The owners were simply ecstatic to be rid of their real-estate headaches and were united in satisfaction that the beasts that were Bessie and Gabriel, if not slain, would soon become someone else's problem.

The people who lived at The Beach House and called that place home were, of course, the real victims of this tragedy of events. Pete and Angel, not that they wanted to leave The Beach House, would be paid out for their property and could easily start afresh someplace else with the proceeds. Bessie and Gabriel would be made homeless, but the consensus was that "you reap what you sow," and this entire mess was down to their crazy out-of-control antics. The remaining tenants were in another situation altogether. With their bad credit, cheap rent deals, police rap sheets, lack of references and short-term horizons, they would struggle to find local digs where certain questions by landlords weren't asked. Tonight there was a residents' meeting with the aim of attempting to halt the redevelopment; but at best this was seen as a feel-good Hail Mary with little chance of success and more likely just an excuse to have a party.

"Fuck me Jesus," were the strong and unchristian words that came from Reverend Randy Showers' mouth as he witnessed a fleet of police cars pulling up all around The Beach House. *They've finally nailed me*, he thought. Randy, from his high-ground vantage point, counted at least six vehicles, half marked, and the rest black SUVs with blue lights bolted onto the roof. He slugged back the remainder of his coffee knowing that, if he were lucky, he would be getting truck stop Joe once they had hauled him to jail. Randy knew there was always a chance that this day would come. Not only was there a likelihood that his past would catch up with him, but there was also a looming menace that his present would bite him firmly in the ass. At the very least, he was reassured that he was wearing a pair of clean underpants and his hair looked good. A man with a C-list celebrity resume and a local standing in the church community needed to look cool and classy in the obligatory police mug shot.

As a young, fresh-faced graduate with a liberal arts degree from a South Carolina university, Randy, like many in his position, had no idea what job he was equipped to do. After deep conversations with the careers department he could only come up with a slush pile of jobs he had no interest in. Needing to pay his way through life, he used his fallback good looks and his given name, and signed himself up with a stripper agency.

It was while working a bachelorette party, undressing as a character cop, that a fortunate encounter would take place. On occasion, upon demand, he would give a little "extra service" for a tip. It just so happened that the guest at this party who had paid to play with his baton and cuffs was a high-flying female television executive with local Charleston network WCIV. Upon getting up-close and personal with his good looks and learning that Randy Showers was his real name, the woman told him, "Do I have a job for you!" Randy was hired as an on-camera weatherman for the local evening news. It didn't matter that he had no meteorological education or television experience. This job was all about looking good in front of a camera and reading a teleprompter. However, the name

Randy Showers was the real clincher for this job, as it was the perfect catchy byline for a primetime local television weatherman.

For twenty-five years Randy was Mr. Weather in the Greater Charleston area. He loved getting out of the studio for big events, such as standing on a beach and being blown around in a hurricane, filing his report from a kayak floating on a submerged street during a flood, or going on air shirtless during a heat wave. For a man with zero formal training in this profession he was the consummate local weatherman's weatherman and won numerous regional awards. However, a local weatherman is also expected to be a trusted pillar of the community, and this part of the gig Randy only half-embraced. He was good at turning on Christmas tree lights, opening new school libraries and being a member of that bright-teethed WCIV team that delivered "dependable news", but he had one major off-screen flaw – he was a crazed womanizer with a chronic sex addiction. Randy was amazed at just how much of a pull being a local television weatherman was to the ladies. Interns, fellow anchors, women he encountered on promotional appearances and generally anything in a skirt he chased. For twenty-five years his employers somehow managed to pay no attention to the ethics clause in his contract, and like a modern-day Don Juan, Randy thought nothing could ever put a stop to his bed-hopping ways.

While Randy kept his looks as youthful as possible with tax-deductable investments in hair plugs, dental veneers and Botox, these weren't enough to defy a changing environment.

It was a slightly sleazy and embarrassing affair that had been brought to the attention of a new generation of station executives that would lead to his downfall.

During a Friday-night live weather report broadcast from a local High School football game, Randy managed to lure and subsequently corrupt two teenage cheerleaders. In his defense, they may have been sixteen but he swore they had the bodies of eighteen year olds and were experienced in the ways of pleasing a man like a woman of thirty. It was not the first time that Randy had descended on the slippery slope of jailbait, but it wasn't so easy in the modern era to get away with it when the girls posted incriminating evidence on Facebook. Possibly it was all used as an excuse by management to bring in a cheaper, younger guy. Perhaps it really was a different era where feminist ethics were not only preached but also practiced. The parents came to a deal with the station. Randy was released from his contract, the cheerleaders were given hush money and the hope was that the authorities and the women's rights attorney Gloria Allred would stay well away. However, there was a statue of limitations that had not expired, and in the eyes of the law it was rape, and a payoff would not save him if the girls ever chose to press charges.

Like many shamed criminals who had escaped hard time, Randy headed to Florida for a fresh start. He knew he would never be hired as a weatherman again, as he was too old and too many questions about his past would be asked. The only other career that he had not tried that fitted in with his catchy name was that of a porn star. Randy was realistic though, and his stamina and girth were just not up to par. Not wanting to put to waste the investments he had made in that artificial television smile and lush carpet of unnatural hair, he did the only thing he thought he was suited for... he started a church ministry.

Reverend Showers, a name he could legally use after the religious crash-course certification he found on the back pages of the *National Enquirer*, had a good ring to it. He chose a poor African-American area of inland Palm Beach County to start his church, as the black community was religious and would be enthralled by a minor white celebrity priest. However, more importantly, ebony-skinned women were not his thing, so he wouldn't have to worry about letting his dick interfere with God's work.

For premises he sublet an underused synagogue. Most of the Jews in that area had moved to better parts of the county and this temple currently sat empty. He had been running his Rainbow Church for just over two years and he would modestly say in public that it had been a great success. In private, though, he would admit that it was all a bit of a racket. Reverend Showers was little more than a smarmy middle-aged snake-oil salesman who, if he weren't selling God to the gullible, would be selling those same people timeshares on the beach.

Randy had one unfulfilled ambition – he wanted to make it big on a national level. Back in his heyday he had applied for network weather jobs but was never successful. He blamed these fruitless attempts on not having a diverse look, never thinking it could have anything to do with a lack of scientific training. So Randy viewed his new ministry as a way of finally becoming a household celebrity. All he needed to take himself into the top division of men-of-the-cloth was to perform a miracle. The one he had in mind was walking on water, and not just any body of water but Florida's own Lake Okeechobee. Randy was certain that if he could make it appear that he was gliding over Florida's largest lake, the national attention would elevate him to the type of riches that even network weatherman could only dream of. Randy was now devoting all his time and money into making this illusion happen. He had reached out to David Copperfield for help and was studying expensive manuals by magicians, as he knew there had to be a way to make this miraculous feat occur.

It was Randy's consuming devotion to performing this miracle that could have been another reason for his impending arrest, as he was guilty of theft and embezzlement from his church. The donations that his devoted parishioners put in his tray were diverted straight into his pocket. Admittedly, some of it was used to keep the lights on at the church, but the majority was for his living expenses and funding the continued exploration of performing his illusion.

As the police descended on The Beach House, Randy's main thought was what lawyer he would use. The charge of statutory rape would be easy to defend, as he could find one of those mud-slinging vultures who would paint a picture of those two fresh-faced cheerleaders as the dirtiest harlots in the whole of Charleston. The church embezzlement charges would be a little trickier to evade. Randy hadn't hidden the money trail very well, often paying for hair-restoration treatment directly from the ministry's checking account. Then there were the escort girls who were on the church books. That would also be a problem. At the start of his "Finding the Lord" phase, Randy had worked out that the best way of staying out of trouble was to relieve any extra holy spirit via paid ladies.

In the light of day, Randy's activities looked uglier than a bag of hairless cats and he might just have to plead guilty and strike a deal. Whatever happened, it would be hard to escape from this monster of a self-created mess. What then for him? A man who had fallen from grace for two heinous successive "lapses of judgment" would be somewhat challenged to find a new place in the world. It would certainly be hard to live off his connection with Jesus again, although he would have name recognition and good looks for a man of his age so he could always try his hand at politics. That seemed to be an eternally forgiving line of work. Randy was amazed just how much clarity he was having in what was likely to be his final thirty seconds of freedom.

The police had made a tactical perimeter around the building. After seeing the phalanx of cops with weapons drawn, the workers at The Beach House realized something big was about to go down. The graffiti clean-up crew got off their ladders and walked to the safety of Andrews Avenue. The surveyors put down their tools and the formerly confused FPL utility worker hit the floor and made himself low so he wouldn't be caught in any crossfire. Randy rested his hands on the balcony railings to make it apparent to all that he was not holding a weapon. The police were now storming The Beach House with guns drawn and were charging up the dual staircases that led to the second-level units. Randy put his hands high in the air and offered his surrender. An approaching policeman pointed at him and motioned for him to hit the ground. He complied and waited for them to place him in custody. He could hear the police all around him. And if he was at all religious at this point, he might have started to pray.

Then, just as Randy thought he was about to be cuffed and dragged down the stairs into an awaiting cop car, a minor miracle occurred and for a brief second he believed in God. Instead of arresting him, the police used a tactical battering ram to smash down the door of Apartment #9. Randy craned his head up and could see the police dragging a naked shouting and screaming Shane Dolman from his home. They threw him roughly to the ground and placed him in handcuffs. A plain-clothed detective read him his Miranda rights before handing him a blanket not quite large enough to fully protect his modesty. Shane was then dragged towards the waiting squad cars by a group of heavily armed police.

Shane's girlfriend Rebecca, who was wearing an expensive-looking green silk negligee, was standing outside her front door engaging in full-on histrionics. Luckily for her she hadn't applied her regular lashings of snooty mascara, as with this level of waterworks it would by now be cascading down her cheeks in a streaky mess. As Shane was thrown into the squad car, Delray's boys in blue clapped and whistled with delight in appreciation of bringing in a notorious local thug. Randy stood up, dusted himself down and thanked his lucky stars that today the police had not come for him.

The talk around The Beach House that afternoon was that Shane Dolman had been arrested, and Rebecca charged as an accessory, for the organization and administration of an international Ponzi scheme. Randy was surprised, as Shane and Rebecca didn't seem like the sharpest duo to operate such a sophisticated criminal enterprise. Shane was taken straight to County Jail and bail set high enough that he would not be seeing daylight any time soon. Rebecca spent most of that day with lawyers in an effort not to end up in an adjoining cell. **Bodie and Ethan** reconstructed the front door of Apartment #9 so it could be put back into useful operation. Randy did offer Rebecca his personal ministering services, but to be fair to the intelligence of The Beach House crowd, his stock as a Man of God was valued at junk level. Most residents viewed Reverend Randy Showers as little more than a smoke-and-mirrors scam artist.

Of late, The Beach House had been jettisoning residents faster than Craigslist could find new blood. Jacob Smith had gone back to St Louis and Shane was now rotting in jail. Colleen Bromefield had not been seen for at least two weeks and no one had any idea where she could be. Her phone had been switched off and she wasn't returning calls. The men of The Beach House were having withdrawal symptoms from not being able to lust over Colleen's tanned and toned body that had been an appreciated poolside fixture since her arrival.

Sally Purdue, or Emily Scott as she was known, was the last of the expected residents to make it down to the patio area for the "Save The Beach House Meeting" that had been arranged earlier. As Sally took her seat with the others, she couldn't help but feel that the flickering light emitted from the mosquito-repelling Tiki Torches gave the gathering a weird anything-could-happen *Lord of the Flies* vibe. Sally had quit her barmaid job that morning to free up time so she could finish off her book before she was forced to vacate the building. Her plan was then to head back home to Santa Fe, decompress and plot her next move in life. Ethan, as the Honorary Mayor, would be chairing the meeting. Angel, Pete, **Rodney**, **Bodie**, Randy and Rebecca were already sat in position and ready to begin. Long Island Iced Tea Bob emerged from Apartment #1 with a tray full of his signature cocktails. He then generously served them out. Pete whispered in Bob's ear to go easy on the booze as he could foresee the meeting descending into a drunken farce, or even worse, everyone grabbing a Tiki Torch, marching to the offices of Surf Way Developments, and burning the place down.

"I have something I would like to say," said Sally, as she got everyone's attention. She then proceeded to take off her self-imposed-disguise glasses, and loosen the hair that had always been tied back during her Beach House residency. The undercover author told the gathered residents that Emily Scott was an alias and she was actually called Sally Purdue, and had been residing in Delray Beach to write a book. And not just any book, but a steamy and erotic travel book about Florida. Rebecca, unsurprisingly, had read Sally's **earlier book** *Sally Does Route 66*, and wanted her copy signed. Pete was a little pissed that he hadn't figured out who Sally really was, as he prided himself on not letting details like this slip past him, although photographs of authors were usually a tough sale so he hadn't missed a lucrative payday. The only writer you could make cash on was JK Rowling, but she hid away in Scotland and was quick to scream "invasion of privacy" and then sue. Randy now realized why Sally had had a revolving door of gentlemen visitors. The other guys at the meeting were just peeved that they hadn't been offered a chance of helping this vixen with her research.

Pete was now concerned that Angel was currently sitting right next to Sally. **Although Pete had technically been knocked back by Angel, who was again wearing Simon's ring, he was determined that something was meant to happen between the two of them.** The last thing he wanted was for any of Sally's loose ways to further dilute Angel's purity. Long Island Iced Tea Bob made another round of cocktails to celebrate Sally's announcement. As they toasted the success of her next book, Ethan decided that with the vested powers that came with his position of Honorary Mayor, Sally Purdue would become The Beach House's official Literary Laureate.

Ethan had just finished a cigarette and was about to get down to the business end of the evening when the grubby white door of Apartment #5 opened. All eyes shifted in the direction of the Garlech's lair. Although invited, Bessie and Gabriel weren't expected to attend. In fact, no one had seen them for days and all feared what they might be plotting. Bessie was dressed in her finest freshly pressed black Lycra leggings and a matching tank top. Gabriel, in a rare wardrobe deviation, wore both a shirt and shoes. There was a groan and a distinct, "They can go and fuck off," from Rodney, as Bessie and Gabriel proceeded to sit down at a table next to the rest of the group.

"Thank you, Bessie and Gabriel, for coming to this meeting. We really appreciate your input," said Ethan in an effort to make peace.

"What meeting?" Gabriel replied.

"We're not here for any meeting. We're just utilizing our rights as owners to enjoy the common area of the condominium," said Bessie, who had a copy of The Beach House rules and regulations to hand.

"So, what you're saying is that you are not attending the meeting, but you are taking in some air on that table and chairs that are, like, a cunt hair away from where we are all sat," Ethan shot back in a loud and husky tone.

"Language, Ethan. We have ladies present," said Pete, trying to bring order.

"Yes, it's a nice night and we want to enjoy the amenities," said Gabriel, as Bessie placed a portable tape machine with an attached microphone on the table and hit record.

"Don't worry about us. Please carry on with whatever you are doing," said Bessie.

Bessie and Gabriel made themselves comfortable on the furniture and acted as if nobody else was sat around them and there was no meeting in progress.

"Awkward," whispered Bodie to Rebecca.

"Well, we will proceed," said Ethan.

"Hold on," said Pete. "These two pricks with their nonstop shit are the entire reason The Beach House is about to be on the receiving end of a wrecking ball. Do we really want to sit here and play nice with these two passive-aggressive psychopaths?"

"He does have a point!" said Angel, backing him up and slugging the rest of her Long Island Iced Tea.

"I don't want to sit here like a fat chick who just bought a big gulp of Diet Coke thinking everything in life will be just swell!" said Bodie in support of Pete. "Gabriel, your petty pissing match with the world is going to leave me without a home. So don't think you can sit here smugly while we're having this meeting and not help us out." Bodie stood and rolled his sleeves up to indicate that his next action would be more than just words.

"We didn't start this!" said Gabriel, squirming in his seat.

"You didn't start it but you certainly made life miserable enough so the owners had no choice but to run! You know what? I will be homeless in a few weeks and it's all down to you two!" said Rebecca.

"Shouldn't you be in jail with Shane, you scammer?" Bessie responded.

Bodie had to hold Rebecca back as she was about to launch herself at Bessie in what would have descended into a hair-pulling catfight.

"We're victims too. We've spent a lot of our money fighting the injustice of the homeowners. Everything we did was for all of you!" said Bessie, defending her case to the combined group of residents.

"The two of you are sad and vindictive!" said Pete to a round of applause from all the others.

"Bessie, Gabriel, we're trying to have a constructive discussion on how we might be able to stop our eviction and the end of The Beach House as we know it. Are you with us or are you against us? If you're with us, join our meeting. If not, just fuck off back to your apartment," said an impassioned Ethan between puffs of a cigarette.

"We'll sit here doing our thing, and you do what you want. We are not breaking any laws," said Bessie waving her book of rules and regulations.

Events were about to turn ugly when Randy, in a wise move, made a less-than-divine intervention. "Let's just move the meeting into my place! It's invite only and you two are in the sin bin," Randy suggested, as he indicated to Bessie and Gabriel to stay clear.

"Can I smoke there?" asked Ethan.

"Sure!" was Randy's no-fucks-given reply.

With that, Randy, Ethan, Rodney Rebecca, Bodie, Sally, Angel, Pete and Long Island Iced Tea Bob, carrying his mobile cocktail cooler, staggered up the stairs into Apartment #12. A checkmated Bessie and Gabriel continued sitting on the patio gazing into the night air.

Upon entering his home, Randy gave the apartment a quick tidy up as the others filtered in. On the apartment's coffee table was a large roll-out map of Lake Okeechobee, a book by illusionist David Blaine and a notepad full of sketches. These items were hastily put in a drawer under the bed before anyone started asking questions.

The inside of Randy's apartment was strange and unlike anything you would expect from a person who marketed himself as a Man of God. One wall was pictorially devoted to Randy's achievements in weather forecasting. The other walls were stacked with expensive-looking abstract paintings to the extent that Apartment #12 looked like an extension of the New York Museum of Modern Art. Nowhere to be seen was anything that could be described as having an affiliation with religion or God. A token Jesus on the cross or maybe a Bible on the bookshelf would have added a veneer of plausibility to Randy's credentials; and it hadn't gone unnoticed by anyone that the magnets on the fridge advertised local strip clubs.

Randy retrieved several fold-up chairs branded with logos from the synagogue that he sublet from. He spaced them out in a circle around the apartment. Pete positioned himself strategically next to Angel, who was by now a little wobbly from her cocktail intake. The others sat wherever they could find a chair or a space on the floor. Long Island Iced Tea Bob went to work in the kitchen and prepared a fresh round of drinks. Ethan started the meeting all over again. He made a long and somewhat rambling speech about his life at The Beach House before passing the floor to Angel.

"Thank you, Ethan, for organizing this meeting and for all you have done for The Beach House over the years," said a buzzed Angel. Pete could not help but notice that the ring on her finger was a good-sized carat, and not only would it be hard to remove, but for him to replicate its size and quality a daunting challenge. However, Pete was in no way fazed by his ongoing mission. Angel presented a state of legal play that gave little optimism of a possible halting of events. She said the sale was all but done and nothing short of a change of mind by the purchaser could stop the proceedings. With the conclusion of Angel's summary, Long Island Iced Tea Bob brought out more refreshments and Angel passed the floor over to Pete.

"Angel is correct. Legally, this is a done deal and it could only be stopped with the cooperation of this man, Noah Furio, the CEO of Surf Way Developments," Pete explained.

Pete took a picture of Noah Furio from a thick file that had been lifted from the Surf Way Developments corporate website.

"I have done work for this guy, and he paid me real quick," said Ethan.

"I've seen him around town," added Rebecca.

"He is a big shot in Delray. He's connected to political circles and, as you know, is responsible for bulldozing and redeveloping a large chunk of the city," said Pete.

"Elwood's makeover was down to him! They ripped the guts out of what was a wonderful place to perform a gig," said Rodney.

"He just bought the Green Owl building," said Ethan as he lit up another cigarette.

"Oh no! That is my favorite diner," said Angel.

"I can't see it remaining there for long. His style is buy, bulldoze and build out the lot," said Bodie.

"Correct, and the 'Coming Soon' signs all over town are evidence of just that," Pete responded.

"The results of his actions are hideous. He has littered Delray Beach with McMansions and parking lots galore," Rebecca shouted out.

"**Huge Organs bar being** flattened to make way for a multi-story car lot was all him," said Bodie.

Ethan interjected, "I know where he lives – ugly starter castle on Marine Way!"

"Guys, I have a full background report on him, but he isn't the kind of man you want to piss off," said Pete.

"Usual rich asshole," chimed in Sally.

"Worse than that. Surf Way Developments is a money-laundering operation for the New England mob," said Pete.

That got everyone's attention and they all took sips of their beverages, prompting Long Island Iced Tea Bob to walk around the room topping up empties.

"They have City Hall and the planning department paid off," Pete added.

Bodie interrupted, "That explains how quickly they get permits approved."

"And how they are allowed to get away with creating such ugly architecture," said Rebecca.

"Exactly. They have a clear path to do whatever they want. One of my sources is a Boca cop, who warned me not to meddle with the affairs of Surf Way Developments. I was told they're a bad company run by dangerous people, and watch my six o'clock if I'm snooping around their operations," said Pete.

"So, that's it. There's nothing we can do," said a bummed-out Angel.

"I think it's best to take the money, walk away and don't ever look back," said Pete.

"That's great for the owners, but us renters are left scrambling for a new home," said Rodney, as Rebecca, Bodie and Ethan hollered their concerned support.

"The Beach House is more than my home. It's my life," said Ethan. "This place is not just crumbling concrete, cheap paint, creaking air conditioning and oversized bugs. The Beach House has soul, personality and a beating heart. I've spent a large part of my existence here with friends and lovers. I feel like The Beach House is part of me and I am part of The Beach House!"

Ethan wiped a tear from his eye.

"It's a special place for me too and I don't want to leave," said Angel in support.

"Have you seen the junk they want to put up on this lot? Demolish a piece of old Florida to make way for six ugly cookie-cutter town homes. We cannot let this happen, we need to make a stand," said Ethan.

There were cheers from all corners of the room.

Long Island Iced Tea Bob was now slumped on a kitchen stool snoring loudly after finally succumbing to oversampling his creations.

Pete felt that the constructive part of the evening might have concluded. He had gone easy on the refreshments, but it was obvious that everyone else wasn't too far behind Bob in the "tired and emotional" department.

"What can we do?" asked Rebecca, who was herself tearing up. Bodie took this as a sign to move closer to her and offer emotional support.

"We cannot take up arms against the mob!" said Pete.

"No, but there has to be something we can do," said Angel. Pete looked at her, and with the sadness displayed in her drunken eyes she looked dramatically beautiful. If he were a less honorable man, now might be the time to take advantage and make a move.

"What we need is a divine intervention, an act of God," said Randy with a tinge of irony.

"Holding out for God, holding out for a hero, same useless waste of time," said Rebecca, who was finishing off what must have been her fifth cocktail.

"I can be your hero, Rebecca," said Randy, as he made a play for the low-hanging fruit of this drunken woman.

"Dude, Shane hasn't even been locked away for a day and you now feel you can hit on Rebecca," said Bodie, who would likely be the one walking Rebecca home that night.

Randy and Bodie now got into a manly stare-off. Rebecca's eye's lit up; she relished attention.

Breaking the uneasy moment, Angel looked around the room before saying, "Who is going to be the hero of The Beach House and save it?" She was herself not far behind Rebecca on the cocktail count and slurring her words.

Pete pulled his chair up closer to Angel. The permutations of how he could be a hero went through his head, but there were no palpable answers forthcoming. *If I could nail Brad Pitt and Jennifer Aniston having lunch together, I would make enough money to buy the rest of the building from Surf Way Developments, and the rest of the block to go with it,* he thought. Pete made a mental note-to-self before grounding himself with the reality that he was more likely to see Elvis pushing his cart down the aisle of Publix than get that holy grail of money shots.

"Angel, you still owe me dinner for the last time I was your hero," Pete replied as he attempted to cash in the chips earned for previous good deeds done.

"Oh yes, my Peter. I am indeed in your debt. You are my resident local hero, dear Mr. Alexander," said a now sloppily drunk Angel as she finished off the last of her drink. "Dinner we will do!" she added following a pregnant pause and a slow rising of her glass in an attempt to make a toast.

"Local hero! That's it. I have an idea!" said Rodney in full-blown limey brogue.

"Uhhh!" said Ethan who had just lit a fresh cigarette.

All eyes in the room were now on Rodney.

"Local hero." Rodney repeated this time more loudly before starting to hum the Mark Knopfler instrumental *Going Home*.

December 17th 2015, from the Orlando Sentinel

FLORIDA MAN EATEN BY ELEVEN-FOOT ALLIGATOR WHILE TRYING TO EVADE COPS

An eleven-foot alligator ate a Florida man being pursued by the Brevard County Sheriff's department on suspicion of burglary. The suspect, who was found drowned in a lake, was missing his lower extremities and a large part of an arm. When authorities recovered the body, they encountered an aggressive alligator. The gator was trapped and euthanized and found inside it were remains consistent with the injuries to the fleeing burglary suspect.

Bad Men from the North

"In the '80s movie *Local Hero*, the residents of an idyllic Scottish seaside town come together to convince a Texan oilman, played by Burt Lancaster, not to turn their little piece of paradise into a refinery," explained Rodney to an eager crowd.

"I remember that flick, saw it on a date with a travel rep down in Doral. That night I was her local hero," Ethan said as he took a pleasing drag of his cigarette and reminisced over times past.

"David and Goliath battle between the big American money and the kooky locals who don't want their way of life destroyed," added Rodney.

"I guess we count as kooky locals?" said Bodie, looking over towards Long Island Iced Tea Bob who had passed out with an empty cocktail glass resting in his hand.

"And Surf Way Developments the corporate meanies!" exclaimed Ethan.

"So, what you're suggesting is that we need to personally convince Noah Furio that we have something special here and he should leave us alone," said Angel, who even in a tipsy state could see Rodney's plans unfolding.

"Exactly! Make a personal pitch, show him what we have is more than dollar signs and sham gentrification," Rodney said before concluding in his rough and ready English. "We need to wow him with passion, exceptionalism, present him our dreams!"

"I'm liking this," Angel said with a grin.

"Not to piss on your idea, Rodney, but what we have is a crumbling cinder-block former roach motel, and I'm not sure how special that is to anyone," cut in Pete. "Another minor detail – the man you're trying to lure into having an epiphany is a hardened mobster!"

"Guys, I remember that film and it wasn't the impassioned pleas from the folksy natives that stopped the development, it was Felix Happer's love of astronomy," added Randy, injecting an extra dose of realism. "He jetted into town, the sky was clear and he could see the northern lights. He liked the view so much he killed the deal and everyone lived happily ever after."

"Houston oil business is a far cry from dealing with the mafia!" said Pete.

"I'm not sure about that, as the oil biz is dirtier than the mob," retorted Sally.

"This all sounds very screwball, guys!" Pete said, trying to quell the crazy talk.

"It will be a one-shot chance. We find his weakness, just like Mac did on the Scottish beach in *Local Hero*, and then make our case and hope it all works," said Rodney.

"Discover what his northern lights are. Find this man's heart, the chink in his mafia armor," Rebecca added.

"From my experience, the guy's weak spot is right between the legs!" said Sally.

"Mentally and physically, and I know, I have cut up a lot of balls and cock in my time." said Angel, slurring out more detail than needed.

"We've seen first-hand what you've done with balls and cock!" mumbled Ethan, not quite loud enough for Angel to hear.

Ethan had always been a little wary of Angel and under no circumstances wanted to end up on her slab at the morgue. He vowed he would die in Broward even if his last act were to drag himself over the county line.

"Guys, you're crazy. What do we do? Go to his office and tell him we want a meeting in his boardroom? Lemon and ice in the water, please. Introduce ourselves, give Noah a slideshow of our beautiful apartments, as we explain what nice people we are, and by the way we really like living near the beach at an affordable price, so can you please work with us!" said Pete in a raised tone.

"No, we don't go to him – he comes to us," said Rodney. "And yes, in a nutshell, that's exactly what we do."

"Bring the mountain to Moses!" Randy added as he looked into the skies.

"Bring the mafia to the mountain sounds more like it," Pete shot back.

"Pete, in your file you have a pretty accurate dial-in on his movements, where he lives, his office address, the regular places he has dinner..." Rodney said before Pete interrupted.

"Sure, where he eats, shits, sleeps, every nugget aside from where he buries the bodies of people who get in his way. That we'll find first-hand if we carry on with this nonsense."

"Oh Pete, you're being such a downer," said Angel, who Pete feared was too drunk for prudent decision-making.

"Guys, what I think I am hearing is that you want to kidnap a mobster, bring him home and tell him his business deal doesn't fit in with your lifestyle. And while you're telling him to adjust his ways, also sweet talk him into not having us all whacked."

"There's a certain chance of risk," said Rodney, as he flicked through Pete's thick dossier and started making notes.

"I would say there is a monster pile of downside on this Keystone Cop operation," replied Pete.

There was a pause at the table, with only the snoring of Long Island Iced Tea Bob heard over the din of the wall-mounted air-conditioning unit.

"I have nothing left to lose. I'm in!" said Bodie.

"Sounds like an adventure," said Sally, no doubt thinking ahead for potential literary inspiration.

"I'm the Honorary Mayor, so I have to be part of it," croaked Ethan, as he emptied the last cigarette from his packet and lit up.

"Count me in. If it goes tits up, I will plead guilty as charged and lie low in jail with Shane," said Rebecca.

"God is on your side," said Randy, indicating he would help.

"I love it, Rodney. You're a great man. I'm with you!" said Angel, as she slowly lowered herself onto Pete's shoulder and simultaneously made herself comfortable and him anxious.

Pete looked down at Angel, who was rested against him with her eyes half-closed. "Angel convinced me. I'm in," said Pete, who was going against his better instincts, but as noted by Sally was not exclusively thinking with his brain. Pete's fatal weakness was always a desire to be a hero and he believed this mission would give him a great opportunity to woo the beautiful Ms. Mancini.

"Guys, there are a few items I need and I suspect between us we will have most of them," said Rodney, closing out this extraordinary meeting of The Beach House.

Rodney scribbled on his wish list: thick rope, handcuffs, Rohypnol and a gun.

Long Island Iced Tea Bob woke up and looked around. "How we doing with the meeting?" said the disorientated man.

* * *

Exactly as Pete's dossier detailed, Noah Furio had shown up for his regular Sunday night dinner at City Oyster on Atlantic Avenue. Pete and Angel were parked up on the opposite side of the street and were using binoculars to watch Noah sat at the bar of the open-windowed eatery. Pete was making the most of Angel being held captive in the passenger seat, and was busily showing off his tricks of the trade. Although Pete had told Angel to wear something discreet, as the need for stealth on surveillance was essential, the head-to-toe black outfit with matching ski hat she'd picked out couldn't exactly be termed Florida casual. The garb made her look more like a Ninja than an inconspicuous local.

"What can I get you tonight, Noah?" said the pretty olive-skinned waitress.

"You should know my order by now, Celia," Noah replied in a thick New England accent.

Noah was a good-looking man for his mid-fifties, and with a little less slouch and a touch more positivity could easily be mistaken for a Wall Street guy who had retired young. He was wearing a blue linen shirt and light grey trousers; the slip-on loafers with no socks would have been a cliché in any other part of the country.

"Of course, your Sunday special – steak cooked medium, with eggplant salad and a glass of California Merlot. Just thought you might want something a little different this week," was the reply from his regular Sunday-night waitress as she took his menu.

"Why would I want to mess with a good thing, Celia?" Noah said. She smiled back. Noah always thought Celia had a flirty disposition, but he hadn't ever gone there.

Noah Furio originated from Federal Hill, Providence – the ground zero of organized crime in the State of Rhode Island. He was a third generation "made man." He moved to Delray Beach a decade ago, not by personal choice but due to decisions forced on him by others. With consolidation of small family gangs in the '70s and early '80s, a centralized mafiosi emerged in Providence. The Furio syndicate came out as regional top dog and became the State's pre-eminent family. In the '90s, business evolved and the Italian families of the North East spun off their low-margin, high-risk drug dealing and racketeering operations to the Jamaican Yardies. Italians moved upscale and got into higher-profit white-collar crime and all together became more corporate within their organizations. Greasing the wheels to win lucrative city contracts and shady HUD-backed land deals made the New England syndicates rich beyond their wildest expectations.

The line of succession left Noah as designated Don for Rhode Island upon his father, Joseph Furio's, retirement. When Joseph unexpectedly died of a heart attack, Noah, as agreed, took the reins of the business. Providence was a mid-market player located between the big league operations of New York and Boston. Unfortunately for Noah, he quickly became the target of a classic hostile corporate squeeze. In a strategy possibly inspired by the 1916 Sykes-Picot Middle East agreement, these two larger players secretly split all the turf controlled from Providence between them. Noah's family operations had succumbed to a hostile takeover and been crushed. Noah was summoned to Manhattan and informed of the new world order. He was told this move was essential, and that "capital efficiency and business amalgamation" were the only ways everyone would stay afloat. Noah wasn't given a say in the matter, "unless he wanted war." He was reassured that he was a trusted Captain, and that they had a top job lined up for him in Miami.

Florida was the historical place that out-of-favor mobsters with friends were sent packing to when their time was up and their usefulness had come to an end. Legend said that Generoso Pope, the infamous owner of the *National Enquirer*, was exiled to Florida by the mob and told if he ever left the

State he would be killed. Noah's new assignment was to set up a franchise of the New England Mafia in Miami. The mob always had connections down there, South Beach being the regular host location for deals with the cartel, but never a piece of the actual pie. Miami was enjoying a property boom and New England wanted in on the action. The Cuban mafia had run Miami exclusively for a decade, and weren't thrilled to see Italians set up camp in their back yard. They gave Noah a respectful choice. It would either be bloody or he could move his operations a little further to the north. Being outgunned and far from home, Noah didn't want conflict with the heavily armed Cubans and relocated himself to Palm Beach County.

In a decade of doing business in Florida, Noah had developed a successful operation. Although backed by mob funds, and being a useful vehicle for cleaning dirty money, he was as legitimate as any other regional development company. Certainly Noah paid bungs to city halls and bought favor with county politicians, but so did every other developer. After all, if kickbacks and corruption hadn't ever occurred, Florida would still be one big gator and panther-infested swamp. Noah paid taxes to the Cubans in Miami and shipped hefty royalties north, but businesswise he stuck purely to real estate and never dirtied his hands with thuggery. He had a good system in place that involved buying cheap land, old distressed houses or fixer uppers and redeveloping them into new shiny special homes. He didn't skimp on fixtures or construction quality and took pride in a first-rate finished product. Surf Way Developments had a regional name for producing the finest real estate around.

Noah Furio was a complicated beast. Growing up as a son of a Don, he had to demonstrate himself capable of the family name. Putting time in for his dad and proving himself on the streets as a young foot soldier, he had taken part in his fair share of action. The faces of all those he had harmed in the name of family pride haunted him. This was one of the reasons he now avoided violence. His exile in South Florida was a fate that he knew could have been far worse. Noah's final instructions when sent packing had been not to visit Rhode Island unless formally invited. He was well aware of what would happen if he showed up anywhere near Providence unannounced.

Now nestled into middle age, Noah was a good-looking and on occasion confident man. He ran a successful business that only those who paid attention to the fine details and knew inside baseball gossip would notate with a cautionary asterisk. Noah took pride in his work and his plan was to make each project more visionary than the last. He had recently been studying the great architects Frank Lloyd Wright, Richard Rogers and Norman Foster. Noah's intent was to make future developments more interesting, flamboyant and less cookie cutter.

Life in Florida for Noah was not just cotton-candy sunsets, land deals and inner angst. There was pressure from all around. The Cubans in the south were slowly marching north and were now established as far as Deerfield. They had also evolved their operations and were getting out of narcotics and investing in real-estate developments. New York and Boston, with their own rust-belt economies in decline, were squeezing Noah for higher payments. He felt they had always held a grudge against him for not standing up properly to the Cubans and staking a claim in Miami. It would only be a matter of time before he wasn't paying them enough, or his face didn't fit any more, or they wanted him to expand into other grubby lines of trade.

When Rhode Island was incorporated into the greater syndicate, Noah was tagged as a "Dead Man Walking." It was his father's reputation, his likeable personality and good business sense that had kept Noah alive for the last decade. He knew that he was living on borrowed time and sooner or later his card would be called in. Noah had been planning for the future. He had put money aside and had acquired documentation in case he needed to get out of town quick. He had no idea where he would go, or even where he could go. The mob had tentacles that stretched into every dark nook and cranny, and they had a habit of finding you wherever you went. One of the reasons that the Feds had such a problem prosecuting organized crime was that witness protection had become a joke. The modern world was a small place and the bad guys knew that you had to be lucky always, and they had only to be lucky once. The life expectancy of a supposedly squirreled-away informant was months, not years.

There was no one special in Noah's life, partly down to his reluctance to get close to someone and bring that person into his world and expose them to danger. There was always a constant threat that he might be taken in the middle of the night and sent to Buffalo or Belize or one of those traditional places where a return ticket wasn't required. It had become a stressful life for Noah and he knew he had to make a change.

"You look deep in thought, Noah," said the always-carefree waitress as she poured him another Merlot.

"I have a lot on my mind. I do envy you Celia. Young, pretty, no ties, your life a blank fabric with boundless possibilities."

Through powerful binoculars, Pete could see Noah Furio was nearly finished with his steak, and a seat at the bar had opened up directly beside him. Pete texted "bombs away!" to Sally, which was her call-to-arms signal. Pete and Angel watched as Sally casually walked into the bar and sat down. Pete could see that she had gone beyond the call of duty in terms of mission preparation. Sally was donning a sexy barely-there black cocktail dress, high stiletto heels, big puffy hair and a face exuding with the application of hot pink lipstick. She looked stunning and could have easily been mistaken for one of the twin staples of pricey South Floridian steak joints – the kept housewife on the trawl for fun or the high-class hooker hunting for business. The uniforms, job descriptions and contractual performance clauses were similar, but to state it bluntly, in terms of mileage and wear and tear, one category of kept lady was carefully raced and the other rallied hard.

Noah would have smelt Sally's aromatic approach before he had a fixed visual on the pretty woman who placed herself just inches from where he sat. As Noah gave her a second not-so-subtle glance, Sally knew she had caught his attention, and it was time to work her charms.

"Are you going to buy me a drink?" Sally asked in that overconfident way that ensures a beautiful woman effortlessly becomes the recipient of all the good things in life with minimal exertion.

Noah introduced himself as a local real-estate developer before ordering Sally a cocktail. Sally gave her real name and told Noah she was a writer of genre fiction. Much of Sally's reeling-in of weak men to satisfy her demonic lust wasn't something she enjoyed but came from deep within and to her felt more like an unexplainable cursed mission of penance than treachery of the heart. Sally was surprised how sweet Noah was and the conversation was easier to keep flowing than feared. Tonight at the bar with Noah, she felt calm and very much at ease.

Angel could see Pete hadn't stopped gawking at Sally since she rolled into their field of vision. "Are your eye's tired yet, Pete?" she asked.

"Uhhh!" mumbled Pete behind his binoculars.

"You've been fixated on Sally's legs ever since she sat down," Angel protested.

"Working the story," he replied. "I have to admit, she does scrub up well."

Angel shot back with a hint of jealousy, "Bone structure. Very good bones. I know a lot about women's bones."

"Perfect bait and he has taken it hook, line and sinker," Pete replied before asking a sulking Angel, "What do you care if I look at her legs anyway, Mrs. Simon Godfrey?"

Sally, just as she predicted, had easily snagged Noah. A little more than an hour after she had first sat down the two of them left the bar together and headed on foot east down Atlantic. Pete started the engine of his SUV and by maintaining a slow speed was able to follow the pair discreetly as they walked along Delray's main drag. Pete could see how well Sally was playing Noah, as the two of them laughed and giggled like flirtatious school kids on the entire stroll to the preplanned destination.

The rehearsal earlier that morning had gone smoothly and everyone knew the individual parts they were to play. With her good looks and experience of artful man handling, Sally was to act in the role of a honey trap. She would lure Noah from his regular City Oyster hangout to the controllable, friendly ground of The Blue Anchor Pub. Rodney was performing a show there that night and from his center-stage vantage position could direct operations. Sally would take Noah to the bar and keep the drinks and conversation streaming. When Sally thought Noah was settled, relaxed and due a top-up drink, she would lower her handbag onto the floor. On seeing this sign, Rodney would launch into his version of Rod Stewart's *Maggie May*. This was the signal for

Bodie, who was tending the bar, to bring Sally and Noah their drinks.

The beverage intended for Noah would be a Mickey Finn; in exact terms it would be laced with Rohypnol, more commonly known as the frat-boy date-rape drug of choice. This vital element was appropriated from The Beach House's Man of God, Randy Showers, who oddly had a bountiful supply sitting in his bathroom cabinet. Once Noah was on the verge of losing all control, Sally would pick up her handbag and put it back on her shoulder. At this movement the band would launch into Rod Stewart's *Sailing.* This was the two-minute warning for Ethan, who was waiting outside on the street to pull his van up to the pub's front door and wait with the engine running. Sally would then drag Noah onto the pub floor and slow dance him around the room and ultimately out of the front door, where he would be bundled into Ethan's vehicle. Once Noah was safely in the van, he would be driven back to The Beach House.

Upon arrival at The Beach House, Rebecca and Randy would discreetly take Noah up to Sally's apartment where he would be undressed and placed in her bed. The next morning, when he had woken up and his head cleared, he would find Sally lying next to him. She would fill in the blanks, letting him know he'd been a "very bad boy," but had redeemed himself by "performing like a champ." At this point Noah, murky-headed, satisfied after a night of passion with a looker, and trapped in the belly of the beast, was deemed to be at his most receptive to hear their pitch.

The Beach House residents had all kinds of activities in place to warm his heart. He would meet everyone, hear their stories, and learn the history of the building and so much more. Rebecca was going to bake cakes, Sally read extracts from her new book, Rodney sing, and Long Island Iced Tea Bob provide refreshments. This was going to be *Local Hero* only with crazier natives, a full cabaret show and warmer water at the beach. The outcome hoped by all was that he would fall in love with their Shangri-La and instead of kicking them out on the street, agree to be their new landlord. Everyone was assured that it would be a success.

However, if Noah wasn't playing nicely and went "hard-man mobster" on them, Bodie, Rodney and Ethan had discussed a half-baked contingency plan. Rodney had commandeered handcuffs, rope and more than enough items of general restraint from Sally's inexhaustible S&M supplies to keep even Harry Houdini from escaping. Although they had the ability to contain and hold Noah, the final plan hadn't progressed to the important issue of what exactly they would do with him once held captive. For of course, a pissed-off freed mobster had the potential to do a number of ugly things. Bodie had a Glock pistol and there was some muttering that if the shit really hit the fan Angel could help with his disposal – although no one had mentioned this "B Plan" to her and if they had, she would have freaked. The Beach House residents were still feeling positive about the "A Plan" and were hoping they wouldn't need contingencies.

That night The Blue Anchor was packed to capacity. Rodney was on stage belting out *Reason to Believe*. Bodie was busy serving drinks, and Sally and Noah were getting along like a house on fire at the bar. Bodie admired how Sally had launched herself "balls deep" into the plan and was playing her part well. While pulling pints on the Harp tap, he managed to hear the occasional sound bite between Noah and Sally. It seemed more like the two of them were long-lost best friends and not two strangers on a faux first date.

Outside The Blue Anchor, Pete and Angel were parked up across the street watching for events to unfold.

"I thought they would be out by now," said Angel, as she viewed Ethan parked up across the street napping in the front seat of his van.

"No shit. This is dragging on. I will text Bodie and see if there are issues," Pete replied. "This sitting back and waiting is ninety-nine percent of the job. Welcome to my world, Angel."

Bodie had served Noah and Sally for nearly two hours, but still hadn't been given the signal to proceed with his part of the plan. Rodney gave Bodie a look from the stage as if to ask if there was a problem as he finished up the tune *Stay with Me*. Bodie looked in the direction of Sally and Noah and shrugged his shoulders to convey he had no idea what was going on.

Rodney made a quick change of the planned set. After thanking the fans, he introduced the subsequent number. "Our next one is from 1969 and a special request from Sally, the pretty young lady at the bar. Make yourself comfy luv, put down your handbag and get dancing gal," Rodney shouted out before launching into the ballad *Handbags and Gladrags*.

Sally looked over to Rodney and gave him a wave.

"Music man's a little familiar!" said Noah, before excusing himself and heading to the John. Seeing a safe window, Bodie approached Sally for an urgent parley.

"Is there a problem, Sally?" Bodie asked.

"Yes, a big one!" replied Sally in a hushed voice before knocking back the rest of her drink.

Angel had been sat in the car with Pete all evening. He could tell she was tiring of the waiting.

"I can handle this on my own if you need to go home," Pete said.

"I want to stay with you."

They had kept the banter businesslike so far, but Pete couldn't resist delving a little deeper, even if it meant ruffling feathers.

"You and Simon – how's that going?" he asked.

"It's all right. Could be better, I suppose," Angel said as she finally took off her ski cap and loosened her hair.

Pete looked over to Ethan, who was still asleep in his car. "You see it working out long-term with him?"

"Do you think I am waiting for something better to come along?" Angel replied

"Are you?"

"You know something I don't?"

As fast as a cowboy gunslinger, Pete reached behind his car seat and pulled out an SLR camera with attached telephoto lens. He brought the piece of professional photographic equipment to eye level, aimed it out of his car's side window and fired off a dozen rapid-fire frames.

"What was that all about?" Angel asked Pete, as she watched him lower the camera speedily into his lap and review the images on the back panel display.

"Just asking how things are going with you and Mr. Perfect, that's all," said Pete.

"That was more than obvious," said Angel. "What I meant was, why did you take those pictures out of the car window?"

"The car parked on the other side of the road with the two men in it has been there for the last two hours. I also noticed it parked outside City Oyster. It has Boston plates."

"You sure do pay attention to everything around you, Mr. Alexander."

"I was waiting an hour for them to wind the windows down so I could get a clear shot."

"I had no idea there was anyone there. What do you think they're doing?"

"If this was a celebrity assignment, I would say they are competition trying to jump my story."

"Could they be Noah's goons?"

"I don't think so. I have passed by his house before and there has never been any apparent muscle."

Angel did not like this at all. "What are we messing with?" she asked. "Maybe you were right and we should have cashed out and moved on with our lives."

"I did tell you that," Pete said, before cheekily adding, "Angel there are several areas of your life you should cash out and upgrade on."

Pete downloaded the pictures he had taken of the two men and a close-up of the car registration plate. He e-mailed the images to his Boca Raton private eye.

"What's the problem, Sally?" Bodie asked as he pulled a pint of Harp.

"I can't go through with it," she replied.

"What are you talking about?" Bodie exclaimed. "You volunteered for this and most of it was your idea!"

"Noah, he's just such a great guy," Sally replied.

"He's a mobster who has bulldozed his way through half of this town. In what way could all of a sudden he be deemed a great guy?"

"I can't explain it."

"A lot is depending on you!" Bodie said as he finished pouring the perfect headless pint.

Rodney was keeping an eye on the intense conversation between Bodie and Sally while finishing off his cover of *Every Picture Tells a Story*.

"Bodie, you may not be aware, but I've led a horrible fucked-up life. Men have treated me like shit since I was twelve. I have treated them like shit since I was thirteen. I have whored my way around the country and never found a man, or woman, I wanted a second date with. Noah is different – we have a connection. I really think I have found my soul mate."

"Are you kidding me?" Bodie said, incredulously. "You only met him three hours ago!"

"He's like Tony Soprano, but with better hair and a fit body. Besides, he's not an old-school scary mobster. He is really more like a regular slick businessman with a sideline in dodgy."

"You are one fucked-up lady, Sally Purdue!" Bodie replied.

"I know, but I just can't do it," she said. "The way I feel with him is different from everything I have ever known. I am so nervous that I am on the verge of something special that I couldn't even sleep with him if he took me home and begged for mad monkey love."

Noah came back from the restroom and took his seat next to Sally at the bar.

"Two Black and Tans coming right up!" said Bodie.

"We should really be going," Sally said to Noah, as Bodie went to the other side of the pub to make their drinks.

"I am good for a nightcap," a relaxed Noah responded.

Rodney broke into *Maggie May*. This had the audience jumping onto the dance floor.

"I don't like this, Pete. What we are doing is crazy," said Angel.

"Kidnapping a mobster and taking him home? You were right behind this bright idea last week," Pete said as he got out of the car and told Angel to hold tight and he would be back shortly. Pete walked across Atlantic Avenue close to where the car with Boston plates was parked. As he was directly next to it, he bent down and tied his shoelaces before walking a block east and doing a loop back to his vehicle.

"What did you see?" Angel asked as Pete got back into the SUV.

"Two nasty-looking pieces of work conducting some shoddy surveillance," Pete replied, as he pulled out a digital scanner from the car's glove box. He then tuned it in and turned up the volume. "More importantly than seeing them is the ability to eavesdrop on them, and track the movements of their car," he added.

"You bugged them?" Angel asked.

They could now hear the results of the small listening and tracking device Pete had attached to the undercarriage of the car.

"What's the plan, Jimmy?" one of the men in the car could be heard asking.

"Just waiting for the word, then take him back to Boston," said the other in a thick regional accent.

"Noah riding in the back seat or trunk?" the second man could be heard asking.

"That depends on orders. If it was down to me I would ditch him in the swamp tonight!" The two men chuckled.

"I'm tired of this job and want to get home for the Celtics game on Wednesday."

Pete's phone vibrated. The incoming text was from his private eye.

"This all makes sense," Pete said speaking down the phone.

"What did you find out?" Angel asked as Pete ended the call.

"That car has been traced back to a Boston waste-disposal company, and of course we know what that is a front for. Those two jokers are soldiers for a big New England crime syndicate and I'm pretty sure they are here to meet with our man Noah Furio," Pete said, as Angel put her ski hat back on and slumped down into the seat of the car.

As Bodie brought out the two drinks, Sally grabbed Noah by the hand and to the beats of *Forever Young* dragged him onto the dance floor. He was evidently not a natural dancer, but was only too happy to play along with his new-found friend. Noah was not the kind of guy beautiful women usually sit next to, chat up and then dance with. In all the years in Delray Beach, or in fact anywhere, he had never had a night like this. Noah was starting to question if this all passed the "sniff test." Sally seemed fantastic and they got on well, but as the saying goes, "If something seems to be too good to be true, it is too good to be true." Noah was wondering if there was going to be a catch, if he had been set up or if she would ask for money at the end of the night. Noah also had bigger concerns. He was aware that if there were not a number on his head now, there would be soon enough if his taskmasters ever got wind that he was hiding money offshore and planning an escape.

"I need a drink," Noah whispered in Sally's ear as they danced away to *Tonight's the Night*.

Noah walked back to the bar and was about to grab his Black and Tan when Sally came from behind, swiped the drink he was about to pick up and shouted, "That's mine!"

"Sure, I'll have the other one. Not a problem," Noah replied with a perplexed expression.

A hot and out-of-breath Noah, who possibly hadn't danced like this since the Reagan Administration, downed his drink and indicated to Bodie he would like a refill. Sally clutched hers without taking a sip. As Bodie gave the thumbs-up to Sally, he winked towards the direction of the band. Rodney made an announcement that this would be their last song of the evening before breaking into *Sailing*.

Within minutes Noah felt light-headed and quickly sat back down on his bar stool. For him, the rest of the evening would be a blur.

"I thought you might do that!" Bodie said to Sally. "So I switched them. I would suggest you dance him out of here pronto, before there's a scene."

Pete and Angel could hear the signal tune of *Sailing* from the far side of Atlantic Avenue. Ethan, although much nearer, evidently couldn't, as he was fast asleep in the front of his van with an unlit cigarette dangling from his hand out of the window.

"Wingman asleep on the job – story of my life," said Pete, who was calling Ethan on his cell phone to no avail.

"Your Boston friends just got out of the car," said Angel, who was keeping tabs on them through a pair of binoculars.

"Perfect timing!" replied Pete, as he gave up on resurrecting Ethan.

"Angel, you grab the wheel and pull up at the front door," said Pete. "I'll go on foot and see what's happening inside."

Pete sprinted across Atlantic Avenue and darted into the pub. The two men from Boston were standing outside their car smoking and checking that their guns were locked and loaded. Angel started up the SUV and drove one block west on Atlantic Avenue before pulling a dangerous U-turn and parking directly in front of Florida's finest British pub.

Once Pete had walked into the pub, the scene awaiting him wasn't what he had anticipated. Noah was slumped on his stool, precariously resting on the bar, and Sally was having an obvious argument with Bodie. Rodney, in an effort to get off stage, had sped up the tempo of *Sailing* and the ballad now sounded like bad Euro pop.

"What's the problem?" asked Pete.

"Sally went all Stockholm syndrome on us and fell in love with our goodfella," said Bodie.

"It's not like that. Noah isn't the man you think he is. He is one of the good guys. He is just like me or you," snapped back Sally.

"You might be right, but there are two bad guys from the north waiting down the street for Noah," replied Pete at double speed. "Best to get him out of here just like we planned and then have a debate about the ethical shades of gray we choose to live our lives by at someplace more comfortable and less dangerous!"

"Randy's stuff was potent, so Noah's beyond dancing," said Sally, looking at the collapsed man.

Pete looked to the front door and saw the two goons enter the bar and scan the room.

"Trouble coming in right now!" said Pete.

Sally grabbed Noah and dragged him to the dance floor. Bodie looked up at the hired hands. He ran to the back of the bar and went straight to the fuse box and tripped the circuits. The lights went down, the pub turned pitch black and Rodney Sawdust's rendition of *Sailing* went raw and acoustic.

"Side door!" Pete shouted. Sally and Pete dragged their charge out of The Blue Anchor's secondary entrance that fed onto Palm Square Avenue. Pete led them to Angel, who was waiting on Atlantic. Once Sally, Noah and Pete were safely bundled into the back of the SUV, Pete gave the order for Angel to "Take us home!"

September 23rd 2016, from the Orlando Sentinel

FLORIDA MAN DUMPS CUP FULL OF SEMEN ON WOMAN AT RESTAURANT

A Tallahassee man is accused of pouring his bodily fluids onto a woman at a local restaurant. The Florida man, after spending a period of time staring at the woman and her friend, went to the restroom. Authorities said he then returned, walked over to the women's table, said, "Here you go" and dumped a cup of semen onto the victim's neck, shoulder and arm. He also left a cell phone at the scene, which contained explicit images taken in the bathroom. Police have charged the man with one count of indecent exposure, two counts of battery, and one count of an unnatural and lascivious act.

An Articulation of Particulars

The saying, "Amateurs talk strategy and professionals do logistics" resonated in Pete's head as he evaluated the events of last night. Sally had gotten cold feet and aborted her mission, Ethan had fallen asleep on the job and was of no use, and the appointed reception committee of Randy and Rebecca weren't in place after getting carried away drinking and subsequently carnally involved. Throw in the two Boston hitmen roaming Delray Beach and the mobster currently passed out in Apartment #11, and Pete knew he had a rather hot mess on his hands.

"Where the hell am I?" Noah screamed as the intense morning sun that seeped through the apartment's plantation shutters brought him back to life.

Sally was sat in a wicker chair watching over him. The gonzo novelist had spent the night contemplating exactly what she would say to Noah when he woke up.

"You came home with me last night," she replied, displaying an obvious nervous tic.

"I don't remember anything after that Black and Tan," said Noah, mentally retracing his movements while rubbing his eyes.

Randy's "roofies" had been industrial strength. Noah was quickly out for the count and the task of getting him into Sally's second-floor apartment hadn't been easy. Pete, Angel and Sally performed a herculean feat, hauling what felt like a sack of concrete across the patio and up the stairwell, while Gabriel stood at his front door trying to compute exactly what was transpiring.

"You were a little worse for wear last night," she said, unconvincingly.

"Something isn't feeling right, Sally. You plant yourself next to me at the bar while I am having dinner. Start up a conversation. Take me out dancing. And then I wake up who knows where with a lost evening behind me," said Noah.

"We were having fun," replied Sally, as she got up from her chair, sat beside Noah and reached out to stroke his face.

He knocked her hand away. "Who are you working for? The Cubans!"

"What do you mean?"

"Your story stinks," said Noah. "You're playing me. Where am I?"

"You are at my place, Noah," said Sally. "The Beach House apartments."

"What! That dump on Andrews I'm in the process of buying?"

"Yes," she said.

"This is weird. Who are you? Tell me the truth?"

"I'm the person you had a great evening with, that's before you passed out," she said.

"I didn't pass out. You drugged me and brought me back here."

"Noah, we have a connection, me and you. Please tell me that," said Sally

"Be honest with me – did you drug me?"

Sally paused before answering. "Yes and no. I was going to, but changed my mind... Someone else did it for me."

"You're working with others? What's this all about? Did you rob me? Do I still have two kidneys?" Noah checked his stomach for stitches and reached for his wallet to see if it still held the mandatory wedge of cash he never left home without.

"Of course not," she said.

"So you didn't rob me, have not taken any vital organs and you're not working for the Cubans? Then who are you, and why did you spike my drink and bring me here?"

"Noah, please tell me you had a good night, enjoyed my company, felt a connection? I had a wonderful time and didn't want the evening to end," said Sally, now close to tears.

"Tell me who you are and what you want?"

"We, the residents of The Beach House, thought that if you came here and met us, saw our community, felt our spirit, you might not want to demolish the building and pave over our way of life," she finally confessed.

"So the way to get me here was with a Mickey. I would then wake up, have breakfast with you, meet your friends and have a burning bush moment. Everyone would live happily ever after," he said with a mocking tinge.

"In a nutshell, yes," said Sally. "The guy from Apartment #3 saw some old British movie and was inspired to copy its storyline. Everyone thought there was a chance if you came here in person we could win your heart, and you would leave The Beach House exactly as it is. I know it is all romantic claptrap, but we thought it would work."

"You're an odd one, Sally," Noah said. "Are you really a writer or was that part of this web of deceit?"

"I am a writer," she said as she threw him a copy of her first book, *Sally Does Route 66*.

Noah flicked through the pages. "What is this? Pulp fiction porn?"

"I do have a kinky streak," Sally replied.

"Did we do any of this kind of stuff last night?" Noah asked after reading the first paragraph of a chapter titled "Dirty Sanchez in Natchez."

"Nothing," said Sally. "I wouldn't take advantage of you, and that's not my regular game plan. Noah, I genuinely had a wonderful evening."

"I knew it was all too good to be true."

"Noah, it was too good to be true, because it is too good to be true, and I'm telling you this from my heart!" Sally then kissed him. "I'm one crazy fucked-up girl, but you're special, and within minutes of meeting you I could tell there was going to be something magical between us."

"Are you just laying this shtick on as part of your *Goonies* gang-thwarting-the-developer nonsense?"

"I really don't care about this place," said Sally. "I was just helping out in the name of community goodwill. I'm only passing through town to finish my book and quite like the project you proposed."

"Fat chance that whatever your redneck friends have in mind means I would scrap my plans for The Beach House. I'm a businessman and have staff to pay and 'shareholders' to answer to," replied Noah.

"Screw your development and The Beach House! What about us?" asked Sally. "We could take it slowly, not that I am too familiar with the concept, but there is a first time for everything."

"It's been a long time since I had anyone in my life," said Noah. "I did wonder when I met you last night…"

Sally cut him off and finished his sentence by saying, "That we're meant to be."

Sally then kissed Noah.

"You don't really know me," said Noah, coming up for air.

"Possibly not, but I know enough and I'll take a chance."

Rebecca barged open the door, looking like she hadn't had much sleep. "Glad you are all up," she said. Coffee and cake are being served."

Sally and Noah dressed and then walked down to the patio. Angel, Pete, Bodie, Randy, Rebecca, Ethan and Rodney were sat around a table digging into freshly baked goodies.

"Sally told me all about your master plan," said Noah, addressing the gathering. "I can safely say that even if you got the Broadway cast of *Hamilton* to perform in front of me, and Donald Trump to sit in attendance, I still wouldn't change my mind about tearing down The Beach House. You're lucky I'm not going to get you all fucked up."

"That certainly wasn't how it played out in *Local Hero*," said Rodney.

"I know you, music man from last night," said Noah, now putting together all the faces and seeing that The Blue Anchor bartender was also in his presence.

"Our plan changed anyway," said Pete.

"We thought you might want some light refreshments before you go home," Angel said, as she offered him a cup of coffee.

"I think I will be on my way, if you don't mind," said Noah.

"Did you tell him everything?" Bodie asked Sally.

"Not exactly!" said Sally.

"Am I missing something?" asked Noah, looking directly at his kidnappers.

"There are a couple of guys from Boston sat outside your house waiting for your arrival," said Pete, as he tossed the pictures he had taken of the two men in front of Noah.

"They were also at The Blue Anchor last night," said Bodie.

"They followed you from City Oyster," added Angel.

"We have audio of them saying they are taking you back to Boston," Pete said.

"In the trunk of the car," added Rebecca.

Rodney chimed in, "There was also some talk about dropping you off at the swamp."

"You're free to go when you want, or you could hang here with your new friends and have some coffee," said Ethan, taking a rest between cancer sticks.

"You guys really are something," said Noah, who made himself comfortable and took a piece of key lime pie.

"They all know about your connections," said Sally, who had talked with Noah the previous evening about his business arrangements.

"But why do these people want to take you up north?" asked Pete. "You're a made man." Pete then played some audio from his planted bug.

"You guys are real good, with all your dirty digging, Nancy Drew sneaky surveillance, drugging, scheming honey traps," said Noah. "I've no idea what your day jobs are, but I'm sure the CIA could put you to constructive use."

"We're just regular blue-collar scammers, dreamers, drifters and crazies trying to get by," said Randy. "Well, they all are. I'm an ordained minister doing the work of God."

Noah's thoughtful reflection of his circumstances was broken by the door of Apartment #1 opening and Long Island Iced Tea Bob approaching with a tray of drinks. He had been asked before if he knew any other original cocktails, but his answer was always, "This is perfection, so why bother?"

Noah had an "Ah-ah!" moment when he realized the money guys in New England had finally figured out that the numbers were not adding up and he had been skimming royalty payments. Noah, revealing his predicament to the group around him, said, "So let's just say that the partnership with my shareholders was more than likely going to come to a mutual end. There was talk of an extraordinary board meeting being called, and I wasn't too keen on attending."

"That doesn't sound good," said Sally.

"Evidently you guys are smarter than I took you for. I'm guessing you'll now present me an opportunity I cannot turn down. Let me rephrase that – if I do turn it down, you have someone in place who will tell the two men sat outside my house where I can be found," said Noah.

"Shit, why didn't we think of that?" said Rodney kicking himself before Pete cut in.

"I do have an idea I would like to present," said Pete.

"While I'm not in the strongest of bargaining positions I'm always open to options, so an articulation of particulars, if you please," said Noah, who was clearly savoring his Long Island Iced Tea and key lime pie.

"OK. If there was a way we could keep you out of the hands of your enemies, and make you totally vanish, would you allow The Beach House to continue in its present incarnation?" asked Pete.

"Not turn this breeze-block barracks into a beautiful luxury piece of prime Florida real estate!" exclaimed Noah.

"Yes, even with its eccentricities, we like it just the way it is," said Angel.

"Most of us like it the way it is," said Pete.

"Have you been inside one of my finished projects? They are beauties," said Noah, as he looked around The Beach House with disdain.

"What gumbo-limbo is to virgin dunes and mangroves, this double lot can be left as a reminder of genuine 1950s old Florida life," said Ethan, who was surprisingly without cigarette in mouth, hand or on the table in front of him.

"I've worked out a possible scenario, where you will disappear and no one will even bother to come looking for you," said Pete.

"It isn't easy to hide someone and I know first-hand what has happened to former 'associates' who thought they were safely holed up and leading a new life," said Noah.

"No worries. We'll not be hiding you, Noah. You will die and disappear," exclaimed Pete, as Noah choked on his key lime pie and spewed up a mouthful of Long Island Iced Tea.

* * *

From tracking the two Boston goons, Pete quickly figured out their pattern of operations. The men were staying at a cheap motel on Yamato in Boca Raton when they weren't watching Noah's house and the Delray offices of Surf Way Developments. They were getting frustrated that they hadn't seen Noah since the power went out at The Blue Anchor the previous night. From listening to the audio of them talking, they had started to worry that Noah had given them the slip, and they were now getting heat from the "Boss Men" in New England.

Pete used their sloppy surveillance techniques to his advantage, and when they went for one of their many piss and food breaks on Atlantic Avenue, he took Noah's Jaguar from the driveway of his house. When Pete listened to the stunned language of the two mob men when they came back from lunch and realized Noah's car was gone, he was reminded of his own botched stakeouts early in his career. The two men would have some explaining to do when they checked in again with their superiors. Lucky for these two hapless fools, what Pete had lined up for Noah would most likely save their own skins.

Noah's car, a late-model Jaguar XF, drove like a beast, and it was going to be a shame to waste a fifty grand ride. However, it had been agreed that this would make their ruse look all the more authentic. At 10 p.m., with Ethan riding in convoy to the rear, Pete drove Noah's car up to the exact spot where just a few weeks ago Jacob Smith had careened into a Boca Raton drainage canal. As Pete pulled up at the location it was evident that Jacob had already done the heavy lifting for them, as there was a clean pathway through the shrubbery and bushes from his crashed car. Ethan and Pete easily pushed Noah's car along that same path and, with a little help from gravity, rolled it straight into the canal. When the car landed it made a satisfying splash followed by a loud gurgle as the cold water cooled down the hot engine.

"That was easy!" said Ethan, as he lit a cigarette and watched the car come to rest in a peaceful half-submerged state.

"Jacob was one lucky crack head getting out of his car alive," said Pete.

Ethan used his cell phone to call a local tow company that had a "no questions asked" sideline in fishing out cars from bodies of water, as most of their customers were drivers who had been a little too happy at happy hour, and had taken a corner wide and then needed their car retrieved before the police rolled up with breathalyzers in hand. As the tow truck pulled out the Jaguar, Pete snapped away with his camera. The money shot he needed showed the car being retrieved with its license plate visible. With the picture cropped and edited, he then uploaded it to a burner e-mail account and sent it to the *Sun Sentinel* news tips e-mail address. They were quick to reply and said if they decided to run the picture they had no budget to pay him. Pete responded as if he were a clueless amateur and said that wouldn't be a problem because he was just happy to see his picture in print.

Pete then called his Boca Raton private eye and put in an order for what he termed "The Special." His man had connections with Russian cyber hackers, and what they couldn't do was far less than what they could. They were not cheap and this level of work would be done for a flat $10,000 fee. His request was simple: he wanted them to hack into the Sheriff's department database and create a police report documenting the fatal accident that occurred at 10.25 p.m. that night on Glades. The most important elements were linked to the ID found in the driver's pocket. The dead body that had been retrieved from the canal in this accident was to be documented as local property developer Noah Furio. The forged and filed police report was so good that perhaps the only giveaway that it was bogus was the speed at which these cyber hackers took care of the task. A typical Sheriff's department report takes hours to process, but Noah Furio's was in the system just sixty minutes after his official stated time of death.

The first question any homicide detective asks is, "Where's the body?" The only way anyone was really going to believe that Noah Furio was dead was if there was evidence of a corpse. Between the hours of 3 a.m. and 6 a.m. the Palm Beach County Coroner's department was technically unstaffed and closed for new intake. It would be this window of opportunity that Angel would use to process the very much alive Noah Furio and present him as if were very much dead.

"Nice office," said Pete, as Angel led himself, Sally, Rebecca and Noah into her everyday place of work. Angel went over to her desk and fired up a computer, while Pete flicked on the lighting. This office was a little more mundane and harshly lit than it would have been if portrayed on a television drama, but from a quick scan around the room it was evident you were standing on ground zero of the business end of industrialized dying.

"This place is creeping me out!" said Noah.

"A mobster freaked out in the presence of dead bodies – that's something new," said Angel in a sarcastic tone.

"He isn't really a mobster," Sally mentioned in a matter-of-fact way.

"Business developer, let's leave it at that," said Noah.

"Former business developer, as you are technically a ghost!" Rebecca pointed out.

"Strip off then," Angel barked at Noah, as she pulled paperwork from a filing cabinet.

"Everything?" asked Noah.

"Does he have to?" Sally cut in.

"We need to make this look real and I can assure you the deceased are without clothes or shame when they arrive at my office. If you don't believe me, open any of the cabinets on that wall and you'll see everyone is sans garments," Angel said, as she filled in the bureaucratic forms that document the newly dead. "Please speed up. I don't want to be busted," she told Noah, who was undressing at a snail's pace.

Sally looked around the room and dreaded to think what was inside the numerous numbered body-sized shelves. Rebecca unpacked her makeup bag, and Pete walked around peeking into places he shouldn't in order to avoid looking at Noah's junk.

"I've seen plenty bigger," Angel shouted with a smirk, as she looked up from her paperwork at a totally nude Noah. Rebecca gave a nodding confirmation as Sally bounced back a dagger stare.

"Lay down on the table," Angel said to Noah.

"Shit! That's cold," Noah growled as his bare flesh made contact with the sterile metal of the examination table.

"You are the first complaint I've ever had," Angel joked as she walked from her desk to what her colleagues called "The slab."

"This place will give me nightmares," said Sally, as she watched Noah lying down.

"At least it doesn't smell like death," said Rebecca.

With Angel's direction, Rebecca applied makeup in order to present Noah exactly as he would if he had been slowly decomposing in the fridge for the last twenty-four hours. With all those years of applying concealer to cover up the bruises of abuse, or mascara to ready herself for a night on the town, Rebecca had become an accomplished makeup artist.

"Nice job, Rebecca," Angel said, as she gave her neighbor a high five.

"What now?" asked Noah.

"Now you look like a proper stiff, I'll photograph you from every angle, just as I would any corpse down here," said Angel as she reached down underneath the examination table that housed her equipment.

"Aaah!" screamed Noah, as Angel retrieved a revving and pulsating power saw instead of a camera, and held it directly over Noah's head.

Pete looked at the situation unfolding and was more scared of the crazed gaze in Angel's eyes than the fear on Noah's face.

"It's on bone-cutting mode, so if I move this two inches lower it will slice right through you skull, killing you quickly, but not as quickly as you would hope," said Angel, as Sally and Rebecca froze in fear.

"Angel! What are you doing?" said Pete, who didn't get a response.

"In theory, Noah, you're dead anyway, so no crime would have occurred and I can easily dispose of you afterwards," Angel added as she menacingly whirred a device over Noah's lower body that looked to a layman like a turbo-powered pizza cutter.

After a further ten seconds of menace, which seemed like much longer to everyone in the room, Angel flicked the off switch and the tool slowly powered down.

"Just kidding. I wanted to vent my inner mobster," said Angel to the relief of everyone. "The expression on your face was priceless, Noah. You really thought I was going to do it, didn't you? I am all about life even though they call me Angel of Death."

"Not cool!" said Sally, as she ran over to Noah, who was visibly shaking.

"I better redo some of that makeup," said Rebecca. Noah's perspiration had left messy streaks over his body.

"Chill everyone. I was just having fun," said Angel, as she grabbed her camera and readied herself to take pictures.

Pete was impressed with Angel as she photographed Noah from all the necessary angles. Angel had a good grip on the camera, a steady hand while shooting and knew the perfect settings for her flashgun. He doubted the close-up shots of Noah's penis were really necessary and put that down to Angel's adorkable sense of humor. Pete could tell from watching her operate that there was the potential for Angel to be a second shooter on undercover assignments in ritzy hotels or big-money tropical missions. The two of them would be a perfect undercover pseudo husband and wife, shooting away at their celebrity targets without ever being made as paparazzo photographers. Pete watched Angel download the images to her computer before adding the needed captions and metadata. He would be the first to admit he found it a turn-on watching her whizzing around the office and going about her work. However, the crazed look in Angel's eyes as she waved around the pulsating power saw was a fiendish vision that would be hard to erase from his mind.

The final document that Angel produced was a release that stated the next of kin had retrieved Noah's body and he was no longer stored at the Coroners' Office. With all the necessary paperwork filled in, the photographs taken and a death certificate created, Noah's case file was now complete and he was legally dead and presumed en route for burial. Angel's final act of the night was to make Noah Furio's file available for internal department release, so anyone following the trail could see that he was more than certainly deceased. The photographs, though not made public, could be accessed by law enforcement. Noah was well aware that the New England mob had dozens of cops on the payroll and they would share the conclusive and shocking photo proof with those who wanted him gone. Once the mob had viewed his file, there would be no doubt that he had died in that car crash.

"Congratulations, Noah Furio!" You have now been processed by the Palm Beach County Coroners' Office and are free to leave," said Angel, in an unusually illogical statement as she threw back to the naked man his pile of clothes.

* * *

The day Ethan Thomas bought a Hunter 356 sailing boat he named *Bow Movement* was one of the happiest days of his life. He knew that some day, when he had finally offloaded this money pit, he would once again feel that same sense of unbounded pleasure. The thirty-five-foot fiberglass yacht hadn't seen open seas for months. It wasn't much more than a pricey ornament that bobbed around the Boynton Beach Marina, extracting cash out of Ethan's pocket for mooring fees, cleaning, taxes and insurance. The only positive part was that it gave him a valid excuse to pop up to the Two Georges pub for a couple of beverages, when he checked on the off-chance that his prayers had been answered and that the yacht had been stolen or there had been a Jewish lightning strike. Tonight, though, his yacht at last would earn its keep and be useful. The plan was for *Bow Movement* to help take a man, who was supposedly dead, out of the country undetected.

Pete, Angel, Sally and Noah rolled up to the marina at midnight. They found Ethan at the Two Georges bar, cigarette in hand, telling fish stories to a flirty barmaid who, two decades ago, might have fitted into the Daisy Dukes and barely there tube top she was forced to wear for work. Aside from the dramatic effect of leaving in the middle of the night, it was the optimal departure time to avoid the daytime coastal thunderstorms that broke out around this time of year. Ethan had spent the day preparing the boat, so as soon as the passengers arrived they could speedily depart. He cast off and motored north along the Intracoastal until they reached the Boynton inlet, and from there he could access the open sea. Once past the reef, Ethan hoisted the sails and set a course due southeast. First light brought the rough swell that comes with crossing the strong Gulf Stream currents. With one hand on the captain's wheel and another holding a cigarette, Ethan pointed the boat in the direction of their destination, only tacking or deviating to avoid heavy rainstorms.

"Look!" said Angel, as she spotted a pod of dolphins in front of the boat.

Angel and Pete ran to the boat's bow and watched the dolphins racing against each other and jumping in and out of the waves. Pete stood behind her making sure she didn't fall overboard as the yacht pitched and tossed in the choppy swell.

"The dolphins are showing off," said Pete.

"For us?" Angel asked.

"For us and for each other. The males are trying to impress the females, looking for partners. The life of dolphins is nothing more than one big mating game," said Pete, before explaining to Angel what was either an unhealthy amount of knowledge about the reproductive cycles of dolphins, or a good recollection of a wordy *National Geographic* article. From the front of the boat they saw manatee, reef sharks, swordfish and turtles. As they left the Gulf Stream current, the ocean turned from a light-aqua color to a dreamy dark blue. As the sun rose to its highest point in the sky, they were in open water and could no longer see the legions of condo high-rises and ugly hotels that distinctly illustrate South Florida's eastern shoreline. Away from land the airborne birds were fewer, and the air without the pollution of sprawl smelled refreshingly clean. The sun sunk in the west, hanging on the horizon for a good three knots as if begging to stay in Florida for just a little longer. To the north, an electrical storm jostled in the thick air.

Pete and Angel sat on the edge of the boat, dangling their feet off the side as day turned into night. The occasional big wave hitting would be enough for a slight wetting of their feet.

Ethan had hooked up the boat stereo system and was blasting out Led Zeppelin's *Over the Hills and Far Away.*

"We pulled it off," said a beaming Angel.

"That's down to you," said Pete. "I would've taken the money and run."

"The Beach House is special. People were relying on us. Rebecca, Rodney, Bodie and everyone else – where would they have gone?" Angel replied.

"They are survivors and would've figured something out. We can't save all of old Florida single handedly," said Pete.

"There will be nothing but McMansions and faux Bermuda town homes if everyone just sells out and stands aside to let the bulldozers roll," said Angel.

"You, better than anyone, should know that you can't stop what is meant to be from happening. Sometimes it is best to let things go," said Pete.

They sat in brief silence, listening to the waves crash on the side of the boat as Jimmy Page's electric guitar screeched into the night.

"That hero halo I saw over your head the last two days: I might just throw it overboard now," said Angel, as she looked into the night before adding, "Why did you do it?"

After a long pause Pete said, "The dolphins."

"What do you mean?"

"Why do dolphins spend their lives performing tricks?" said Pete, who now finally revealed his playbook to Angel.

"To impress me, or some big mating game?" she asked.

"I would've been banging on the doors of the church if I had to," said Pete, looking directly into her eyes.

"Why me?" asked Angel.

"Why wouldn't I? Hello?" said Pete, in an inadvertent tribute to the late Tim Flanders. "You're beautiful, smart, sometimes classy and mostly honorable."

"When not on all fours making home movies," Angel interrupted.

"Nobody is perfect, but yes, like the dolphins, I was along for the ride because of you."

"Should I be flattered or freaked by your dogged pursuit?" she asked.

"You tell me?"

He then leant over and attempted to kiss Angel. Being a regular-looking guy with minimal dating experience for someone past the age of fifteen, this wasn't the type of movement he had a bountiful amount of practical familiarity with. At best it was going to be a coin toss as to the outcome. Pete had taken into consideration that they were in a confined environment, and if he were on the losing side of the gamble the consequences would be awkward and unpredictable.

Angel saw Pete's less-than-slick move approaching faster than an out-of-control freight train rumbling over the Delray railroad crossing. Angel had always been intrigued by her neighbor, but possibly not enough, under regular circumstances, for events to have turned romantic. In contrast, Simon Godfrey had, on paper, been an embodiment of any girl's dreams. Worse things could happen, she thought to herself, as Pete launched his kiss. Angel didn't push his advances away, possibly due to the moment, the fresh sea air or maybe she had been inspired by the dolphins earlier that day. The kiss was sloppy, a touch wet and far from anything Taylor Swift would pen a song about, but at that exact moment it was just perfect and for a brief second she felt more special than ever.

That went better than I imagined, Pete thought to himself as she received the kiss without a hint of protest. Pete knew from the first day he met Angel that she was "The One." It had been one hell of a slog to get to this point, but it was worth it. As his tongue worked its presumed magic in the dark night, he moved his hand gently towards her chest and caressed her soft right breast. This seemed to Pete how this scenario ought to progress.

"Mr. Alexander – is that your hand on my tit!" said Angel in an alarmed tone, before grabbing Pete's arm and uncoupling from their embrace.

"Yes, sorry. I got a little carried away," stuttered Pete, as he thought to himself *Women way too hard to read*!

"I am officially dead now!" roared Noah, as he came running up the cabin's stairs clutching Sally's phone in his hand and disturbing Pete and Angel's moment.

On the phone screen was a news story about Noah's tragic demise from the *Sun Sentinel* website. "Local Developer Meets Fishy End" screamed the headline to an item that heavily alluded to Noah's affiliation with the mob. The writer couldn't help but insert into the story that Noah Furio was found "swimming with the fishes." Noah was pleased they described him as a "successful developer responsible for much of the Palm Beach County's urban renewal." The story was illustrated with Pete's picture of the car being hauled out of the canal and a full verification of the grisly findings from the Coroner's report. The story tagged cause of death resulting from a combination of head trauma and subsequent drowning. The quote from the police report described how Noah Furio would've died a slow and agonizing death as the water level rose in the car.

"I read it on the Internet so it must be true," said Pete, now scrolling through the story on his own phone.

"We did it, Noah. You're free and don't ever need to look back," said Sally, as she came on deck from the cabin, put her arms around Noah and kissed him.

"Land ahoy!" shouted Ethan, after briefly taking a cigarette from his mouth.

The lights that lit up the sandy dunes of Bimini Harbor could be seen on the distant horizon. After a journey of sixteen hours they had reached their destination.

Angel turned to Pete and said, "I think, my hero, I owe you a dinner."

The introduction of Led Zeppelin's *Thank You* belted out from the boat's sound system as Ethan readied the fenders for port.

December 17ᵗʰ 2013, from the Sun Sentinel

FLORIDA MAN TRIES TO TRADE ALLIGATOR FOR BEER

A Florida man walked into a Miami convenience store and tried to pay for a 12-pack of beer with a live alligator. He had just caught the four-foot gator at a local park. The store clerk called police and instead of a cool-beer barter, the man received citations for illegally catching and attempting to sell the alligator.

The Beach House

The Beach House, with its kooky and ramshackle splendor, was saved from the wrecking ball. The tenants' eviction notices were voided and the residents, with the exception of Bessie and Gabriel, were told they could stay. The four owners who had initiated the building's sale were paid out as per the financial terms of the original Surf Way Developments deal. There may have been bells ringing and an extra round of whooping it up at The Beach House, but the feeling in the local neighborhood was that this pocket of blight would continue to drag property prices down and exaggerate local area crime reports. It was also deemed a roadblock for the city elders who wouldn't be happy until the entire town was cleaned up, gentrified and made to look like new. Ultimately, the saving of The Beach House was a small victory for Florida Man, Florida Woman and a redneck way of living that was the soul and heartbeat of the great Floridian State.

Matthew Knight Esq., in a complicated arrangement with more lateral moves than the legendry final play of the 1982 Cal vs. Stanford Big Game, had transformed The Beach House into a cooperative, registered under a Bermudian shell company that used his Malibu practice as a business address. This set-up meant the property was not listed on the books of the New England Mafia and had no connection whatsoever with the recently presumed deceased mobster Noah Furio. The other benefit of the multi-layered paper trail that had been created was to make everything purposely over-complex in order to shield the fact that a corporation from Antigua with an unnamed director living in the Bahamas owned a ten-twelfths share in the building. Pete and Angel owned a share each and were appointed co-directors of the new cooperative board. The plan was for Noah, over time, to discreetly divest himself of the individual apartments, as he had no intention of dealing with the problems that come with a crumbling building inhabited by cranks, crooks and crazies.

Bessie and Gabriel Garlech were not aware of the new deal that had been worked out until they had vacated the property. Once their U-Haul had safely left the zip code, the first order of duty was to paint their dirty white door flamingo pink. The second task was to hire an industrial cleaning crew to make Apartment #5 fit for human habitation once again. The unfortunate team tasked with this job said the carpet was the most disgusting three-hundred-and-ninety-six yards of cheap polypropylene flooring they had ever bared witness to. The pool was refilled with water and a heating system installed in time for winter. The building's roof was fixed and, slowly but surely, Angel and Pete brought the building back up to code and transformed it into a wonderful livable place. The only challenge they were never able to overcome was making the walls soundproof. However, it was believed that the residents were so used to this way of life that they wouldn't be able to sleep at night without the ambient noise of the person next door flushing the toilet, watching a loud movie or getting frisky with a significant other.

The additional benefit of being a cooperative was the ability to pick and choose new tenants. Now anyone who applied to live at The Beach House had to be vetted by a panel of all the other neighbors to make sure they fitted in perfectly with the oddballs who called this place home. The Beach House was now technically run by the tenants for the benefit of the tenants, and had become a happy place for all, although a casual observer might say it was damn close to putting the inmates in charge of the asylum.

On the one-year anniversary of Tim Flanders' death, reports of his ghost-like spirit started popping up. At first, people thought Long Island Iced Tea Bob had had one too many of his signature drinks, and it was all in his head when he said a ghost that looked like Tim was sat on the sofa of Apartment #1. Adding to the strange factor, a *Two and a Half Men* episode was airing on Bob's television at the same time. Then others started seeing this strange apparition. Rodney Sawdust said he witnessed a ghost in the laundry room and swore it was Tim asking for quarters. Not long after that, Brenda Smith and her wife called 911 when the spirit of Tim chased the pair around their bedroom demanding to be orally pleasured.

Sporadic reports of the ghost were reported over the subsequent months. The consistent element of all the accounts was that the ghost was wearing tennis whites, had a cocktail in hand and a cheeky smile on its face. In a twist of ironic karma, Tim Flanders' brother-in-law died not long after Tim. He was playing tennis in California and dropped dead on court of a heart attack. He had no prior medical history of any related ailments.

Rodney Sawdust of Apartment #2 made a change to his regular set of gig songs by adding a selection of Elton John tunes. He initially gave it a punt as a one-off at a concert in Boynton. With the aid of some big glasses and a flamboyant hat he belted out *Rocket Man*. The crowd was a little stunned and confused, but seemed to appreciate the unexpected program and asked for more. Now at each performance he added at least three Elton John songs. This public appreciation for his personal passion was enough to make Rodney a happy and satisfied man in all aspects of life.

Ethan Thomas from Apartment #6 stayed at The Beach House for the remainder of his days. It was his happy place and he liked the lack of duties that came with the position of Honorary Mayor. The one change he did make to his life was finally settling down with a woman. Sarah Summer, who worked at the watch department of Macy's, reeled in Ethan and wore him down to a near model of domesticity. Sarah got him to quit smoking, womanizing and to stay away from happy hours at The Hurricane. Weaning him off his addiction to porn and gospel choir music was a bridge too far, but the pair was happy to have found each other.

Colleen Bromefield from Apartment #7 was eventually located, but unfortunately for her when finally found she was in several mutilated pieces bobbing in a three-set of Samsonite suitcases off Key Biscayne. Through articles in the *Miami Herald* it was learnt that she had been filling her days by double-dealing with the South Beach Cuban Mafia and a section of Barbadian Triads. Her pretty smile wasn't enough to save her when both parties worked out they had been played. Colleen's grisly death proved to be a lucrative opportunity for Pete. The New York tabloids purchased the sneaky shots he had taken of her laying poolside. The eye-candy art went great with the headline: "Headless Body Found With Topless Parts." From here the story was picked up internationally and known as the "Barbadian Triangle Mystery."

With The Beach House's pending demise and the fear of becoming homeless, or worse still living on his dad's sofa, Bodie Miller from Apartment #8 did what anyone else with a terrible run of luck would do – he purchased a lottery ticket. He did not win the jackpot, but he was pretty close. After taxes he had $2.7 million dollars in his pocket. Being the honorable man that he was, he went about paying everyone and anyone who had lost money in his bankrupt carwash business. He then bought a one-way ticket to Hawaii and banged on Nani's door. What she saw once again was the at-ease man she had originally fallen in love with. They were remarried in a small ceremony on the rugged North Shore of Oahu. Hawaii at first was a culture shock for Bodie, and he was amazed at just how cold the Pacific Ocean was compared to the warm Florida waters, but over time he slowed down his pace of life, learnt a little Pidgin and fell in love with the emblematic rainbows that became his daily vista. Bodie was surprised just how few car washes were in Honolulu, so he built himself a state-of-the-art facility in the ritzy suburb of Kahala. Bodie's business second time around was a great success.

Shane Dolman and Rebecca Gravois from Apartment #9, with assistance from the Federal authorities, finally went their separate ways. Shane, on poor advice from his court-appointed lawyer, pled guilty to all charges. Under heavy pressure from the Florida Governor, who was fed up with his State being tagged the home of Ponzi schemes, the book was thrown at him. Shane was given a twenty-year sentence. If lucky, he would be out in fifteen. It was commented in press reports that most people in Florida get less for murder.

Rebecca was luckier, as once again her family came to her rescue and paid for a quality defense. Her legal eagle put plenty of distance between her and Shane, resulting in Rebecca getting away with just probation and a lifetime ban on running a business. The court case also led to Rebecca finally having a happy ending. Once the trial was complete, her lawyer asked her on a date. He was everything that all her other boyfriends had never been - good looking, with a professional career, a stable personality and unmarried. They hit it off and soon Rebecca was living the dream. She had a

Lexus in the driveway, an oversized McMansion with a pool under mosquito netting, and the carefree life that comes with being a kept woman dwelling in a subdivision on the western extremities of Boca Raton.

Jacob Smith from Apartment #10 never went back to Florida, as for him it held nothing but bad memories. His first winter home in Missouri was depressing and he planned a speedy escape. He cashed in his school pension, sold his St Louis house after several price reductions, and then dragged his wife to the warmth of California. Jacob purchased land in Riverside County and started a small organic citrus farm. He didn't ever again contact Celia, but he was sure he saw her just once. It was at a four-way stop sign in the city of Redlands. Their eyes met and she smiled, that same smile she always gave. He couldn't be sure and his wife was in the car so he didn't want to cause a scene, but in his heart he felt it was Celia. Citrus farming was good for Jacob and he stayed clean and remained happy and married.

Randy Showers from Apartment #12 slowly expanded his church. He moved from his sub-let synagogue and eventually through donations built his own premises on the site of a former carwash in Lake Worth. He was careful not to get greedy with his parishioners' money and remained content to live a shabby middle-class life. Randy's only extravagance was the maintenance of his hair plugs and dental veneers. He spent all his free time trying to perfect the walking-on-water miracle that was his dream, thinking that if he could pull it off it would land him in the big league of sham Men of God.

Bessie and Gabriel Garlech took their money from the sale of Apartment #5 (minus liens from unpaid lawyers) and, due to their fear of banks, converted it to digital Bitcoins. They were both quite bitter about the manner in which they had been outflanked and crushed by the board of The Beach House. They couldn't understand why they weren't offered the same opportunity to stay put along with Angel and Pete. After all, they saw themselves as reasonable people who had been terribly wronged. Bessie and Gabriel rented themselves an apartment in West Palm Beach, from where they regrouped and planned their future lives. The humiliation they were subjected to was something so painful that they vowed they would never let it happen again. With her law degree in place, Bessie set herself up as a practicing attorney. She was extremely good at her craft and became an advocate to owners of condominiums who were facing victimization by their boards. Gabriel spent his days roaming his new apartment complex's pool and gym, ogling women and looking for a new war to wage. He spent his evenings keeping his wife's books and trolling the Internet becoming more paranoid, radicalized and in fear of the entire world. Bessie and Gabriel never went back to The Beach House and couldn't imagine how beautiful the building looked with twelve matching flamingo pink doors.

If Bimini was a good enough place for cannibal Hannibal Lecter to lay low, it was certainly the ideal hideaway for a mobster meant to be swimming with the fishes plus a nomadic writer of soccer-mom porn. Sally Purdue from Apartment #11 had lived her life by the mantra "love is a series of acts."

Unfortunately, her lifelong problem was never being able to string more than one act together to create a personal and meaningful narrative of love that she could own. The casual sex never filled her void or yearning for what she needed.

That night at the bar of City Oyster, Sally instantly knew she had finally found herself a partner. Noah Furio was dark, dangerous and, much like Sally, leading a secret double life. Sally was perhaps a little consumed in her literary fiction alter ego and chose to ignore the fact that Noah's persona as a mobster about to be "rubbed out" was a few leagues of crazy above that of her own. Sometimes for a full-time writer with a troubled edge, separating larger-than-life fact and top-of-head fiction becomes a flaw. For Sally, though, it all ended beautifully. Over that forty-eight hours they had spent together while they plotted Noah's faked demise and ultimate escape, Sally knew she was in love and would spend the rest of her life with this man. Ms Purdue's long-in-the-works book *Sally does the Sunshine State* became an instant bestseller. Sally told her agent that her next work would be pure fiction, set in the colonial Caribbean and of course riddled with her trademark dirty sex. Under this cover she would live as Ernest Hemingway had in this exquisitely beautiful part of The Bahamas.

On the mobster scale, Noah Furio was a soft five in mean and hardness. However, that wouldn't have saved him from the Boston hit squad that had been sent to make him disappear. He was unaware that his number was up and thankful for being rescued by the ragtag residents of this Delray Beach building he was about to raze to the ground. Now in The Bahamas, without the pressures of running a criminal enterprise and the fear of having a target on his back, he could start again. Finding a partner in Sally had made his new life appealing in a whole different way. Upon reaching Bimini, he bought Ethan's yacht and so returned him a favor. Noah and Sally sailed around The Bahamas until they found themselves a perfect little house to rent. For the first time in their lives they both felt they had finally found a place they could call home.

The Beach House had changed Angel Mancini beyond her wildest dreams. As a newly arrived first-time homeowner she was awkward and nervous of her surroundings. In Angel's world, where death and tragedy were a constant, something fundamentally needed to change. A slow warming to and finally embracing of her new neighbors transformed her perspective and allowed her, even with odd eccentricities, for the first time to be one of a gang. In a world of no privacy, an unlikely hero came to her rescue. If only everyone had that chance of scrubbing a piece of their past that had come back to haunt them. Angel was not blindsided with love, but slowly worked into submission. With his everyday looks and generic dress, Pete was not the type of man Angel had ever dreamed could sweep her off her feet. That moonlit kiss on Ethan's yacht was a little wet and over-tongued, but even with that clumsy grab of her breast, it was perfect for the moment. As Pete would tell her, life is all about timing and he had spent much effort working his way to get her into that sweet spot on the boat and in a position to go for the girl. Angel gave Simon his walking papers and returned the engagement ring. His lack of emotion summed up that it wasn't meant to be, and what she thought they had was mostly in her imagination. Angel's romance with Pete was slow and steady, but unexpectedly all that she could have ever wanted.

Pete Alexander had chased Angel much like he would a news story. The obstacles thrown in front of him were just challenges that made him want to make it happen even more. He wasn't rich or good looking, and lived an unconventional life, so it was always going to be the back story, the effort, the game and ultimately seizing the moment that would give him a chance. It would take Pete several months to work his way to the explosive antics that he had witnessed on Angel's now voided tape. He was in no rush and just happy that in the man-bites-dog world of Florida that he lived in, a good guy was able to steal the heart of a beautiful woman like Angel.

Pete had always admired and feared the couples who called The Beach House home, but swore he would never join their ranks. Those apartments were just not big enough for two, especially with the added complication of Halo, who also needed a little space to stretch out her paws. A year after helping to save The Beach House, Pete and Angel purchased a cottage a few blocks north on Waterway Lane. It was a modest sixteen-hundred-square-foot 1920s house built of rugged Dade County pine. Angel sold Apartment #2 of The Beach House to a single girl with a cat that reminded her very much of herself when she had first moved in. Pete kept Apartment #4 and used it as his office. In that way, Pete and Angel could check into The Beach House when they liked for as long as they wanted and then make the quick walk back to the sanity of their quiet home.

Pete and Angel were perfect together. They would spend the evenings recounting their workdays, detailing which unfortunate soul had been on the sharp end of Angel's pulsating power saw and who Pete had hosed down with his telephoto lens. It was always a close-run thing as to whose day was the more shocking, strange and bizarre. Their only rule in life was to end each day with a smile and live the next like it was their last day on Earth.

Postscript

Florida man, Florida woman and the everyday mayhem that occurs around the State of Florida inspired this work of fiction. The initial genesis came during a moment of clarity bobbing in the warm waters of Delray Beach while drinking cocktails with the late Tim Anderson. The story outline was drafted at The Beach House during its final days of existence. The first chapters were written at The Kahala Apartments ocean-view library in Honolulu and on numerous Hawaiian Airlines flights between Oahu and Oakland. The final chapters and editing were completed in Berkeley, California, and St Louis, Missouri.

The real Beach House was sold in 2014 to a developer who, I might stress, has no ties to the mafia. There now stands in its place six-luxury townhomes.

The Author

James Aylott was previously a Hollywood paparazzo photographer who sold his successful news agency in 2016. He received his education from the University of California, Berkeley, and King's College, London. A prior resident of Delray Beach, Florida, he now splits his time between Berkeley, California, where his cat resides, and St Louis, Missouri, where his family currently live.

Made in the USA
Columbia, SC
02 July 2020